Monster

Monster

Ben Burgess Jr.

www.urbanbooks.net

Urban Books, LLC
300 Farmingdale Road, N.Y.-Route 109
Farmingdale, NY 11735

Monster Copyright © 2021 Ben Burgess Jr.

ISBN 13: 978-1-64556-171-2
ISBN 10: 1-64556-171-2

First Trade Paperback Printing June 2021
Printed in the United States of America

10 9 8 7 6 5 4 3 2 1

*This is a work of fiction. Any references or similarities
to actual events, real people, living or dead, or to real
locales are intended to give the novel a sense of reality.
Any similarity in other names, characters, places, and
incidents is entirely coincidental.*

Distributed by Kensington Publishing Corp.
Submit Orders to:
Customer Service
400 Hahn Road
Westminster, MD 21157-4627
Phone: 1-800-733-3000
Fax: 1-800-659-2436

Dedicated to my daughter, Jaelynn. There are real monsters out there. When the time is right, I hope this book will encourage you to choose wisely.

"To attempt the destruction of our passions is the height of folly. What a noble aim is that of the zealot who tortures himself like a madman in order to desire nothing, love nothing, feel nothing, and who, if succeeded, would end up a complete **MONSTER***!"*

~Denis Diderot

The poem that inspired the novel, Monster, *from the poetry book,* Times Have Changed and Life Is Strange, *by Ben Burgess Jr.:*

UGLY

There's a darkness inside me hidden deep within my psyche, causing me to act in a manner that's unlike me. I have turned into a lustful monster that conquers to alleviate my emotional hunger, preying on women like a hunter to add to my sexual numbers. Always on guard, this side of me is a mask used to put up a façade, disregard, and protect me from the feeling of being empty.

I spent many dates gazing into eyes and holding hands. My only plan was to add to my statistic of one-night stands and becoming legendary in women's beds. I messed with many heads to get them to spread their legs and relished the feeling of being intimate. No longer into it, my feelings for the situation became intricate while she's still smitten by the way I caressed her. My feelings changed the moment I undressed her. Under no pressure, I address her with full force, showing no remorse as I tell her I felt nothing, and this was all just a fling. To me, she didn't mean anything. I could've never been committed. I didn't have to wonder why I did it. The answer was simple; I just wanted to "hit it."

I slept with many women, some I didn't even remember their names, but no matter how many I slept with, I could never get rid of that initial pain. Back then, "she" had manipulated and hurt me, so I decided to show no mercy, do the same, let women feel my pain, and become a player in this game. Her method of deception left me suspended in a state of depression, affecting my judgment and affection. I was wounded with emotional scars. From bathrooms in bars to backseats of cars, I would go with the flow with any woman that tempted me. I would have sex and hop to the next, and still feel empty.

After my heart was destroyed, I felt all of those women would help fill that void and make everything clearer, until one day, I didn't recognize myself in the mirror. What have I done? What monster have I become? How could I ever expect anyone to love me, with my heart being this ugly? When did my heart turn to stone? The path I was leading was deceiving and would eventually leave me all alone. What I did was wrong and was done with evil intent. I decided to forgive myself as my first act of atonement.

I've grown and stopped being vindictive, trying to "get them." I've stopped feeling like a victim and returned to the man I was meant to be, forever keeping that evil part of me in captivity.

Monster

by

Ben Burgess Jr.

Chapter One

Weak

"Bri, please, don't do this to me. I love you. What did I do wrong? I can fix this. Just tell me what to do," I pleaded over the phone.

"It's nothing we can fix, Kenny. I'm sorry. I'm just not feeling *us* anymore. It's over."

I sat up in my twin-sized bed, trying to reason with Bri not to break up with me.

Bri sighed. Obviously, she was bored with our situation and was ready to end the call and move on.

"Look, we're still cool. We'll still hang out and stuff as friends."

"Friends . . ."

"Yeah, friends. It's not like I don't care about you, but we got into a relationship way too fast."

I was heartbroken.

The first thought that came to mind when she called me at three thirty in the morning to break up was that she was fucking David. She and David grew up together and were very close . . . too close if you ask me. He was some big-time pretty boy drug dealer in Glen Cove that she was friends with before we started dating.

He was about six foot five, had a chestnut complexion, hazel eyes, and was in decent shape. He had a souped-up S-Class Mercedes-Benz.

David never wore the same outfit twice. He had money and walked around the neighborhood like he was the king of New York. All the girls in the area were sweating him. He always had a different one on his arm, and I guess Brianna was one of them too.

When we first started dating, I made sure to ask her if she had feelings for him, and she laughed it off. The first time I suspected something was going on with them was after one of our dates when David was sitting on her front steps, waiting for her to come home. He walked up to my car when I pulled up, pointed at it, and laughed. Bri struggled to crank my windows down manually.

"Hey," she said, smiling hard.

I wanted to knock David's fucking head off when he gave Bri a peck on the lips in front of me.

"Hey, I was waiting for you," he said.

"I was out with my boyfriend, Ken," she said.

She faced me. "Ken, this is my boy, David. David, this is my man, Ken."

He gave me a halfhearted wave and didn't bother to look in my direction.

"All right, I'll holla at you later since you're busy right now."

She smiled. "We'll talk."

"Later, beautiful."

I sat there in my car, livid.

"You mad?" Bri asked.

"You and David look like y'all are more than just friends," I said.

Bri laughed and shook her head, but I didn't find shit funny. Back then, Bri swore to me he wasn't my competition, and I had nothing to worry about.

"Look, if you want, I can back off until you figure things out with him. I don't want to keep this going, catch more feelings, and—"

"It's not like that. Nothing is going on between him and me. I'm with you. David is like my brother. He's fucked too many of my friends for me to ever look at him as anything more than that."

At the time, I believed her, and she calmed me down, but subconsciously, I always felt David was better than me. He drove a Mercedes, while I drove a broken-down 1989 Ford Escort. He sold dope, so he had money. I worked at a food store as a cashier and made nine dollars an hour. He had an apartment, and I still lived with my parents.

"It's late. What made you call me right now to break up? Are you with him right now? You fucking him?"

"Whether I'm with him doesn't matter. I don't appreciate you making me sound like a ho."

Her lack of an answer confirmed I hit the nail on the head.

"Look, I gotta go. If you ever want to talk or hang sometime, give me a call," Bri said.

She hung up without saying goodbye.

I sat in the dark, crying, looking at the pictures on my rickety nightstand of us together, and feelings of loneliness hit me.

For the next three days, I didn't eat, sleep, go to work, or school. I stayed holed up in my room, depressed, and listening to sad love songs. I had Brian McKnight's "Anytime" playing when Donna, my friend that matched Bri and me up, called.

"Hey, Kenny? I heard about you and Bri, " she said.

"I know she cheated on me. Why else would she call me so early to break up? I'd bet money she's fucking David."

"Stop that. She's not sleeping with him. I'll find out what happened, but trust me, I've been seeing David for like five months now, and we're about to make things official soon. She's known David and me since we were kids. She wouldn't do that to you, and she definitely wouldn't do that to me."

Donna sounded confident, but in my heart, I knew I was right.

"Plus, you guys only went out for nine months. At least you didn't waste too much of each other's time. Well, Kenny, you know I'm here for you if you need me. Keep your head up, and I'll talk to you later, sweetie. Bye."

We ended the call. Talking with Donna didn't help me. It only upset me more.

It was true, Brianna and I didn't date long, but I felt she was the one. Before her, I was in a cluster of shitty relationships. There was Chanel. I liked Chanel until her friends convinced her that she shouldn't limit herself by having a serious relationship with anyone since she had just started college. They told her she needed to "find herself," and she wouldn't do that by staying in a committed relationship with me. She was weak-minded and listened to them. I was bitter about that one.

Then there was Leysha. Leysha was fun, and we got along great until she decided to leave me and go back to her ex-boyfriend. She explained that they had broken up on good terms, and while she liked and cared for me a lot, she loved him and wanted to see if they could work things out.

Again, I was hurt and alone. I went on many dates, but I couldn't find a woman I truly connected with until I met Brianna. I loved Bri more than I loved myself. I didn't want anyone else. I didn't *need* anyone else. As long as I had her, I didn't desire another girl. I felt Bri brought out the best in me. I didn't have much, but anything I had, I gave it to her because I always wanted her to be happy. I felt she completed me and thought she was the woman I would eventually marry, but I guess I was wrong.

I drove to Centennial Park in Roosevelt to play basketball and clear my head. The park was deserted. It was windy, and the clouds looked like it was about to pour, but I didn't care. I missed shot after shot. I just couldn't focus.

When I got home, I thought of going inside and wallowing in my sorrow, but I decided to walk across the street to my friend Ray's house since I didn't feel like being alone.

I knew Ray since junior high. He was good with cars and landed a steady job with BMW right after he finished trade school. Out of all of my friends, Ray was the most logical. While my other friends, Perry and Adam, would tell me to do typical stupid guy shit, Ray always gave me advice that was sensible and mature. I valued his friendship and his opinions.

Ray was a stocky six foot one. He was heavy, but his balanced mix of pudginess and muscle helped him not to look sloppy. He had a copper-colored complexion, always wore a goatee, and had a slightly receding hairline.

I knocked on his door, stood in front, and felt like a loser. When he opened his door, his reaction showed he knew something was wrong.

"You all right, brotha?"

"Nope, I'm a single man again."

"Shit. Come in, man. I'm guessing she broke up with you?"

"Yup."

He gave me a brotherly embrace. We walked into his living room and sat on his tan fabric sofa. Ray muted the TV while I brought him up to speed about my breakup with Bri.

"Damn, bro, I didn't see that coming. You all right?" he asked.

"Nah, I loved her."

"I know you did, brotha, but dwelling on it isn't gonna help. Try focusing on other things in your life right now. Put more energy into those things, so they'll take your mind off her."

He was right, but when your heart is aching, your mind doesn't listen to logic.

Minutes later, Ray's girl, Lucy, and his younger sister, Kim, came home with shopping bags from the mall. Lucy looked as beautiful as ever. She's petite with a chestnut complexion and long, wavy, jet-black hair. Kim had the same copper-colored complexion that Ray did. She's shapely with huge tits, so Ray was always protecting her from the knuckleheads that hit on her.

Lucy and Ray had been together since third grade. She lived with Ray in his grandmother's house since they were in high school. Lucy was smart and landed a job with an accounting firm that paid for her to go to school at NYU. Their relationship is what I always wanted for myself. They complemented each other perfectly, and being around them always reminded me that true love does exist.

I ended up repeating my drama to Lucy and Kim. Lucy sat on the sofa next to me.

"I'm sorry, Ken. I'm not trying to be a bitch, but I think she was fucking too. She wouldn't have called you at that time unless something was up. I can't stand cheaters. I don't understand how anyone could be so selfish. I could never do that."

"You can do better than that skank, Kenny," Kim said.

I won't lie, I still loved Bri, so I didn't like Kim calling her a skank, but I knew she only said it because she cared.

"Thanks," I said.

I vented more, and they all chimed in with their thoughts and advice. I wondered if I'd ever feel whole again.

***

I went back to school and work. The first week went by slowly because I waited by the phone like a chump, hoping Bri would call. That was wishful thinking. The next week went by quicker, but there was still no call from Bri. I started to realize she wasn't coming back.

I was having a good day. I got As on all four papers for my classes. I was off from work, and for the first time since the breakup, I felt relaxed. I sat in my living room, watching TV when my cell phone rang. I answered on the third ring.

"Yo."

I heard crying in the background.

"Who's this?"

There was no answer, just more crying.

"Hello?"

"It's me, Ken."

Confused, I asked, "You okay? What's wrong, Donna?"

"You were right, Ken. She *is* fucking David."

When she sprang that shit on me, there went my good day. I sighed.

"What happened?"

"Bri called me and asked if I wanted to hang out, so I was like, 'Sure, girl, where you want to go?' She was like, 'I don't know. We can figure that out later. Let me pick you up.' The next thing I know, I see David's car in front of my house."

I felt my anger rising in me. A part of me didn't want to hear that shit, but I needed to. Donna continued.

"So I went outside, and I was surprised Bri didn't say anything about David being with her. She usually moves to the backseat so that I can sit in the front with him, but she didn't this time. I thought that was weird, but I let it go and sat in the back. When I went to kiss David, he turned his face, and I ended up kissing his cheek.

Something didn't feel right. We drove around. It got quiet, and they kept smiling and looking at each other all lovey-dovey. As we drove on, Bri turned around, gave me a sorry-ass look, and said, 'We couldn't think of a way to tell you, but David and I are together now.'

"I asked her, 'You mean y'all are in a committed relationship, or he's just fucking you?' She stammered over her answer. I ignored her bullshit and faced David. I asked how long they've been fucking. Bri answered for him and said—are you ready for this, Kenny?—'six months.'"

I felt sick to my stomach. I was sweating. I felt like breaking anything I could get my hands on. I repeatedly punched a wall in my living room. My hand throbbed and bled. The skin ripped off my knuckles, but the physical pain was nothing like the emotional pain I felt inside. How could I be so blind? How didn't I see that?

Donna went on.

"I asked him, 'So you were fucking me and fucking her behind my back?' I wanted to smack the fucking smirk off his face. I asked, 'How could you do this to me?' He didn't answer. I turned and faced Bri. 'You were supposed to be my homegirl. You knew how I felt about David. Out of all the men out there, why did you have to fuck *him?*' Kenny, don't get mad. This part is gonna hurt."

"I don't think I can feel worse than I do right now."

I was wrong.

"I asked Bri how could she do this to you when she knew you loved her. She said, 'Ken is too weak. He never has money. He can't even take care of himself. How can he take care of me? What does he have to offer? He can't treat me as good as David can.' David was grinning like he was the pimp of all pimps. She said you're nice, but you're nowhere near the man she needed."

I couldn't talk. I wiped my eyes with my sleeves and told Donna to keep going with her story.

"You sure? Are you okay? We can talk about something else if you want," she said.

"I'm fine. Keep going."

I could hear in her voice that she was emotional too.

"Kenny, I couldn't even look at them. I asked why they took me out to tell me this, and they said they felt they owed it to me. I told them I was done with them both and to take me home. They sucked their teeth and were like, 'Okay, let's get you home then.' When we got back to my house, this heifer tried to hug me. I stopped her dead in her tracks. She tried to justify what she'd done, telling me everything would be okay, and we'd get over this. I let her know she was dead to me, and I'd get her ass back. Are you all right, Kenny?"

"I'm good," I said, holding the phone to my ear and my left hand to my face.

"Ken, let's go out tonight, just me and you like we used to."

"The way I'm feeling, I'd be shitty company."

"Kenny, please. I don't want to be alone right now. I need you."

Somehow, she convinced me to agree to pick her up around five o'clock. I thought about canceling. I was angry and hurt, but Donna told me she needed me. Maybe I needed her too since this all started with her.

Before Donna hooked me up with Bri, I wanted to be with her, but she had a boyfriend at the time. We used to hang out regularly and were close friends, but I wanted more than that.

Since there weren't many good guys like me around, Donna felt she'd hook me up with her best friend since Bri was tired of meeting bad boys.

***

At five o'clock, I was in front of Donna's house. I hoped Bri was close by to see me pick her up so she could be jealous, but I'm sure I wasn't even on her mind. I honked the horn. Donna's front door opened, and she stepped out of the house looking amazing. She had on the tightest black jeans I had ever seen, and they accentuated her shape perfectly. Donna wore a low-cut red shirt that showed off her tits, and her makeup was done to perfection. I felt underdressed. All I had on was a blue and white polo shirt, blue jeans, and blue sneakers.

"You look great," I said.

"Thank you, sweetie."

"Where do you want to go?"

"A motel with you," she said with a wink.

I laughed. "Seriously, do you want to see a movie or something?"

"Let's get something to eat first. We can see a movie afterward."

We ended up at Buffalo Wild Wings in Hicksville to unwind, watch the Yankees' game on TV, and have a few drinks. We ate, talked about how shitty love had been to us, and laughed about old times. I noticed she was tossing back drink after drink, so before she got sloppy and we had to cut our night short, I had the waiter stop bringing her drinks. I didn't know if it was the liquor or all in my head because I was vulnerable and lonely, but Donna kept giving me flirty looks. I tried to ignore it. I didn't want to do or say something stupid that would ruin our friendship.

After dinner, we went to the movies. Once the lights went off, she was all over me. Between how good she looked and her stroking my dick through my jeans, I hardened instantly.

"Damn," Donna said.

I needed that confidence boost. She smiled and inched closer to me until our lips touched. She opened her mouth, and it felt good to have her lips on mine. It felt good to be wanted and desired. We couldn't keep our hands off each other and cut our movie short. I had to have her.

We ended up getting a room at the Yankee Clipper Motel in Freeport. After I paid for the room, I noticed Donna seemed hesitant and looked like she was in deep thought, but her eyes darkened, and before I knew it, she was yanking me to our room.

I opened the door, and there was a neatly made king-sized bed in the middle of the room. We kissed, and in the back of my mind, I questioned if I could go through with it. Would this hurt our friendship? Would anything come from this? Would this take away the heartache Bri had given me?

We undressed each other. Donna stepped out of her black, lacy, Victoria's Secret thong. Seeing her flawless, curvy, shaved, full-figured body had me hard as a rock.

She pulled off my shirt, rubbed her hands down my chest, and traveled down to my dick. She moaned as I sucked on her neck. I looked into her eyes, and I could see she had doubt. I knew the look because I felt the same way. As hot as Donna was, and as much as I hated Bri at the moment, I couldn't go through with it. I couldn't fuck Donna out of spite. I kissed her and said, "We can't do this."

"I *need* to do this. She didn't give a shit about your feelings or mine. If I go through with it and tell her what happened, it'll hurt her, and I want her to feel it. As horrible as she has been to you, I know she still cares. She knew I was feeling David, and she knew you loved her. She's a selfish bitch that thinks you're weak. In her mind, she can get you back anytime she wants. You're just her backup plan if things don't work out with David. She wants a man that'll pamper her."

Everything she said pissed me off because I knew she was right. I pulled her to me and looked into her eyes. Both of us wanted revenge. We both wanted a release, but in our hearts, we knew this wasn't right. I held her naked in my arms.

"We can't do this. We're not going to use each other," I said.

Donna's eyes were full of tears as she looked up at me and nodded her head in agreement.

We spent the rest of the night talking, and before falling asleep, she looked at me and said, "Thank you for everything. Anyone else would've just fucked me without remorse or thinking twice, but you care about me and didn't take advantage. I respect and love you for that."

I went to bed feeling good about myself. In the morning, we dressed each other and held hands as I drove her home.

When we got to Donna's house, David's champagne Mercedes S500 was parked in front. I looked over at Donna, and she smirked. I guess she was going to get her revenge one way or another.

The driver's-side door of the Mercedes swung open, and Bri stepped out. Donna stepped out of my car and shot Bri a look. Donna smiled at me, licked her lips, and said, "Thank you for everything last night. I was definitely satisfied with how our night went."

She smiled at Bri, said, "Bye, bitch," and walked into her house.

The flush on Bri's light skin showed me she was furious. She walked to my car and, without asking, flung the door open and got in.

"What the fuck was that, Ken? Did you fuck her to get back at me?"

"Are you serious right now? You've been fucking David for six months while we were together, and you're asking if I fucked Donna last night? I loved you."

Bri looked at me in disgust.

"I *never* loved you. When I'm with David, I always wonder why I wasted so much of my time fucking with you. You did nothing for me, and sexually, you're wack. Sometimes when you used to kiss me after work, I had just finished sucking David's dick before you came over. So how'd his dick taste, Ken?"

I was falling apart. My hands doubled into fists.

"Sometimes, I'd let him fuck me raw and come inside me, then laugh to myself when I'd watch you eat me out minutes later after he left my house."

I curled my bottom lip and leaned my head back to hold my tears at bay, but I was losing that battle. As she went on, she stopped talking shit long enough to observe my face.

"Aww, are you going to cry? You're a pussy. I need a *man* in my life, not some punk-ass, broke little boy. I don't care if you fucked Donna. She can have my weak leftovers. I never needed your black ass."

I was so hurt and angry that I couldn't even hear her insults anymore. Once she realized she broke me, and I wasn't arguing back, she flung my car door open and walked away without shutting it. She started up David's car and drove past me with the windows down, giving me the finger.

I got home, and my parents were in the living room watching TV. I quickly walked past them and went straight to my room to avoid a long, drawn-out inquisition and conversation.

My mother, noticing something was wrong, knocked on my door. "Kenny, you look upset. What's wrong?"

"Nothing. I just need to be alone right now."

I loved my mom, but there were certain things I couldn't talk to her about. I wished I could get fatherly advice from my dad, but the only person my pops cared about was himself, and my relationship with him was nonexistent.

Other than sports, we rarely talked. I held a lot of hatred toward him because he regularly left my mom to be with his side chicks. He used my mom for everything. He didn't work or help her with bills or responsibilities. He just leeched off her, and when he got bored, he'd leave for days, weeks—even months—without calling or stopping by the house.

Once he had his fill with his other women, he'd come back home. My parents would argue, and somehow all would be forgiven, and things would go back to normal like nothing happened. I never understood why my mom always forgave him, and I hated her for being so weak when it came to him. I guess I was weak too because before today, if Bri said she would've come back to me, I would've forgiven her and taken her back with no questions asked.

Everything Bri said in the car replayed in my head and brought back painful memories from my childhood—a period in my life I worked hard to move on from. Growing up in Queens back in the day, the other Black and Hispanic kids made fun of me relentlessly for being very dark-skinned. Every day, they'd call me names like "tar baby," "midnight," and "black monkey."

Back then, my self-esteem and confidence were shot, and there were times when I was borderline suicidal. I didn't have many friends, and being depressed all the time had me stress eating. By fourth grade, I ballooned to

185 pounds, and that literally and figuratively only made me a bigger target to tease. I became a hothead and daily got in fights. I took up jujitsu and boxing with the sole purpose of beating the asses of those that were hurting me emotionally and mentally, but the disciplines ended up helping me lose weight and taught me how to control my temper.

Although I was no longer overweight, they still made fun of me for being dark. Once puberty started, all I wanted was for girls to like me. I gave them the little money I had and gifts, but even though I did whatever the girls asked, none of them wanted me, and some of them still made fun of me despite everything I did for them.

After years of being called dark and ugly, I accepted it as the truth by junior high. As fate would have it, I met a pale Polish girl named Vera, who changed my life. She was the only person at the time to tell me my dark skin was beautiful. If it weren't for her, I wouldn't be who I am today. We lost our virginity to each other, but our relationship was short-lived because I eventually moved from Queens to Long Island and had to start all over again, making friends at a new junior high school. I didn't have Vera to boost my self-esteem anymore, but meeting her helped me learn how to like myself.

It took years for me to become secure. While we learn and most times move on from the past, we still remember it. Sometimes the past hurts, and Bri reminded me of those times I tried so hard to forget. I wasn't secure or confident anymore. What had taken me years to fix about myself, Bri destroyed in a matter of weeks. I felt lost. I needed to change.

I lay in bed and reflected on myself and my past. I was tired of hearing that I was such a "nice guy" and only meeting women who ended up disappointing me. I didn't want to care anymore. I didn't want to feel anything anymore. I decided from then on that things would be different.

I thought about calling in sick and not going to work again, but I changed my mind. I needed to stay busy. I needed to take my mind off the pain. I was done with feeling sorry for myself. I wouldn't let anyone ever hurt me again.

Chapter Two

Change

Going to work was a good idea. The food store was busy, so that helped to keep my mind off Bri.

One of the girls who worked with me, Kianna, winked at me. She was heavyset with big breasts, thick thighs, a cute, round face, and pretty hazel eyes that matched her brown skin complexion.

There was a ten-year difference in our ages, but she didn't seem to care about it, so neither did I. Usually, when she flirted, I'd smile and laugh it off, but this time, I winked back. When our shift was over, we walked to the back office to count our registers.

"I saw you looking at me," she said, joking.

"Is that right? I could've sworn you winked at me first."

"You're right. I was checking you out, but I don't think you're ready for all this yet," she said, rubbing her hands down her body.

"That's big talk, but I'm more about action."

In the past, I would've never said shit like that, but the old me wasn't working. I needed this change. Kianna looked taken aback but sighed and said, "Is that right? I'd love to prove it to you, but I forgot you have your little girlfriend."

"That's over with, so what's up?"

I thought she'd back down, but she didn't.

"Really? What are you doing after work?"

"Umm, nothing."

"Good. So hang out at my place."

I already talked shit. I couldn't back down now. "All right, cool."

After work, we got in my car.

"So what happened with you and your girl?" Kianna asked.

I didn't want to get into that, so vaguely, I said, "Things just didn't work out."

She smiled. "Her loss, right?"

"Yup."

We pulled off, and I drove to her apartment building. I was nervous, excited, and curious about what was going to happen next.

"You coming or what?" Kianna asked.

I nodded and walked with her to her building. Once we got inside the elevator, she immediately started kissing me. Kianna's soft lips trailed from my mouth to my earlobe.

"I can't wait to feel what you got. I've wanted you for a long time," she confessed.

I smirked but kept quiet.

She opened the door to her apartment. Kianna quickly grabbed my hand, waved to her sister sitting in a shirt and panties watching TV, and dragged me to her bedroom.

As soon as the door closed, Kianna dropped to her knees. "Let me see what I'm working with here," she said.

She slowly unzipped my jeans, and I could see the approval on her face as she pulled my dick out, stroked it, and put it deep in her mouth. Holy shit, it felt good. Each time she moved her mouth on me, she tried to get more of it inside.

"Jesus, you're about to give me lockjaw here," she said, joking briefly as she filled her mouth again.

I felt somewhat guilty because I had no feelings or intention of ever being in a relationship with her. I pushed those thoughts aside and focused on the task at hand.

"Your lips feel good on me, but let me return the favor," I said.

I took off her clothes and slowly laid her down. I could tell she was self-conscious about her weight when she tried to cover the little stretch marks on her stomach with her arms. I held her close and said, "You don't have to hide from me. I like you just the way you are."

With that comment, she relaxed, kissed me, and spread her legs apart. I licked the inside of her thighs, and her body shivered. My tongue touched everything but her vagina, and I liked hearing her beg me to eat her. When she couldn't take me teasing her anymore, I sucked on her clit, licked her southern lips, and slowly worked her with two fingers. Hearing her loud moans was a real turn-on for me. I worked my fingers in and out and kept a steady suction on her clit. She looked down at me, eating her out, and her breathing quickened. She gripped my head firmly, came hard on my face, and lay in the bed shaking. I enjoyed seeing that I pleased her.

Without asking, she turned around on all fours and bent over. I grabbed a condom out of my pants pocket and rolled it onto my dick. Then I grabbed her waist and eased inside her. With each thrust, I wanted her to feel every inch of me. She gripped the sheets and pressed her face hard into the pillow to muffle her moans. She laid me down, took off the condom, and went down on me.

"Oh, shit, I'm about to come," I shouted.

She kept her rhythm steady until I came in her mouth.

We shared smiles. I pulled her close to me, held her, and we talked.

"You're a thin guy. I didn't think you'd put it on me like that."

That was a big boost to my ego and turned me on again. "You ready for round two?" I asked.

She nodded.

When it was over, she had the look of a very satisfied woman.

She walked me to the door, and we promised each other this wouldn't be a one-time thing.

For the first time since my breakup, I felt happy. Even if it was just temporary, I had a feeling of redemption.

I went home, showered, and got ready for bed. I lay in bed, stared at the ceiling, and wondered if Bri enjoyed herself like I did today.

I forced myself to stop thinking about her. I was mad at myself for being so weak. I'm sure I didn't even cross her mind. Bri only cared about herself, and I need to look at life the same way. Being in relationships wasn't working for me, but what I did today was harmless. No commitment. No attachment. We both got what we wanted, and no one got hurt because we knew what we were getting into. From then on, I decided I only wanted to have experiences like that.

The next day while in my business math class, I realized dating was like investing in stocks. Whether it's to be in a committed, monogamous relationship or to get a piece of ass, guys invest a lot of time, energy, and money buying women drinks, jewelry, and gifts during the courting process for one purpose—a high return in which case is to get the girl.

Rachel, the girl who usually sat next to me in class, poked me with her pen and broke my train of thought.

I smiled and asked, "What's up?"

"You look deep in thought," she said.

In the past, I was so caught up on being loyal to Bri that I never realized how pretty Rachel was. She had a deep chocolate-brown complexion with a curvy, toned body that turned heads. Everyone knew her because Briarcliffe was big on softball, and she was the star pitcher for the team.

"I'm just thinking about what I want to do this weekend," I lied.

"Yeah, I want to plan something too. I'm from Oakland, so I don't know anything out here in New York."

"You should hang out with my boys and me."

"I'm down for that."

"You have any single friends?"

"I can bring Kelly from my team."

"Cool."

We exchanged numbers. In the past, I would've never been so direct. I was proud of myself for breaking out of my comfort zone.

I went to my other classes and drove straight to work afterward. When I got there, everyone was smiling at me.

My coworker, Sa'Rita, came up to me, smiling.

"So, I heard you and Kianna had fun last night."

I was a little embarrassed. She told everyone but figured it was a good thing since she said she enjoyed it. I smiled and played it off like I didn't know what she was talking about.

Kianna was talking to her friend D'Asia by the time clock. I wasn't sure how I should act toward her now that we'd been intimate. Should I wave, or should I kiss her on the cheek? I decided to wave and move like I usually did. D'Asia flickered her tongue at me. I laughed, and we walked into the back office to get cash bins for our registers.

When Kianna wasn't looking, D'Asia slipped a piece of paper into my jeans and motioned for me to keep it quiet. Confused, I nodded and didn't think much of it.

The shift went by fast because the store was busy. I was finally able to take a break, so I went outside to get some fresh air. I reached in my pocket for gum and found the note D'Asia stuffed in there.

It read:

Hey, Kianna told me you wore her ass out. I want to experience it for myself. When and where can we do this? P.S. Don't tell Kianna.

This was new and exciting for me, but I wondered if it would be smart to take D'Asia up on her offer. I didn't want to hurt Kianna or ruin their friendship. I shook my head, feeling weak that I gave a shit about any of those things. Why should I care? I wasn't committed to either of them. The old me would've left the situation alone, but fuck that. I welcomed this new change.

Hugo, the store manager, asked all the cashiers if they could stay later for overtime, but only a few of us remained. Kianna went home on time while D'Asia, two of the new cashiers, and I stayed.

Once the midnight crew came in and relieved us, we all went to the back to count out our registers. D'Asia sat next to me. She whispered in my ear, "Meet me in the back near the bathrooms."

She got up and walked away. *Don't be a pussy, Ken.* I gathered my nerve and went to the back of the supermarket. The store was empty, and the back area was deserted at that time of night. Only George, the midnight manager, was on duty, and his lazy ass usually never left his office.

I didn't see her at first but finally noticed her in my peripherals poking her head out of the women's bathroom doorway. She waved for me to come to her. I quickly went to her, and she grabbed my hand and took me inside the handicapped stall.

I groped her tits as we kissed. She grabbed my dick and stroked me through my jeans. I quickly unbuckled her belt. She kicked off her shoes, and I slid her jeans and panties off. The only thoughts in my mind were to take her right here in this bathroom and gain another memorable experience. I sucked on her neck, held a breast in one hand, and slid my other hand down between her thighs. She shivered when I pushed my middle finger inside her. Her wetness saturated my finger as I worked it in and out of her and rubbed her clit with my thumb.

I pulled my hand away, reached for my wallet, and pulled out a condom. D'Asia took it from me and rolled it onto my dick. I lifted her and held her against the tile wall. She wrapped her legs around my back, and I rammed my length inside her, smiling at the sight of her eyes rolling back. We fucked loudly in the stall.

I put her down, and she bent over and put her hands against the wall. I grabbed her firmly by the waist and thrust deep inside her. She pushed back to match my rhythm. She came loudly, cursed, and put her hand on my chest to slow me down, but I wanted to come too. I kept thrusting. The sound of our moist bodies slapping against each other turned me on.

"Come for me, baby," she said.

I pulled her hair, and with one last, hard thrust, I released. *Thank God for condoms,* I thought to myself. I turned her around, and we laughed and panted as we leaned against the wall.

After a few minutes, we dressed and walked out of the bathroom.

"That was good. Kianna was right about you," D'Asia said.

"I aim to please."

I felt proud of myself. Bri made me feel like I was nothing, and now these new women were enjoying fucking me. I loved this feeling.

I put my house key in the door, opened it, and heard the sound of my mom crying. She sat on the living room couch in the dark. I wasn't surprised. Mom was always depressed when my pops ran off to be with his side pieces.

I was used to seeing her in that state, but I still felt sorry for her. I comforted her and cursed my dad. I remember once, when I was 10 years old, eavesdropping in the hallway during one of their arguments.

"James, come back here. Where are you going?"

My dad didn't answer. He just grabbed his bags, went into their bedroom, and shoved his clothing inside them.

"James, you gave me chlamydia. You're having sex with these women unprotected. What if you had given me AIDS?"

"Calm down. The doctor said you'd be fine once you start taking the medication."

"Fine? James, the doctor said it's been in me too long and made me sterile because of you. I'll never be able to have children again. Do you ever consider or care about how I feel when you cheat on me?"

"Oh well, so you can't have any more kids. Good. I didn't want the one we have now."

Hearing my dad say that only reinforced my hatred for him. Our family meant nothing to him. My mom sobbed.

"I wanted more kids. Why is it always what you want? Why do you always do this to me?"

He looked her in the eyes and said, "Because I can."

Mom begged him to stay, but he ignored her and kept packing. Out of desperation, she held on to his leg to stop him from leaving, but he forcefully kicked her to the floor.

"Please, don't leave me," she cried.

He didn't look back or show remorse. He left her weeping on the cold, living room floor. I could never forgive him for the shit he put us through.

As the years went by, he never changed. He didn't give a shit about anything going on in my life. He didn't care that my mom was an emotional wreck. His family was never a priority for him.

My mom blowing her nose brought me back to the present.

"Why do you always let him do this to you?" I asked her.

She stared at the carpet. "I . . . I . . . love him. I don't know why I put up with it. There are times when I hate him and wish he'd stay away for good, but when he comes back to me, all the anger goes away, and I fall for him all over again."

I figured it was just something I couldn't understand unless I were in that situation.

"I hate seeing you cry over him. That's not love. If he loved you, he wouldn't stress you out like this."

Bookwise, my mom's a smart woman. She had her doctorate in education and received numerous commendations for teaching, but my father's stress had its effects on her. When he left, she rarely cleaned the house. She'd leave stacks of old newspapers and self-improvement books all over the place, cluttering the house almost hoarderlike. Mom was always religious, but whenever my father would leave, she'd drown herself in it. For some reason, she believed if she prayed hard enough, God would bring him back to her. I hated that my dad had that effect on her. I hated him. I spent my life trying not to be anything like him. He was fat. I was in shape. He couldn't keep a job. I've been working since I was 15. The list went on and on.

While listening to my mom vent, I ended up telling her about my breakup with Bri.

"I'm sorry, Kenny. I thought she was a good girl. Don't worry. You'll find the right one."

I didn't respond to that. I kissed her on the forehead, said good night, and went to bed. I had no intention of finding "the right one," at least not anymore, but she didn't need to know that.

Chapter Three

Transformation

The weekend was here, and my boys Adam and Perry were chilling in my room while I finished getting ready. We met in junior high, playing on the basketball team together, and have been tight ever since.

Adam was a lean six foot with a mocha complexion. He wore designer frames for his glasses and sported an Afro. Perry was five foot ten. He had deep brown skin and a stocky build.

I told them all the details of my breakup with Bri and the adventures I'd been having since then.

"I never said shit because you were so sprung on her, but I didn't like that bitch. I don't know, but I always got a sneaky vibe from her," Perry said.

"I cosign on that," Adam added.

"I know you're in your feelings right now, but look at all the new ass you've been getting. Keep doing your thing. Soon, she won't even be an afterthought," Perry said.

Adam rolled his eyes. "Don't listen to this fool. Instead of fucking around, you should try finding everything you want in one girl. Perry's right, though. I always got a shady vibe from Bri too."

That annoyed me. Everyone else saw Bri for the snake she was, but I was oblivious to see what was happening right in front of my fucking face.

I let those thoughts go and focused on the night at hand. Since I wasn't sure if Rachel was bringing another girl besides Kelly, I told my boys that Rachel was off-limits, and they could battle over Kelly. They were cool about the friendly competition and were up for the challenge.

"I'll drive. Yo, Adam, may the best man win, brother," Perry said with confidence.

Adam laughed, and they fist-bumped.

My car was run-down and always in and out of the shop. I had no problems letting Perry drive since he had an X5 BMW. His pops owned his own construction company, so Perry was well-off.

We drove past campus to the softball house. The softball team had a massive place off campus that most of the team lived in. I guess the coach thought it was easier to watch them that way, but everyone knew the softball house was notorious for throwing the wildest and craziest parties.

We parked, and I rang the doorbell. One of the girls from the team answered the door wearing a white T-shirt and flannel pajama bottoms.

"Who you?" she asked.

"Hey, I'm Ken. I'm here for Rachel," I said.

"Hold on."

She left the door open, shouted up the stairs, then walked away. I looked inside, and Rachel walked down the stairs dressed to kill, wearing a lacy, white blouse and dark, tight, blue jeans.

"Hey, Kenny, come in. Kelly is just finishing up getting ready. She should be down in a few. Hang out in the living room and watch TV with some of the girls. Are these your friends?"

I nodded and introduced them.

"These are my boys, Perry and Adam."

"It's nice to meet you guys. Do y'all want something to drink?"

We all said no.

"Well, I'm going to hurry Kelly's ass up so we can go. Make yourselves at home."

Rachel went back upstairs while we went into the living room. Perry walked in and quickly introduced himself to the girls in there. They smiled, and he turned on the charm. Adam was laid-back and more of a "go with the flow" type dude. He wasn't aggressive when it came to women, which is why he didn't date much. Perry, on the other hand, was fearless. He used his humor, wit, and confidence to draw in women. He was never intimidated and didn't care how pretty or popular they were. If he thought they were hot, he'd spit game.

Rachel and Kelly came down into the living room to meet us. Perry and Adam couldn't keep their eyes off Kelly's huge tits. She had on a low-cut black blouse and form-fitting Capris that showed off her thick, full-figured frame.

We left the house and made our way to Perry's car. Kelly sat next to him in the front. Adam, Rachel, and I sat in the back. Since we wanted to talk, get to know each other, and didn't feel like doing the whole club scene, we decided to go to Strike in New Hyde Park because we figured we could eat, drink, bowl, and do a little of everything there. On the way, we laughed at corny jokes and sang Sir Mix-a Lot's "Baby Got Back" at the top of our lungs.

Walking into Strike, I held Rachel's hand, and I was curious to see if I could get her to be my newest conquest. I was so busy trying to put the charm on her that I didn't notice Kelly come to my other side. She grabbed my left hand and smiled at me. I looked back at Perry and Adam. They waved at me to go on.

We started with bowling, and Rachel went first. By her form, you could tell she wasn't new to the game. She hit a strike on her first try.

"Good throw, bitch," Kelly said.

"You jealous, huh?" Rachel laughed.

Perry bowled on our high school team, so there was no question he'd have a good game. He followed with a strike of his own.

It was my turn.

"Whew, look at that ass," Rachel shouted.

I laughed, and when I looked behind, Kelly winked at me. I knocked down seven pins, and while getting my ball, Kelly grabbed my ass.

"Rachel and I share everything," she said.

I didn't know what to think of that. I looked at Rachel, and she nodded in approval.

Perry talked to Kelly for a while but lost interest once a group of girls wearing practically nothing walked in. He dropped his conversation with her and went to them. Adam talked to her, and I thought there was a connection there, but that ended as soon as she took out a cigarette. Adam hated girls who smoked. I did too, but I could put up with it. For Adam, it was a deal breaker.

Perry hit it off with the group of girls who had arrived earlier and convinced Adam to be his wingman, which left me alone with Rachel and Kelly. While joking and laughing, Kelly grabbed my face and kissed me. Rachel kissed me immediately after, and then they kissed each other.

The girls rubbed my dick through my jeans while I felt their tits. We explored each other's bodies in the open. Adam looked over at us and nudged Perry.

"That's my boy," Perry yelled.

We didn't pay him any mind. We just kept doing what we were doing.

Perry drove us back to the softball house. He and Adam made plans to meet up with the girls from Strike after dropping Rachel and Kelly home.

"Since we're having a good time, and your boys have their plans, why don't you spend the night here? I can get one of my teammates to drop you home in the morning," Rachel said. She leaned in close and said. "If you stay, I'll make it worth your while."

"That sounds like a great idea," Perry answered for me.

Perry and I looked at each other and laughed.

Rachel searched in her purse for her keys while Kelly held my hand.

"Don't do anything I wouldn't do," Adam said.

We all laughed. Perry and Adam drove off, and the girls and I went inside the house. Kelly ran upstairs before Rachel and me. I was surprised at myself. I thought being in this situation, I'd be tense or afraid, but I was excited.

Rachel led the way to her room, and Kelly was already undressed, sitting on her bed. Rachel started taking off her clothes.

"I told you, Rachel and I like to share everything."

"Lucky me," I said as I stripped.

They laughed.

Rachel said, "Yup, lucky you."

We all sat on the bed naked.

"We don't believe in anyone being left out, so we all have to be involved at all times when we do this. Agreed?" Rachel asked.

"Agreed," I said, smiling.

Kelly stroked my dick while Rachel and I kissed hungrily. I stopped kissing Rachel and fingered Kelly. She moaned, smiled, and kissed Rachel. Rachel put her soft, dainty hands on my chest and pushed me down. Kelly handed her a condom, and she swiftly put it on me and positioned herself on top to ride me. Rachel gasped, and her ass clenched when she put my hardness inside her. She started a slow grind. Kelly crawled over to my face and positioned her body so I could eat her out. Rachel increased the speed of her riding. They moaned in unison. Rachel wailed and shivered on top of me. She rested motionlessly on me until her orgasm finished blasting through her. Kelly moved Rachel off me, kissed her, and we switched positions.

"I want to feel you inside of me now," Kelly said.

Rachel spread her legs, and Kelly ate her out while I entered Kelly from behind. She pulled her mouth off Rachel's clit and gasped. Rachel quickly pulled Kelly's hair to bring her back. I stroked and stroked and stroked. Kelly vigorously shook her head. I ran my fingers down her back and felt the shiver run down her spine. Kelly's vagina spasmed, and I felt it squeezing tightly around my dick while she came. I pulled out of her. Kelly turned around and pulled the condom off me. She went down on me eagerly. Rachel crawled under her. Kelly opened her legs wider so that Rachel could eat her out. Rachel fingered, slurped, sucked, and licked Kelly thoroughly like she was a porn star. The stimulation from Kelly going down on me, watching Rachel going down on her, and just being in this situation made my orgasm sneak up on me.

"Oh shit," I said, lying there, panting.

We spent the rest of the night touching and pleasing each other. When it was all over, I lay in the bed with both of them nuzzled comfortably on my chest. I felt like the king of the world.

I didn't know it then, but my wild threesome with Rachel and Kelly changed my college reputation forever. By Monday, the word was all over campus about the deed.

Antoine, a classmate in my business math class, walked up to me.

"Yo, Ken, I gotta talk to you about something, bro," he said.

"What's up?" I asked.

"Everybody is saying you banged out Rachel and Kelly. You know Rachel is Owen's girl, right?"

"Shit. Are you serious?"

I had no idea she was with him. Owen and Antoine played on the baseball team, so I knew I needed to tread lightly in the situation. I didn't need a whole bunch of drama with the entire team.

"Yeah, bro, I don't know how serious they are, but I know that's his girl. If I were you, I'd talk to him."

I met Owen at the beginning of freshman year when people kept mistaking us for each other. Both of us wanted to see if the resemblance was real or if everyone was exaggerating, but we both admitted we did look very similar. Since knowing him, we'd been cordial and hung out a few times, but we weren't close enough to be called good friends. For as long as I've known him, he never mentioned going out with Rachel and vice versa, but I needed to let him know I had no idea they had a relationship.

I went to the gym on campus and found him working out there.

"What's up, Owen?" I said.

A couple of his teammates laughed and said something under their breaths. I tried to read his face as he walked over to me. He didn't look angry at all.

"What's up, Ken?"

"I'm good. I need to clear something up, though. Is Rachel your girl?"

He laughed. "Ken, relax, man. I know about you and Rachel. I'm not mad at you, brother. I do my thing too. I don't take things with her seriously. She's the one that wanted to give us a title. I use her as a steady fuck buddy, and that's it. So, no worries, man, I have no beef with you."

"All right, cool. I didn't want you to think I purposely did that shit."

"Yeah, we kept things on the low, so there was no way you would've known. Rachel's spiteful ass probably fucked you to get me jealous, but little does she know I was fucking one of her teammates that same night," Owen laughed.

We changed the topic and made small talk. I was convinced that he didn't give a shit about her, or he was a great actor because he showed no signs of giving a shit about me sleeping with her. I admired that.

I've always been soft and had strong feelings for any girl I slept with in the past, but she was nothing to him. I knew that to prevent myself from getting hurt, I needed to learn to detach my feelings too.

After going to my classes, I drove to work. My manager, Hugo, was standing by the sign-in clock and asked me to come to the back office.

"Have a seat," Hugo said.

He looked serious, and I didn't know what this was all about. He looked at me skeptically and said, "There have been rumors that you've been intimate with one of your coworkers here in the store. As you know, that type of action can lead to termination. George and I have reviewed the security tapes from the night of the alleged incident, and it showed you and one of your coworkers going into the women's bathroom for a substantial amount of time. My question to you is, why were you in the women's bathroom? Before you answer, understand I have already talked to D'Asia, and I have a statement from her."

Shit. He had already talked to D'Asia, so I didn't know if I should lie or tell the truth. He said that being intimate in the workplace could lead to termination. I needed my job, so I went with lying. I hoped I could get some sympathy from him.

"Hugo, my girlfriend broke up with me recently, and I've been depressed. D'Asia told me she liked me, and I was vulnerable. We didn't want people to recognize us making out in the parking lot, so we thought the bathroom would be secluded enough. No sex, though. I'm sorry. I just had a rough couple of weeks."

Hugo looked me dead in the eyes and leaned back in his big chair behind his desk. "I understand that you may have had a rough couple of weeks, but D'Asia admitted she had sex with you in the bathroom in her statement."

I was stunned and speechless, but I guess my face said it all.

"With that being said, Ken, I'm going to have to let you go. I think you're a good guy and a competent employee, but I have to set an example that this type of behavior will not be tolerated here."

"I know. Just out of curiosity, did you hear people openly talking about it or something?"

Hugo took a long, deep breath and sighed. "No. Another employee approached George and me about it and insisted that we look at the cameras from that day. We investigated the incident and saw the two of you enter the bathroom. Once we confronted D'Asia, she told us about the incident. She was terminated today as well, so I don't want you to think we were only targeting you."

"I understand. Well, thanks for talking to me privately."

I shook his hand and then punched my time card out. I said goodbye to a couple of people I befriended while working there, and as I headed for the door, I saw Kianna on a register. When the lady she was helping looked down to bag her groceries, Kianna gave me the finger. I knew she probably tipped Hugo and George about D'Asia and me and got me fired out of spite. I didn't care about her enough to lose sleep over the end of whatever you'd call what we had, but I was mad that she caused me to lose my job. I needed to work to help pay for my tuition, books, and car.

I remembered the bookstore and library on campus were hiring. I knew I wouldn't get a lot of hours from either one, but with the combined wages from both jobs, I'd be able to stay afloat. I lucked out and got both jobs. The managers knew each other and created a schedule for me that worked around my classes.

I lost my friendship with Kianna, but I didn't care. Since D'Asia knew what was coming and said nothing to warn me, I was done with her too. Despite everything that happened, I was in a good place mentally. I gained experience being intimate with both of them and found new jobs on campus. Working on campus would be advantageous because I wouldn't have to travel back and forth for work and school. Most importantly, I had new ways to meet women on campus. It was time to stop being the nice guy and start being a man.

My threesome with Rachel and Kelly set off a chain reaction. Once they bragged about my performance in the sack, other girls from their team and around campus wanted to see if the hype was real and experience me for themselves. It wasn't long before I slept with almost half the team.

I dated all types of women. I didn't care what color, race, or size they were. I fucked them all. If they were into music, movies, or books, I used what I learned from all the women I slept with before them and applied those things to become whatever type of guy the next one wanted. Using my book and street smarts made seducing them easier. I paid attention to all their likes—both sexual and intellectual—and used that knowledge to make myself more appealing.

In high school, I had many girls who put me in the friend zone and thought it was "so cute" how I remembered little details about them that every guy they dated didn't give a shit about. Back then, whenever a woman I liked talked about her flaws, I always made them feel positive by uplifting them and complimenting their strengths. Now, I turned that talent into strength to get them to spread their legs for me.

Most guys tried to impress women with material things, but the real power came from mental stimulation and listening. By showing women that I paid attention, cared about what they said, and understood them, I was golden. Once I put it in their hearts and minds that I was different, that I'd treat them better than any other guy in their past did, everything else fell into place.

I still saw Rachel and Kelly now and then, but I was so busy fucking women around campus that my relationship with them eventually phased itself out. Being a novelty with women around campus felt good. I shared all of my adventures with my friends. Perry encouraged it. Adam thought I needed to stop and find a new girlfriend. Ray and Lucy felt I was going through a selfish rebounding phase and figured I'd eventually stop my man-whoring ways and settle down with a nice girl, but I knew that wasn't happening anytime soon.

I thought Lucy would be disgusted with me, but surprisingly, she understood. When I asked her why she was so understanding with what I was doing, she said, "I know you. Even though you're acting out right now, this isn't who you are. You're hurt. It's only natural that you'd do things like this to stop the pain, but eventually, you'll see that until you chill out and take the time to really heal, no number of women you sleep with will fill that void."

I appreciated her words of wisdom, and I was glad she didn't see me as a total asshole. Deep down, I knew she was right, but I didn't want to admit it. I slept with more than enough women to get over Bri, but every time the thought crept back into my head of her fucking David behind my back, I needed another random woman to fuck the pain away. It was only a temporary fix, though. For some reason, I couldn't let that memory go.

Chapter Four

Unleashed

It was the start of a brand-new week. I walked to my car, put my books on the passenger seat, and put the key in the ignition to head out to my first-morning class. My damn car wouldn't start. I tried over and over, and it still wouldn't crank over. Adam was already at his college, and Ray was at work. I dialed Perry's number and hoped he didn't leave his house already to go to his classes.

"Yo," he answered.

"Did you leave your house yet?"

"Nah, not yet. Why? What's up?"

I let him know what was up with my car.

"You seriously need to junk that shit. Give me ten minutes. I'll drop you off."

As soon as he pulled up, I rushed to the car. I was already late. We talked the whole way there about women and relationships.

"So, Adam thinks I'm nuts and need to stop fucking around and find one steady girl."

"Man, he doesn't know what he's talking about. He can't even find the right girl for himself. You're taking advice from a guy that gets no pussy? It's all about the rule of two."

"The rule of what?"

"You heard me, the rule of two. Since you're a little slow this morning, I'll explain it to you. Men and women want the same two things—money and sex—but men and women prioritize these things differently. Men work to make more money to buy nice clothes, cars, apartments, and houses. We take women to nice places and buy them expensive gifts for one purpose—sex. Women have sex with these men to secure a good future. Women want nice things in life and a man who can give them those things. So while we're working on getting that ass, they're working their ass to find that right guy for security. Again, it all comes down to those two things—money and sex. We both work what we have to get what we want. Everyone uses everyone."

His analogy immediately made me think of Bri, and I realized there was some truth to what he was saying, but I didn't want my thoughts about her to further affect my shitty morning, so I shook my head, laughed it off, and said, "You're a fool."

He laughed. "It sounds blunt, but it's the truth. At some point, we'll all use somebody, and we'll all be used by somebody."

"So are you saying women don't care about sex, that they just want money?"

"Not at all—they care about sex almost as much as we do, but it's not their main priority. Women love sex, especially when it's with me."

I rolled my eyes.

"So you don't believe there's a woman out there for you who legitimately just loves you for you and doesn't want anything material?"

"If a woman like that exists, and I highly doubt it, I'd marry her."

"What do you call what Ray and Lucy have?"

"A fucking miracle."

We laughed hard at that.

He dropped me off at my school, and I thanked him again for the knowledge and the ride. Then I rushed inside to start my day.

The day felt overly long. Between working my two jobs and going to classes in the morning and evening, I was exhausted.

I sat in my business ethics course, and it felt like it would never end. The professor broke the class into two groups, and I was paired up with a woman named Gina. The exercise was about office romance. One of us had to be pro and the other con. I chose to be the latter. We got to know each other before starting our assignment. I found out she also lived in Freeport and was divorced with three children after fifteen years of marriage. We shared laughs about the neighborhood before working on our debate. We put on a heated discussion, which had the class cheering and laughing. She won the debate with her strong, heartfelt arguments, and I had to admit her passion for the topic turned me on a little. She was a very attractive 45-year-old with long, golden-brown hair that matched her complexion. She had a full figure and a no-nonsense attitude. I liked that.

When class ended, everyone was still talking about how good our debate was. I picked up my things and headed for the bus stop. I hated taking the bus, but when your car is DOA in your driveway, what choice do you have?

I was waiting for the bus, and a black Q35 Infiniti with tinted windows pulled up. I figured it was someone asking for directions, but when the windows rolled down, I saw it was Gina.

"Do you need a ride? I'm headed to Freeport anyway. I can take you home if you want."

I didn't hesitate to take her up on the offer. "Hell yeah."

"Hop in. You can put your bag in the trunk."

"Thanks."

"No problem. Hey, I'm a little hungry. Do you mind if we stop by a diner for a quick bite to eat?"

"I don't care. You're my ride. I'm in no rush to go home. We can go anywhere you want."

"Good."

We went to the Imperial Diner in Freeport. We ate and talked about school, relationships, and life in general. She told me all about her job as a secretary at Optimum cable near campus, her love of Egyptian culture, and how her dream was to visit the pyramids someday. Most importantly, she told me about her ex-husband, who belittled her and cheated on her throughout their marriage. I sympathized with her, comforted her, and told her a little about my relationship with Bri. Through experience, I'd learned that women appreciate a guy who could admit he'd been hurt and show emotion—though only to a certain degree. A woman still wanted a man to be a man. He couldn't be too soft, or she wouldn't find him attractive. She'd only pity him. A woman would rarely fuck a man she pitied. My high school life taught me that much.

I told her just enough to let her see I understood what it felt like to have your reality and trust betrayed.

I let her do most of the talking. I listened, making sure she saw that she had my full attention and interest in the conversation. Then we stopped sharing our sad stories and talked about some of the people in our class.

"I like you, Ken. You have an old soul."

"Thanks. I like you too."

"Talking to you today, I feel like I've known you for years."

"I know. We have a lot in common."

"You know, I work close to campus. Since your car is acting up, I can drive you to school in the mornings and take you home at night since your last class is with me."

"Wow, thanks. I'd really appreciate that."

I didn't know what was wrong with my car or how much it would cost to fix it. It would be at least another month until I could muster up enough money to get it repaired, so getting a ride from her to and from school would be a blessing.

While walking to her car, Gina stopped me and gave me a soft kiss on the lips. "I don't have a lot of people I can vent to. You really listened to me tonight, which is a rare find because, in my experience, most men usually only want to talk about themselves, but you let me open up to you. I like that. Do you mind if we go to the Nautical Mile and talk a little more?"

The Nautical Mile was a mile-long strip of bars and nice restaurants in Freeport. I had nothing else to do, and it wasn't too late, so I agreed. Besides, I could tell Gina was feeling me, and I wanted to see how far we'd go that night.

We drove to the end of the strip and faced the water. It was secluded, and our talking led to kissing. I knew what that was about. I'd been in her position before. She was vulnerable and upset with her ex-husband. She needed validation, someone to show her she was still attractive and desirable. I felt somewhat guilty because I took advantage of her vulnerability, but that feeling quickly went away. My conscience was becoming nonexistent.

We moved to the backseat of her car. She climbed on top of me and kissed me all over. I squeezed her firm ass. She rubbed her hands all over my chest and down to my crotch. She unzipped my pants and pulled out my dick. Then she quickly pulled down her pants and got a condom out of the armrest storage compartment. She stroked my hardness and gently put the condom on me.

In the past, I would've felt weird being in a situation like that, but I felt nothing now. I stayed calm and let everything take its course. Gina eased down on top of my hardness and did a slow ride. She kissed me. The look on her face was so eager and wanting. I could tell by that look and the way she was riding me, she didn't want to feel like we were just fucking. Right now, she wanted that feeling of being made love to, even if it was only temporary.

I moved my hips up and down as she rocked on top of me. Our bodies were in sync. I opened her shirt, unhooked her bra, and pulled out her breasts. I pushed them together, licked all over her areolas, and sucked on her nipples. Her soft moans let me know she was enjoying it.

She sped up her rhythm and held me close as she was about to come. She put her head on my chest and moaned loudly. When that feeling of complete ecstasy subsided, she smiled and kissed me. She got off me and removed the condom. She went down on me, but her mood changed. She was sucking on me like she was paying her husband back for all the women he ever cheated on her with. The increased swiftness was driving me wild.

"Shit, Gina, I'm close," I moaned.

She ignored me and kept her rhythm going until I exploded down her throat.

We lay in her backseat, half-naked and winded.

"I hope you don't think less of me for this. I'm—" I stopped her by rubbing her hand.

"You don't have to say anything. I understand. I don't think negatively of you at all."

She looked relieved. "Thanks."

I held her, and we sat in comfortable silence. I felt our connection was more of an emotional release for her than just lust. We got dressed, talked, and she took me home. I was irritated instantly at the sight of my dad's champagne Cadillac Coupe DeVille parked in the driveway.

Gina told me she'd be there bright and early in the morning to pick me up. We kissed and said our goodbyes.

I walked inside my house and climbed the stairs hearing my mother crying and my parents arguing. Their bedroom door was shut, but I heard them bickering.

"This is bullshit, James. You always do this shit to me, and I'm sick of it," my mother shouted.

"Baby, you know you're the only one for me. I fuck other women from time to time, but I only have one family, and that's with you. There's a difference between lust and love. I fuck them, but I make love to you. I can't help what's in my nature. I want you to understand that I love you."

He laid his whack game down thick. As many bullshit lines that I've said to women to get them in bed, I never used the "I love you" card. To me, saying that was a dangerous way to play with someone's emotions. I knew my mom was angry, but I also knew they'd be back together by morning, and things would go right back to the way they were. My eventful night ended with me going to sleep to the sound of my mom crying.

Things with Gina were working out perfectly. She wasn't too clingy or demanding, and she never got jealous if she saw me talking to other women. She knew what our arrangement was, and she was okay with it because she didn't want a commitment either.

We spent a lot of time together after our evening class, and our sex was always passionate. She taught me what she liked as far as massages, foreplay, and other things that added to intimacy.

Before I met her, I usually tried to fuck women's brains out, but Gina liked variety and explained its importance to me. Sometimes, she'd like it slow, romantic, and passionate. Other times, she'd like it hardcore and rough. Being with her helped me to become a more well-rounded, seasoned lover. When I wasn't with Gina, I found another girl that sparked my interest—Tiffani Barrett.

Tiffani was one of the few girls I hadn't slept with from the softball team. She had a smooth, caramel complexion and a hearty booty. A lot of women tried to pull off short hair and failed, but it worked for Tiffani.

I met Tiffani in my human anatomy class. We joked around in class all the time, and I realized I wasn't pretending to be what I thought she liked. I was just being myself. She knew about my reputation around campus and never judged me. Despite knowing everything, she still hung out with me.

Every guy on campus who approached her had been shut down. She had a man back home in Seattle and was faithful to him. I admired that.

At first, I wanted to bed Tiffani because it would've made my legend around campus even greater, but after getting to know her, I found myself falling for her. We became close friends. I even introduced her to my mother.

"Oh my God, is this Kenny?" Tiffani asked while holding my baby picture album.

"Yup, that's him," my mother said with pride.

"Aww, look at that little butt," Tiffani teased.

"Does she have to look at these old pictures?" I groaned.

"Yes," they said in unison.

They continued to laugh at my old photos and embarrass me.

"Can I help you with dinner, Mrs. Ferguson?" Tiffani asked.

"Of course, girl. I'm making macaroni and cheese, ribs, and collard greens."

"Oh my God, I can't wait. I'm gotta come here to eat more often."

My mom smiled. "I'd like that."

They hit it off immediately and hung out regularly on their own. I liked that because my mom didn't have many friends.

Tiffani was smart, funny, athletic, and sexy, but she had a boyfriend. As always, anything I wanted ever had a fucking catch to it.

"Hurry up, man," Adam yelled at Perry.

Perry ignored him and continued to trim his beard in his bathroom. Perry never left the house until his hair and beard were on point.

"Chill out. It takes time to look this good," Perry replied.

"Oh, shut up," Adam said.

We sat in Perry's bedroom, getting ready to go to a campus party at Adam's school, Molloy College. Adam was in a rush to get to the party because some girl from one of his classes was going to be there, and according to him, she was "the one."

Adam was always looking for that one woman to be his queen and never dated more than one at a time. He got his heart broken a lot whenever things didn't work out in the past, but he was adamant about dating his way.

He paced around Perry's room and started doing Tai Chi. That always made me laugh because whenever Adam was nervous or bored, he would randomly do Tai Chi in the middle of nowhere—sometimes even in public. Perry peeked out of the bathroom and saw him.

"Tell Bruce Leroy to cut that shit out. I'll be out in a minute," he said.

Perry finally got out of the bathroom. We looked in the mirror, and we were dressed to impress.

"Brothas, we look good," Perry said.

Adam and I nodded.

"Now, let's get to this party. I made the women wait for my presence long enough."

We laughed, and Adam drove.

The party was cool. The food was great, and the DJ was on point with his playlist. He was all about having everyone out of their seats and on the dance floor.

Scanning the room, we noticed there were a lot of pretty women around. We talked to girls we thought were hot and interesting and laughed amongst ourselves.

Adam and Perry found girls to dance with, but I decided to sit one out and get something to drink. I left the dance floor, and a pretty Hispanic girl walked up to me.

"Hey," she said.

"How are you doing tonight?"

"Good."

"I'm Ken. What's your name?"

"Liza. Look, my friend is really shy, and she's been checking you out all night. Can you go over to that table over there and talk to her? She's nice."

She pointed, and I saw a plain-looking blond girl hiding her face and smiling. She had dark brown eyes, wide hips, and a round ass. She wasn't pretty, but she wasn't ugly either. She was attractive enough where my decision wasn't a hard no.

"Sure," I said.

I walked over to the girl. I wasn't interested, but I wasn't going to be rude.

"Hi. I'm Ken. How are you doing?"

"I'm Heather." She looked nervous and embarrassed.

"Would you do me the pleasure of dancing with me, Heather?"

"I'd love to."

We walked to the dance floor, and like clockwork, the DJ put something slow on.

"This is a slow jam for all the couples out there. If you're single, grab someone new and get on the dance floor," the DJ announced.

I didn't let it stress me. I grabbed her by the waist and pulled her close to me. Heather smiled back at her friends. My hands drifted past her waist and held on to her round ass. She smiled, leaned her head against my chest, and looked so comfortable being in my arms. We danced to a couple of songs, and I was impressed. She had good rhythm.

"Wow, are you a professional dancer or something?" I asked.

She laughed. "No, but I've taken dance lessons since I was 5. It's one of my hobbies."

We walked back to the table with her friends, talked, and got to know each other better. Like Adam, she was studying computer science. She was smart and nerdy but in a cute way. There was an innocence about her, a pleasantness that attracted me to her.

We exchanged numbers. I didn't know if I'd ever call her, but she was nice.

Perry was getting another girl's number. As expected, Adam focused on one girl all night, but what shocked us all was witnessing him tongue down the girl he was with. He always took things slow, so seeing such a bold move from him completely surprised Perry and me.

Later, we walked to Adam's car and talked about the night.

"I got a few prospects tonight. There was a lot of talent out there," Perry said.

"That girl I met was nice," I added.

"She was a moped," Perry replied.

"A moped?"

"Yeah, she's fun and nice to ride, but you don't want your friends to see you with her."

We laughed.

"Looks fade, brother. The right woman needs to have more than looks."

"I think I found my queen, guys," Adam said.

"Oh Jesus, every time you meet a girl, you think you're in love or that she's your queen. You need to chill with that shit," Perry told him.

"You didn't meet her, man. She's perfect. She goes to school, she's close with her family, and she goes to church. She's everything I'm looking for in an ebony queen."

Perry and I snickered.

"I have to say, Perry is right on this one. You have to stop falling for every girl you meet."

"I know I got to work on that, but this one is different."

"You say that about *all* of them," Perry stated.

We talked more about the party and hung out at Perry's house for a little. Afterward, Adam drove me home. I could see in his eyes he was going to fall hard for this girl. I just hoped everything would work out.

The next morning, I met up with Gina, and we got our usual room at the Freeport Motor Inn. Our grunts and moans gave everyone in earshot an early wake-up call.

Afterward, we got lunch but cut short our time together because she had to run some errands. We went our separate ways and made plans for another romp later during the week.

I called Tiffani, and we met up at the mall. We looked in a few stores, she did a little shopping, but she had to head back to campus because she had a paper to do that was due Monday.

It was only 6:00 p.m., so it was still pretty early, and I was bored. I decided to call Heather to see if she was doing anything. I could hear the excitement in her voice over the phone when I told her to meet me in Wantagh at The Cup. The Cup was a quaint place with pastries and different types of coffees and teas.

I got out and leaned against my car so she could see me when she got there. She looked ecstatic to see me as she pulled up in the spot next to mine.

As soon as she got out of her car, we hugged, and she gave me a peck on the lips that caught me off guard. We walked inside and got a table. I asked her the usual date questions.

"So, you're originally from Connecticut?"

"Yeah, my parents wanted to be closer to their families here in New York, so they got jobs at Winthrop Hospital."

"What do your parents do?"

"They're both orthopedic surgeons. When I was younger, they pressured me to be a doctor, but I was more into computers."

"Damn, that must've pissed them off."

"Yeah, but I eventually want to create my own medical software firm that makes applications for hospitals. Sort of like a consolation prize for them."

We laughed.

"So, what do you do for fun?" I asked.

"Well, you already know I love programming. I love to dance, read, and I'm really into movies. I'm a big movie buff."

"Me too."

"When you have free time, maybe you can hang out at my house, and we can watch our favorite movies together."

"I have no problem with that," I smiled.

Heather couldn't take her eyes off me, but I played it cool. Her body language, facial expressions, and the little things she said while flirting let me know I could probably have her that night, but I decided to take it slow with her. She was genuinely nice, and I didn't feel like preying on her just yet.

Over the next few weeks, Heather and I went to different museums, movies, and parks together. I liked her because I could be nerdy around her, and I didn't feel like I had to simplify things when I talked to her, which was a big plus. My intellectual side was pleased. She kept me mentally aroused, and that added to her appeal. I could tell she didn't have much experience sexually, but what she lacked in experience she made up for in willingness. She tried everything in her power to please me.

The first time we had sex was on a Saturday afternoon. Heather invited me to her parents' house while they were away for the weekend.

"So, what do you want to do today?" I asked.

"You," she said, getting right to the point.

She held my hand and took me to her bedroom. Her bedroom was so neat that it looked like a hotel room. All of the furniture in her bedroom was made out of mahogany and looked expensive. Her hands were shaking. I didn't know if it was out of nervousness or excitement.

We undressed each other. Heather got down on her knees, her hands still shaking, and grabbed my dick. She took a deep breath and eased my erection into her mouth. She suckled on it and licked all over the sides and head. She worked her throat muscles to try to take me in whole.

Heather looked at my face to search for my approval. My eyes rolled back as she went back to deep-throating me. I lightly caressed her face to let her know I had enough and wanted to be inside her. I picked her up off her knees and placed her on the bed. Then I quickly rolled on a condom, positioned her knees to her breasts, and entered her. She winced and moaned. She was tight, which was great for me, but I knew I'd have to break her off slow until she got used to me. I stroked her with a moderate pace, each time trying to get more of my dick inside her.

"Oh my God . . . You're so deep . . . so deep," Heather moaned.

I held under her knees, spread her legs, and continued stroking her. Heather buried her face in my chest. Her breathing was so hard it sounded like she was hyperventilating. I pulled her face from my chest so I could watch the expression of both pain and pleasure across it. Her face was flushed.

"You feel so good . . . so fucking good," she said.

Her mouth formed the letter O. Spasms rushed through her, and her eyes were glazed over. She clenched her teeth—that beautiful face of a woman coming surfaced. I pulled out of her, and remnants of her orgasm continued to move through her as she squirmed on the bed.

She positioned herself to ride me. Since she didn't have much experience with that, we didn't stay in that position long.

Surprisingly, she liked it hard. I thought she'd be prissy and want it slow and romantic, but she liked it rough and loved talking dirty.

As time went by, I could see Heather was catching feelings. She'd continuously buy me expensive gifts and do anything and everything I asked—financially or sexually. To save her from eventual heartbreak, I told her about Brianna, so she understood I was not looking for a relationship any time soon.

"Ken, I get it. Brianna hurt you. I know you don't want to open yourself up and trust another woman like that again, but I'd never do that to you. I've dated other guys before, and none of them made me feel the way you do. I don't want anyone else. I only want you, and if I have to wait until you finally trust me enough to commit, I'll do that."

While that sounded nice, and I loved that she was so loyal, she couldn't say I didn't warn her.

"I already know I got this. You should give up now before you embarrass yourself," Perry said confidently.

"I'm trying to be a better Christian, so I won't curse you out, but you know where you can go," Adam said.

We laughed.

We were on our way to Roosevelt Field Mall, and Perry and Adam were debating who was better at picking up women in public. I seriously didn't feel like playing, but peer pressure got the best of me. The winner would be treated to the movies and dinner by the losers, and I planned on putting in as little effort as possible.

As a challenge, we each had an hour to go around the mall, talk to as many women as possible, and get their numbers. We walked around the mall, and Perry went first. There was a beautiful Hispanic girl near the food court—long, black hair, nice firm ass—I knew she'd be a challenge, but I also knew Perry was up for it.

"Excuse me, miss . . . my name is . . ."

"Save it," the girl said.

"Oh, that was cold-blooded," Adam laughed.

Perry rolled his eyes and shrugged. He never cared if he didn't get the girl he hit on. Perry felt any woman he dated benefited from being with him and never the other way around. He didn't care how pretty they were or who they were. If they didn't want him, it was their loss. I admired that.

Next was Adam's turn. He found a cute brown-skinned girl that looked like Nia Long. He walked over to her with a confident stride and said, "Excuse me, miss . . . Do you have the time?"

The girl laughed in his face and pointed to the watch on his arm. Perry laughed at Adam's failure. The girl kept laughing and walked away. It was my turn. I saw two women sitting at a table and introduced myself. They both smiled but told me they had boyfriends. I didn't care. I didn't even feel like playing this stupid game.

There were only five minutes left. None of us had any numbers yet. It was my turn again. I saw a nice, brown-skinned girl with hazel eyes and a killer body. Even though she was gorgeous, I decided I still wouldn't put much effort into trying to get her number. I walked up to her slowly and put on a corny smile. She immediately spotted me and chuckled as if she knew I was about to say something stupid. Reaching her, I said, "Excuse me, miss . . . Did you know that racecar spelled backward is racecar?"

She looked puzzled as if she had to think about it and then started hysterically laughing. I laughed too.

"I'm just kidding, but seriously, my name is Ken. I just wanted to know if there was anyone in your life that would mind if I called you some time to get to know you?"

"No, I don't have anyone that would mind. I'm Denise. I didn't expect you to try to pick me up with that line," she laughed.

"I wanted to be spontaneous and different."

"Well, you definitely were."

I reached in my pocket and pulled out my cell phone. She grabbed it from me and put her number into my contacts.

Perry's and Adam's faces were priceless. They couldn't believe what just happened.

"What? Hell no. I know that bullshit line didn't work. Shit, if dumb-ass jokes like that work, check this shit out," Perry said.

He walked up to a random girl in front of Foot Locker and said, "Excuse me, miss . . . What's better than roses on a piano?"

The girl looked confused. "I don't know."

Perry replied, "Tulips on my organ."

"*Pervert*," she yelled as she stormed away.

We all laughed.

I faced Denise.

"I don't know if you had plans or if you're busy now, but if you aren't, you can hang out with us if you want," I said.

"I actually have nothing going on right now. I just came here to return some things at Victoria's Secret. I was going to have a nice quiet night at my house, but I think you guys are hilarious, so I'll take you up on your offer," she shrugged as if to say, *why not.*

Again, Perry's and Adam's faces fell. They couldn't believe what they were hearing. I laughed to myself.

"We're going to get a quick bite to eat and see a movie. Is that cool with you?"

"Sounds good."

"Luckily for me, my boys here are going to take care of our expenses for the night."

"Let's go . . . lucky bastard," Perry mumbled.

We went to TGI Friday's. Adam and Perry were still annoyed that they were paying for my evening with Denise, but we had a good time getting to know her. Denise was into designing clothes, so she studied fashion at FIT in Manhattan. She was an only child and lived with her mom in Uniondale.

We went to the movies and saw the latest installment of *Final Destination*. I felt comfortable with Denise, and for the next couple of weeks, we were inseparable. She was into clubs, so we club-hopped a lot. I still saw Gina at least once a week, but she never pressured me for more time. If I could see her more, she was happy. If not, she understood I was seeing other women.

Meeting Denise was unexpected, but she had a sense of humor and was gorgeous. While I liked having Heather around because she was safe and caring, I was getting bored with her and found myself breaking our plans regularly to chase other conquests.

Heather had a lot of positive qualities, but being with her exclusively would bore me. She took care of my emotional and intellectual needs, and I knew she cared about me, but I also knew we'd never have a relationship more than our fuck buddy one.

I kept Heather on ice by talking to her on the phone daily and sending candy and flowers to her job sporadically. I made time to see her at least two times a week, even if only for a few hours.

Denise and Heather were night and day. While Heather was more of a homebody and loved to dance, she wasn't into the whole club scene. Denise loved the club life and was a live-in-the-moment type of woman. Every day with her was an adventure. We never planned our time spent together, which made our dates and sex together great because she was down for anything, anywhere, any time.

Every time we had sex, it felt like we were in a porno. That kept me interested and coming back instead of getting bored with her and disregarding her like I had done with so many others.

The first time we had sex was on a Wednesday. I picked her up after she finished her classes, and we planned to hang out that afternoon into the evening. She usually took the train home, but I agreed to pick her up to maximize our time together.

I pulled up on Twenty-Seventh Street and Seventh Avenue, and Denise got into my car wearing a black leather miniskirt and matching top. The heels she had on made her legs look even sexier.

I took the Midtown Tunnel, then got on the LIE Route 495.

"Want some road head?" she asked, licking her lips.

I was taken aback by that. We hadn't done anything sexual yet, so hearing that caught me off guard.

"Fuck yeah," I said.

Denise unbuckled her seat belt, reached over, and unzipped my jeans.

"Push your seat back some," she said.

I quickly complied. Denise held my dick in her hands and positioned herself so one side of her head was on my stomach and the other side was on the steering wheel. She immediately sucked me up like a Hoover—long licks and hard sucks on the head. She deep-throated me so deeply that I could feel the back of her throat. I jerked and moaned to every lick. I swerved and drifted off into other lanes of traffic. I kept my left hand on the steering wheel and put my right hand on the top of her head. I moved her to my rhythm, slowing down her speed so I could savor the sensation. She playfully slapped my hand and used both hands to jerk me off while she sucked me vigorously. The combination of her jerking and sucking me felt so good that I had to pull over. I let out a loud moan and came down her throat. She continued her combination of jerking and sucking, and just watching her swallow it all without even flinching intensified my orgasm.

"Is your mom home?" I asked, panting heavily.

"Nope."

"Good. I gotta have you."

I sped to her house. We rushed inside, and I followed her up the stairs. When she opened her bedroom door, we didn't even make it to the bed. I pulled a condom out of my pants pocket. Denise got on her knees and put the condom on me with her mouth. I fucked her right there on the floor. She was the most flexible woman I'd ever been with. She put her legs behind her head, and I was able to get every inch of my hardness inside her. With her in that position, it was perfect for stroking her and rubbing her clit. Denise bit her lip and swayed her head from side to side with her eyes tight.

She came all over me. I pulled out of her and watched her moan and quiver in elation.

"I want more of that." She pointed down to my hard dick. "Put it in my ass."

That caught me off guard. I tried anal with women before, but it was very rare that they requested it.

She slowly picked herself off the carpet and went into her dresser drawer, where she pulled out a big bottle of K-Y Jelly, tossed it to me, and bent down on all fours. She spread her knees, showing me more of her flexibility. I poured the lube in my hands and applied it to her anus with my fingers. I poured a good amount on my dick and spread her cheeks. Then I slid the head in her ass slowly, and bit by bit, worked my whole dick inside. Her ass was as tight as a vice grip. She seemed to love it. She was relaxed and showed no signs of it hurting her. The sensation it gave me felt heavenly.

"Pull my hair and fuck me hard," Denise demanded.

I pumped away at her, working her anus like it was a pussy.

"Yes, yes, yessss," she screamed. "Fuck me harder."

I was amazed at how much she was enjoying this and how hard I was penetrating her. Watching her come from anal was both satisfying and amazing to see. The tightness of her ass became too much for me. My floodgates opened, and I busted my load inside her. We lay on the floor dripping with sweat, our breathing heavy.

After that day, we did it everywhere. We fucked in her friend's pool, in bathrooms, in movie theaters, in my car, on the beach. We even did it on her balcony in the middle of the day.

"What? Are you scared?" Denise asked.

"Your neighbors are gonna see us."

"So let them be jealous. Now come here and give me that dick."

"You know you get me hot when you talk like that."

"Good."

Denise pulled me close to her and kissed me.

"You know how I want it. Don't punk out," she said.

I quickly turned her around, pulled down her skirt and panties, and bent her over the metal railing of the balcony.

"I want you so bad right now," she moaned.

I quickly ripped open the condom wrapper and got ready to wear her out. Denise swayed her ass from side to side, rubbing it against my hardness. I arched her body over the railing, grabbed my dick, and entered her. She grunted. I gripped her breast and thrust my hips. I pushed into her so hard, her whole body moved, and the balcony railing vibrated.

"Yes, fuck me," she demanded.

"Shhh. People are gonna hear you," I whispered.

"Good, I want them to hear me getting fucked."

Her neighbor's blinds were moving. The mailman stopped and looked up. He stood next to his truck to hide that he was watching, but I saw him. Denise saw him too. She got wetter. She put one leg over the top of the railing, and I was able to get more of my dick inside of her.

Denise's eyes were closed now. Her breathing was thicker. I felt that pressure building inside her, getting ready to reach its peak. I continued to slam into her, my hips colliding with her ass. Her head tilted forward. She yelled out, letting the world know she was coming. I think the feeling of getting caught amplified her orgasms.

Heather and Denise both had their quirks. Heather was smart, affectionate, and would do anything for me, but she was kinda dull. Most times, when I was with her, I felt she just said "yes," to anything I wanted out of fear of losing me. While this was probably cool for most men, I wanted more than that. Denise had her flaws too. She was very impulsive, and while it could be a turn-on, it could also be dangerous. I couldn't predict what she'd do next, which meant I always had to stay on my toes. She didn't pay any of her bills and didn't think they weren't important.

"Fuck bills. I'd rather live in the moment than to be a slave to paying bills," she always said.

That was a turnoff because she didn't think about her future. Again, I recited the whole overused story I used on Heather and told her I was too "damaged" to be in a relationship.

"Honestly, I'm not looking to get into a relationship either, but I know down the line, I want to be with you," she said.

So nothing came to bite me in the ass later. I told her it was fine with me if she saw other guys. It wasn't my fault she chose not to.

While hanging out with Gina, Heather, and Denise was fun, I still felt myself wanting Tiffani. Our chemistry was perfect together, and I felt like I'd known her my entire life. Perry and Adam saw firsthand how much I cared for her, especially after a party at the softball house.

"Yo, Ken, you know your girl Tiffani broke up with her man, right?" Owen said.

"Yeah, right."

"Yes, man, yes. She's free game. You think you got a shot at fucking her?"

"I guess."

"Good, because everyone on campus is betting on it, and I put up five hundred that you'd tap that ass, so win me some money," Owen laughed.

I looked over at Tiffani. She was with her friends playing beer pong. I stuck my tongue out at her. She smiled back at me.

A couple of hours later, and after a lot of drinking on Tiffani's part, she was all over me. We kissed. Our hands were groping all over each other. I guess that old saying was true—a drunken mind speaks a sober tongue. Me, I rarely drank. I liked always to be conscious of what I'm doing and in control of my actions.

Tiffani kissed my neck. Everyone was watching us. All the jocks were going back and forth, talking shit. Some were rooting for me. Some were pissed off.

Tiffani grabbed my hand and took me to her room. I could've easily had my way with her and won the bet, but I didn't. Her words were slurred, and when I looked in her eyes, it was apparent she was shitfaced drunk. If and when I got her in bed, I wanted her to be completely aware of what she was doing.

Before I knew it, Tiffani was throwing up all over the room. I quickly took her to the bathroom. She threw up in the toilet and kept apologizing to me.

"I'm so sorry, Kenny. I really did want to do it tonight."

"Don't worry about that. Just relax."

A little vomit was on her face and in her hair. With any other girl, I would've been disgusted, but with her, I didn't mind as much. I genuinely wanted to make sure she was okay. I walked down the stairs and went into the kitchen. Kelly and Rachel were in there playing cards.

"Hey, guys, do you have any aspirin or ginger ale? Tiffani is in bad shape upstairs," I said.

They looked at each other, shared a grin, and said in unison, "Nope."

All of the jocks were looking at me for confirmation to see if I had done the deed. Unless I was a two-pump chump, there was no way I could've had sex with her in that short time. I shook my head, no. There were some sighs and some hi-fives shared. Perry and Adam were sitting on the couch, talking to girls.

"Yo, I got to go to Walgreens real quick to pick up some stuff for Tiffani. Do you guys want to come with me?" I asked.

"I'm busy talking to these lovely ladies," Perry said as he winked to the two girls on the couch with him.

"I'll go," Adam said.

He was still infatuated with the girl he was seeing anyway, so he decided to come out with me. As usual, Perry drove.

"Can I get your keys so I can drive to the store?" I asked him.

Perry reached into the pocket of his black peacoat and tossed me the keys. When I went back upstairs, Tiffani looked worse than before. I cleaned her face up, dampened a paper towel, and let it rest on her forehead.

We slowly walked down the stairs.

"Tiff, I'm gonna get you something from the store to help her feel better, OK?"

She nodded.

Adam helped me put her into Perry's car, and she immediately went to sleep in the passenger's seat.

When I got to Walgreens, I talked to the pharmacist.

"I wouldn't recommend giving her aspirin. It could magnify the drunken effects. It's best to let her rest and drink Gatorade," he said.

I thanked him and bought her a fruit punch Gatorade and nursed her into drinking it. She was shivering. In my rush to take her to the store, I forgot to bring her coat.

"Can you drive us back? I'm gonna sit in the back with her," I said.

"Yeah, I got it."

I held her while she finished the Gatorade and went back to sleep in my arms.

"You really like her," Adam said.

"Yeah, I do."

"Did you hit it tonight?"

"Nah. I wanted it to be—"

"Special," Adam interrupted.

I thought about it for a second. "Something like that."

We got back to the party, but I stayed with Tiffani. Perry came outside and saw me with her.

"Wow, dude. Usually, you would've said, 'On to the next one' and moved on to another chick, but you're missing the party to take care of her. You trying to wife this one?"

"Maybe one day. You guys go on. I'm just going to take care of her."

"You sure, man? I can chill out here with you," Adam said.

"Nah, I'm cool. Enjoy yourself. I'll see you guys later."

I sat in Perry's car with Tiff and held her while she slept. Before I knew it, I nodded off, and when I woke up, it was 8:30 a.m., and I was still sitting in Perry's car. I woke Tiffani up.

"Tiff, baby, wake up."

She squinted at the sunlight, hitting her from the window.

"Shit. My head is killing me. What happened last night? Where are we?"

She was sober now, so I told her what went down.

We walked inside the house. People from the party were passed out all over the place. Adam was sleeping on the couch while Perry was in the kitchen, knocked out on the table with three girls from the softball team.

I walked up to Tiffani's room with her. Her roommate, Angela, was passed out holding a bottle of whiskey, lying across her boyfriend.

"I shouldn't have drunk so much," Tiffani said, holding her head in her hands.

"What happened with you and Josh?" I asked.

"I don't know. He had a hard time dealing with the distance. He was always saying how this is too hard for him, and he missed me like crazy. The bottom line was he wanted me to come back home, and I can't do that right now. I'm getting a free ride for school to play the game I love."

"What did you say when he asked you to come home?"

"I told him that couldn't happen right now, and it wasn't fair for him to put that stress on me when he knows how much I love him. He didn't like anything I was saying, so he broke up with me."

"You think he'd cheat?"

"Nah, I don't think so, but at the same time, who knows. I see guys and girls here call their girlfriends and boy-friends back home. They tell them how much they love them, then go out and screw somebody else five minutes later. Seeing that makes me paranoid, and I worry about it a lot. I have needs and temptations too, but I'd never cheat on Josh. I've been with him since we were 10. I've always known he was the one for me."

She confided in me and told me all the reasons why she loved him. I knew she was upset and would've slept with me the night before to try to escape her stress—acting similarly to what I'd been doing.

"You need to call him ASAP and patch things up. If you love him that much, you should fight to work it out."

"You're right."

She called him right there on the spot. They talked, and it sounded like they both overreacted and were getting back together. While I was glad to see her happy, she was going back to him, and I was back to square one.

I whispered to her I was going to go. She quickly nodded and waved to me. She told him to hold on and put the phone on mute.

"Thank you for everything. I was really drunk last night. If I were like that with any of the guys downstairs, I would've made a stupid mistake and wouldn't be able to make this call right now. Thanks for taking care of me."

"No doubt, Tiff. You know I'm here for you."

"I know."

I left the room and closed the door behind me. As I walked down the steps, with each step, I regretted telling her to go back to him.

I woke Adam and Perry up, and since they were still hungover, I drove.

"Damn, man, I was going to fuck all three of those girls I passed out with," Perry said.

"This was the last time I'm gonna be your wingman. I hate having hangovers," Adam said.

"Whatever. Your goofy ass can't hang anyway."

Perry faced me. "Did you get to bed that girl, Tiff? You were with her in my car all night."

"Nah, I just took care of her while she was messed up. She's talking to her man right now, trying to patch things up."

"What? And you didn't tap that ass last night? You feeling sick or something?"

"I'm good. Tiffani isn't the type you fuck and run. If we did get to that point, I'd want it to be more than that."

"That's what I'm talking about. See, Perry, all he needs is that one girl to keep him on the right path," Adam said.

"Oh, shut your silly ass up, man," Perry replied.

"I'm serious. Look, Lilly said she has two single friends. Maybe we can all go out. Her two friends might be the women you two need to settle down."

"So, your mystery lady's name is Lilly, huh?" I asked.

"Yeah, and after hanging out with those girls yesterday, it's even clearer to me that she's a woman I can see myself having a future with."

"Here we go again with this shit," Perry said.

"No, seriously, she has friends she said are just as good as she is. I'll ask if her girls are free, and maybe we can all hang out this weekend."

"I have enough on my plate as it is. I don't know if I need to have another woman in my life," I said.

"You need a good woman more than any of us," Adam replied.

He continued to try to persuade us to hang out with these girls this weekend.

"Fine. Set it up," I said.

Chapter Five

Trouble in Paradise

A week passed. Adam set us up to meet his new girl and her friends. We waited for them at the AMC Empire 25 on Forty-Second Street in Manhattan. The girls finally got there, and I have to say I was impressed. Lilly walked up to Adam, hugged, and kissed him.

"These are my boys, Ken and Perry."

"Hi, guys. Adam has told me so much about you."

She was pretty, about five foot five, had a dark complexion similar to mine, and flawless skin. Her body was on point too. She was thin but had curves.

"Good things, I hope," Perry said.

"Very good things." She stared at me for a second and smiled. "These are my friends. This is Jessie, and this is Kristen."

"Please call me Krissy," Kristen said. "Kristen sounds too formal."

Jessie was sexy. She was light-skinned with green eyes. She was about five foot four and had a well-proportioned body. Perry nudged me to let me know he had dibs on her. Krissy had a sexiness about herself too. She was about five foot seven, with huge breasts and a nice ass. She wasn't fat, but she wasn't a toothpick either. She had a tan complexion and hazel eyes, which made her look like she could pass for a Dominican. The expression on her face let me know I caught her eye too.

"This line is crazy. I don't want to be standing out here all night," Jessie said.

"Don't worry, baby girl. I know people. I'll get us to the front of the line," Perry said with confidence.

I looked at him like he was out of his damn mind.

"Hold this, baby." He handed her all of the snacks he bought for them at the concession stand. "I'm going to work my magic."

He looked at me, smirked, and said, "When I text you, come to the front of the line."

I nodded.

A good three minutes passed. Finally, I got a text from Perry saying to come to the front. I told everyone to follow me, and sure enough, Perry was the fifth person in the line, laughing with the guy in front of him. All of us joined him in the line, and no one complained or commented. Adam and I looked at each other in disbelief. The girls were impressed. I pulled Perry to the side.

"How the hell did you pull this off?"

He whispered to me, "You find someone who works here and ask a question. Then start up a conversation with someone in the line. People will think you're with that person you're talking to. The person you're talking to will think you're with the people you just skipped and think nothing of it when you bring more people to the group. This shit works every time."

We both laughed to ourselves.

After the movie, we decided to go to the Pulse Karaoke Lounge on Forty-First to sing and have a good time. We got a private room and searched in the giant books on the tables for songs we wanted to sing.

"My girl Krissy can sing her ass off. Every time she does this, I swear it's like she's in concert," Jessie said.

"Yeah, we always tell her she should try out for one of those singing shows," Lilly added.

"You guys are putting me on the spot," she smiled.

"Since your girls are hyping you up like that, you know you gotta go first now," Perry said.

"Oh Jesus," she said, sounding nervous.

She set up her song and picked up the microphone. Her first song was "Dangerously in Love" by Beyoncé. Her voice was so powerful none of us could deny she had talent. She came off as shy and timid, but once she started singing, you could tell she put her heart and soul into it. We all took our turns singing afterward, but we paled in comparison to Krissy.

My boys and I seemed to be hitting it off with our dates. Heather and Denise called, but I quickly sent those calls to voicemail, and I got a text from Donna, but I ignored that too. We walked out of Pulse, debating where we should go to eat.

"Why don't we walk to Fifty-First and Broadway? We can go to Ellen's Stardust Diner. The food is slammin', we can chill, and the staff dances and sings songs from Broadway plays," I said.

"Walk?" Jessie asked, making it sound like what I said was blasphemy.

"Yeah, walk. It'll give me time to know the woman behind that pretty face of yours," Perry told her.

She tried to hold in her smile and said, "OK, corny."

"It's corny, but you like that shit, girl."

They laughed together. Nobody else had any objections, so we walked to the diner. I took that time to get to know Kristen. Adam and Lilly were in front of us while Perry and Jessie were behind us. Lilly turned around and winked at me. She looked me up and down and said, "You two play nice now."

Kristen smiled.

"So tell me about yourself," I said.

"What do you want to know?"

"Everything and anything."

"That's a broad statement, don't you think?"

"True, but for now, I'll start with some easy questions. Do you go to school? If so, what are you studying?"

"Yeah, I'm in school. I go to Five Towns College. My major is music. I've been singing, playing the piano, and guitar since I was a little girl. I hope and pray that I'll get signed to a record deal someday, but if it never happens, I want a job where I can help teach kids to appreciate music."

It was obvious she loved singing. I saw her eyes glow with excitement when she spoke about being signed.

"That's cool. Do you work with kids now?"

"Sort of. I work in the piano section at Sam Ash in Garden City. When I'm not working there or at school, my side job is teaching people, mostly kids, how to play the piano. To me, it's rewarding because it makes me remember how my momma taught me to play."

"Does your mom still play?"

"Nah, she died of breast cancer when I was 13. It's just my dad and me."

"Damn, I'm sorry. I didn't mean to bring that up."

"It's not your fault. You had no way of knowing."

"Yeah, but I know that must've been hard for you."

"It is, but when I sing or talk about her, it keeps her spirit alive to me. My mom was Black, so I got the singing from my soul thing from her."

I smiled at her.

"What's your dad like?"

"He's your everyday regular Cuban, deaf father."

"He's deaf? What's that like?"

"Well, growing up, it was easy to sneak into the house, and he can barely talk, so he doesn't yell at me. We have a great relationship."

We laughed.

We finally got to the diner. Perry open held the door for Jessie and stopped her before she went through the door. He had a concerned look on his face.

"This is important. Before you go in there, I need to know what color panties you got on."

Jessie laughed out loud. "What? Get the hell outta here. You're out of your mind."

"What if there's a horrible fire and everybody except me is killed and burned beyond recognition? I'm going to have to identify your body. How will I know it's you if I don't know what color panties you have on?"

She playfully slapped his hand and walked in.

"By the way, they're red."

Perry grinned. We laughed at him.

We were all chilling, talking about our colleges when something unexpected happened. My player ways came back to bite me in the ass.

"Wait, you said your name's Ken Ferguson, right?" Jessie asked.

"Yeah, what's up?"

Jessie's face went from smiling to frowning instantly. "My girl Liza is friends with your white girl, Heather. Heather confides in her and tells her all the time how you dog her out. Isn't that your girlfriend?"

Shit. It hit me that Liza was the girl that introduced me to Heather. I didn't like this situation because one, I was feeling Krissy, and two, I didn't know how much Jessie knew about Heather and me.

"I don't have a girlfriend. I went out with Heather a few times, but we're not in a relationship."

"So, you just fucked her a few times, and that's it, huh? It doesn't matter that she bought you shit and cares about you, right? Liza and I go way back. We talk about wannabe players like you all the time." She turned to face Perry. "I hope you're not a dog like your friend here."

Perry looked her dead in the eyes and said, "I'm not a dog, and neither is he. If she wanted to do stupid shit with him without having a title, that's her choice, but don't look down on us like you're all holier than thou. I'm not having that shit."

A fire was in both of their eyes, but it looked like Perry being loud back at her turned her on. She calmed down and smiled at him, but she went back to frowning when she looked up at me.

"As far as me lashing out at you, Perry, I'm sorry. I just don't want my girl Krissy to catch feelings for him and get hurt or played like that girl Heather."

"I'm not playing games with Heather," I said sharply.

"Whatever."

Krissy didn't say a word.

"Look, Ken is one of my best friends. He's not perfect, but none of us are. Trust him. He has a good heart. He's not a bad guy," Adam said, defending me.

Perry faced Jessie.

"You called me corny before. I think Adam here took the crown."

Perry and Jessie shared a laugh.

Adam shook his head.

As the night went on, things calmed down, and we enjoyed the rest of our dinner. My boys and I exchanged numbers with our dates and agreed we'd hang out again soon.

"Did you get those pants on sale?" Perry asked Jessie.

"No, why?" she asked.

"Because if you come to my house, they'll be 100 percent off."

"Oh my God, you're *so* corny."

They laughed together.

Perry and Jessie were hitting it off. She thought he was corny, but she also felt he was charming. They couldn't keep their hands off each other. Adam and Lilly were off to the side, holding hands and laughing.

"I know Jessie can be a little blunt, but she doesn't mean it. Her bark is bigger than her bite," Krissy said.

"I get that she's trying to look out for you, but I'm not lying. I don't have a girlfriend. I'll be honest, I'm not looking for one right now, but I'm not the guy she thinks I am."

"I know. I wouldn't be talking to you if I thought you were."

"I hope she didn't change how you see me now."

"No. Maybe we can meet up for lunch sometime this week."

"Sounds good to me."

I started spending less time with Heather and Denise to make time for Krissy. I loved that she took care of me. She did little things that made me feel like a king, like washing my clothes, cooking me dinner, and giving me massages after work.

While it was hard to read Denise's actions, it was easy to read Krissy's. I knew what to do and say to get her to do what I wanted.

The first time we had sex was on a Sunday. We had gone to the cemetery to visit her mother's grave.

"You miss her a lot, don't you?" I asked.

Krissy's eyes welled up with tears. She nodded, and I held her close.

"Can you give me a minute? I don't want you to think I'm crazy or anything, but I like to talk to my mom alone when I visit her grave."

"I understand. Just give me a shout when you're ready."

I walked away to give her time alone with her mom.

After about twenty minutes, we headed back to her house.

"I'm happy you came with me today. I've never taken anyone there before, not even Jessie or Lilly."

"I'm happy you shared that special part of your life with me."

"I'd share anything with you." She smiled at me. " I was thinking, every Thursday at Nakisaki's in Hempstead, I practice singing in front of a crowd there for open mic night. Would you come out to hear me sometime?"

"Of course."

"It's good practice for me, and I know I'll sing better with you in the audience."

"I'll definitely check it out."

We pulled up to her house, and her dad's car was parked outside. She walked me to her room, and I was trying to be as quiet as possible.

"My father's deaf, Ken. He won't hear you," Krissy said.

"Shit. I forgot about that."

"I want to share something else with you today."

She took off her shirt, and she wasn't wearing a bra. Her breasts were firm and perky, and her nipples were hard enough to cut glass.

Next, she pulled off her Capris and panties. I got undressed as well.

"The best thing about my dad being deaf is he can't hear me scream, so we can be as loud as we want."

We held each other and kissed. I put a condom on as she crawled on the bed on all fours.

"Just so you know, I'm not the prissy type. I want it hard."

That turned me on. I entered her, firmly grabbed her waist, and plunged into her rapidly. I slapped her ass, pulled her hair, and gave it to her the way she wanted it. I laid her on her back. With the back of her legs hooked on my shoulders, I entered her swiftly.

"Oh my God . . . I'm so close. Choke me . . ." she begged.

"What?"

"Choke me."

I did what she asked and choked her.

"Harder."

I squeezed a little harder around her neck and increased my penetration. She gasped and came so hard that she bucked and almost pushed me off her. I released my grip on her neck, and she smiled at me as she twitched on the bed. I loved seeing her so satisfied.

I continued to slam deep inside of her. She gritted her teeth, and I saw the whites of her eyes as she moaned loudly. She was sweating and worn out, but I wasn't done. I wanted to see that big ass of hers in reverse cowgirl.

"Get on top. I want you to ride me," I told her.

She quickly mounted me backward and slid down on my dick. The feeling of my thickness stretching out her walls was incredible. She circled her hips and rocked up and down. I held her ass and slapped it. The curve in my dick must've repeatedly touched her spot in that position because she came twice. She was exhausted, but I wanted more. I bent her over and hammered her doggie style again. As I watched her firm, round ass vibrate from my thrusts, I got more hot. I pulled her hair hard and plunged into her deeply as I came inside.

"Holy shit, that was intense," she said.

"Hell yeah," I laughed.

After that day, that's how our sessions usually went.

We hung out regularly. Jessie still talked to Liza, so Jessie and I fought a lot. Heather and Krissy learned of each other.

"Kenny, what is Kristen to you?" Heather asked one day.

I sighed. We were hanging out in her room. With the little time I spent with her, I didn't want to ruin it with this conversation.

"She's just a friend."

"Are you fucking this friend?"

"I'm not going to answer that."

"Why? Because you are or because you don't want me to know?"

"Because I'm not having this conversation. Just a reminder, we're *not* in a relationship. I told you when we first started hanging that I'm not ready for all that. If you're jealous that I have other friends who happen to be women, by all means, see other guys. I'm not stopping you."

"No, I don't want other guys. I want you."

"Then stop stressing me when we're spending time together."

I think Heather felt she wouldn't find someone better than me.

It was a seesaw battle trying to keep Heather and Krissy happy because Liza would tell Jessie things that Heather and I did, and Jessie would tell Krissy. Krissy would get jealous, but I always calmed her down and got her to forgive me.

Jessie constantly insulted and belittled me and what made shit worse was she and Perry were joined at the hip, so she hung out with us on the regular.

Juggling Heather, Denise, and Kristen took a lot of time and energy, and sometimes it was stressful, but they all made me happy in different ways. Instead of continuously seeking out new girls, they were my go-tos for now.

When I needed a break from them, Gina was always there to make things better. Gina still took me to school even after Heather gave me the money to fix my car. Since she was older, she schooled me on younger women's thoughts and behaviors.

My life wasn't perfect, but it was far from boring. I couldn't find one perfect woman, but I found a little of what I wanted in the four I had.

I couldn't believe I was in the middle of this shit.

"Ken, this is my husband, Terrence."

"So, you're the guy my wife is always talking about," Terrence said with a pissed-off look on his face.

He was bald with a full beard, had dark skin similar to mine, and was built like a linebacker. Gina's husband squeezed the hell out of my hand when he shook it. I tried to smile and act like I was cool, but this guy's grip felt like pliers. He looked me square in the face and stared me down.

Out of the norm, Gina asked me to come to her house. For as long as I've known her, I'd never been to her home, even when there were times when she said she had the place to herself. I figured she never invited me there because she had three kids and didn't want any of them to know what we were doing.

As I put more thought into the situation, things started to make sense. Gina and I never talked on the phone. We always communicated through text. *She was still married.*

Gina had a spiteful smile on her face. "Yep, this is him," she said.

Terrence never took his eyes off me. I looked around the house to try to break eye contact, noticing there was nothing but trophies with his name on them for martial arts. The scariest thing that caught my attention was his picture in his NYPD Police Officer uniform. Now I was *really* uncomfortable.

"Well, we better get going. Kiss me before I leave, honey."

"Really? Get out of my face with that bullshit," he mumbled.

"Oh, don't be mean. If you don't, I'll have to kiss my friend Ken then."

Gina grabbed me off guard and kissed me right on the lips in front of him. I saw the anger in his eyes.

"Bye, honey. Don't wait up for me tonight," she said with a smile.

Gina grabbed my hand and yanked me out the door with her before he could react.

She was laughing when we got in the car. I was ready to scream at her for putting me in that situation, but her laughing quickly turned into crying. She cried so hard that after traveling three blocks, she had to pull over.

"What's going on, Gina?" I asked, trying to sound sympathetic.

"That was my husband."

"I thought you said you were divorced."

She sighed. "I was tired of him always cheating on me. I'm sorry I dragged you into this, but seeing him angry lets me know he still cares about me. I still love him. We have a history together. We have three kids. I can't just throw all that away. Maybe after meeting you today, he'll smarten up, and there's a chance we can save our marriage."

I was still mad, but I saw the desperation in her face. While we had fun together, what we had wasn't real. She'd been married to her husband for years. She loved him, and if it meant doing something drastic to get his attention, she didn't care what it took.

"So, what are you going to do now?" I asked.

Gina wiped her face and put on her sunglasses.

"I don't know. Hopefully, that'll wake him up to what he's missing."

We drove the rest of the way in silence, both of us lost in our thoughts. We got to the school, and she kissed me. It felt loving, like she wanted it to be real. I smiled.

"Thanks for that. I'll see you later tonight," I said.

"Okay, . . . Ken?"

"Yeah?"

"Thanks . . . for everything."

"No doubt."

I waved and headed to my first class.

"All right, everyone, that's it for today. Have a good night," the professor said.

Gina and I hadn't said much to each other the whole time, but she texted me during class to let me know she wanted to see me afterward.

Ken, I need to de-stress tonight. Can you forgive me for this morning and help me out?

Yes.

We walked to her car. She smiled and held my hand.

"Do you want to go to the usual spot?" she asked.

"Yeah," I nodded.

We said very little on the ride to the motel. Gina paid for the room and handed me the key. I knew she didn't want to be fucked tonight. Today, she wanted to feel loved. I kissed her passionately, looked her in the eyes, and gradually took off her clothes. I sucked on her neck, held her hand, and led her to the bathroom.

I turned on the faucet to the shower and adjusted the temperature of the water. Then I undressed, held her hand, and we both got into the shower. The water cascaded down our bodies as Gina stood in front of me with my manhood pressed comfortably against her backside. I squeezed the cloth and allowed the warm water to flow down her back. After several minutes, I took a washcloth, lathered it up, and washed her back. Her eyes were closed. She always enjoyed it when I was sensual with her. I turned her to face me and washed her breasts. I rubbed some soap on my hands and ran them all over her curves. My hands went down her thighs, and I teased her pussy with a finger. I continued to wash her entire body and touch the zones that I knew made her moist.

I toweled her off, lifted her, and took her to the bed. There I laid her on her stomach and went to get the lotion I knew she kept in her bag. When I opened her purse, I saw a picture of her and her husband smiling together. I understood I could never replace the love she felt for him, but I wanted her to feel desired and appreciated.

I poured the lotion into my hands and rubbed them together. As I began to rub the cream all over her skin, I dug my fingers into the small of her back and worked my way up to her shoulder blades, massaging and working the tension out of them. I poured more lotion on and rubbed her thighs and calves. Her body felt so relaxed. I turned her over on to her back and massaged lotion on her breasts.

I kissed her stomach and licked down to her thighs. Gina grabbed the back of my head. She couldn't take me teasing her. I knew she wanted that release. I licked her pussy. I made circles with my tongue before sucking on her clit. I licked and hummed, creating that added vibration that drove her wild. I curved my fingers and touched the roof of her pussy, working my fingers. Gina's head thrashed from side to side. I could feel her vaginal muscles tightening around my fingers. Her nails clawed on the sheets as I continued to make circles with my tongue and worked my fingers. Soon, Gina was pounding the mattress with her fists. She arched her back, and her body convulsed. She screamed out, holding my face in her treasure. Her juices were all over me. I got up to get a towel to wipe my face. She stayed in bed, smiling and twitching nonstop.

I put on a condom. Gina wrapped her legs around me, and I felt that the incredible feeling of my penis spreading her lips apart. I maneuvered my arms around her shoulders, so I had the leverage to grind in her hard. Gina's eyes rolled back, her breath thick on my neck. She moved her hips to increase the rhythm and exploded all on me. She violently jerked and yelled out her appreciation as I continued to pump inside of her. She held my hand as we breathed heavily.

"Thank you. I needed this," Gina said.

"I learned how to be more sensual from you."

I wasn't trying to flatter her. I meant it. Before I met her, I would try to sex every woman into submission. She taught me that women didn't want sex one way all the time; they liked variety. She helped me become a better lover.

"I was so stressed, Ken. Terrence called my job all day, cursing me out. He's threatened by you."

"What do you think will happen?"

"I don't know. I hope he comes to his senses. At one point, he was my heart. I miss that."

I knew she was hurting. I knew I was only there to satisfy her emotional and sexual needs. I didn't take offense by it.

"Maybe you guys need to work it out," I suggested.

"Maybe."

Gina got up and started to get dressed, which I thought was odd because she usually showered before she went home. She kissed and dressed me. Then we were in her car on the way to dropping me off. She looked like she had a lot on her mind.

We pulled up to my house.

"Are you going to talk to him tonight?" I asked.

"Yup, as soon as I get home."

"All right . . . Well, good luck with everything."

"Thanks. Tonight was perfect. You gave me the strength to be able to go home tonight."

We kissed and said good night. I headed into my house, and she headed into war.

The next morning, Gina didn't come by to pick me up for class. I called her cell phone.

"Hey, Gina—"

"This isn't Gina. This is her husband. I know you've been fucking my wife. She came home smelling like sex last night, and I know you were with her. I'm only gonna tell you this once. Stay away from my fucking wife."

I knew it was weird she didn't shower. She wanted him to know she was with me. At the same time, I wasn't going to admit to this man I was screwing his wife.

"I don't know what you've heard or what you think you know, but Gina loves you."

"I know she loves me, and I know I fucked up, but that's in the past now. We're going to work things out, so find your own way to class and stay away from my family. Gina is dropping out of that college, so she isn't tempted to see you again."

"Look—"

"No, *you* look. I'm warning you—stay away from my wife. We're gonna make our marriage work, and you're not needed."

He ended the call, and just like that, she was gone. Gina didn't come to class. She didn't call me or stop by my house. After two weeks of not communicating with her, I called her job number.

"Hey, Gina."

"Hi, Ken."

"How are you?"

"I'm really good. I don't want you to think I used you or didn't appreciate how you made me feel."

"I know."

"Terrence needed a wake-up call, and seeing you as a threat made him want to stop fucking around and appreciate me."

I knew this was the end. "I'm going to miss you," I said.

"I'm going to miss you too," she replied, sounding emotional like she was on the verge of crying.

"Will I ever see you again?"

"If that bastard cheats on me again, you better believe you will," she laughed.

I laughed too but only a little.

"Goodbye, Gina."

"Goodbye, Ken."

We hung up and returned to our worlds. Gina returned to her family, and I continued to drown myself in the affection of my three women. I wondered if either of us would ever get what we wanted.

Chapter Six

The Game

Adam, Perry, and Ray wanted to hang out and asked if I could get away from my busy schedule of seducing women to hang out with them. I agreed, and we decided to go out to dinner and play pool. I met them at Applebee's in Bellmore.

When I got there, I saw an attractive redhead at the table. I sat down and said hello to everyone. I figured she was one of Perry's recent conquests. I prayed that was the case, so I didn't have to see Jessie anymore. I just waved and moved on.

Perry looked at me and said, "Hey, you remember Ashley, right? She graduated with us from high school. I saw her at the mall today, and she decided to come out with us tonight."

"Oh, that's cool. Hey, Ashley. How've you been?" I said.

I'd seen her in passing, but I never really got to know her in high school.

"I'm good. Going to school. You know, the usual."

"That's what's up. What school are you in?"

"I'm going to Fordham for my degree in philosophy. What I plan on doing with that degree, I have no idea," she said.

We laughed and told stories about the crazy things that happened in our current lives. Ray went on and on about Lucy, Perry bragged about being an electrical genius, and Adam talked about his auditions in martial arts movies.

Ashley went to the bathroom. I quickly questioned Perry about her.

"Yo, you trying to hit that?" I asked.

"Nah, she's hot and all, but she's too much of a challenge. I like a challenge, but I don't need a headache. Plus, I just made things official with Jessie. I'm going to rock with that for a while."

"Oh God, why? I mean, oh my God, I'm so happy for you," I said sarcastically.

"I know you guys can't stand each other, but that shit has to end now because you're my boy, and she's my lady. Anyway, you can try working your magic with Ashley, but I don't think you can get this one."

"I second that," Ray said.

"Yeah, I think you've met your match with this one, Ken," Adam added.

Since I had the green light to move forward with talking to her, I looked at it as a challenge. I wanted to prove to them, and myself, that I could get any woman to fall for me. She came back, and I nodded at Perry.

Let the games begin.

We decided to play pool at RAXX in West Hempstead. Everyone piled into Ray's Chevy Malibu. I asked Ashley if she wanted to ride with me since they were all squeezing into his car. She agreed.

"Ugh, your music sucks. What are we listening to?" she asked.

Common's song "The Game" was playing on the radio. Ashley turned the station. I never let *anyone* touch my radio, but I made an exception with her.

"Don't tell me you don't appreciate good music. Only because you're a guest will I allow you—and only you—to touch my radio."

"If you think that's good music, then you need your hearing checked, and you didn't have a choice, booboo. I was going to touch your radio regardless of whether you gave me permission."

I laughed at her spunk. She was smart and witty, and I liked that.

We pulled up into the RAXX parking lot. When Ashley wasn't looking, they all shook their heads and laughed at me. I gave them a devilish grin and held the door open for her.

Ashley wiped the floor with all of us. On the drive over, I figured I'd let her win a couple of games so that she could feel good about herself, but that wasn't necessary. She *was* good and ended up hustling all of us.

"Rack 'em up," she said while chalking up her stick and brushing the blue dust off her shirt.

As soon as I saw her break shot, I knew I was going to lose.

While we played, I tried to distract her by flirting. I danced in front of her, told her corny jokes, and bought her drinks—all to win a game and to get her to fall for me. None of it worked. She continued to sink solids in pockets and cleaned the table with us every game.

My boys and I laughed at how bad she beat us and talked more about the past and where we wanted to be in the future. Since it was getting late, we decided to call it a night.

"Do you mind if I drive you home?" I asked her.

"Nah, that's cool. You can drop me off."

We said goodbye to the guys and went to my car.

"You guys suck at pool. Why didn't you pick a game you're good at?"

"Ah, we let you win. What kind of man wouldn't want a woman to feel good about herself?"

She smiled. I knew she wouldn't be easy, but I also knew she found me cute and interesting.

"Sure, you let me win. Keep telling yourself that."

She gave me directions to her apartment, and we talked more along the way. Step one of understanding her was to learn about her likes and dislikes. She told me about her family. Her mother was Puerto Rican but very fair-skinned. She could pass for white. She stayed at home and took care of the house while her Irish father worked for a computer programming company. She had two brothers and one sister. One brother was in the air force, and the other one was still in high school. Ashley and her sister lived together in an apartment in Freeport. Her sister worked with the disabled at South Oaks Hospital.

We pulled up to her place, and I continued to listen to her. She explained that her family was very dysfunctional and never showed her or her siblings affection growing up. I could empathize with her on that because my relationship with my father was similar. Her family put her down a lot and told her she wouldn't amount to much. To fight the negativity she faced at home, she put all of her energy into learning and doing well in school. Ashley was well-versed. She could talk intelligently about almost anything, and that drew me to her.

"I was wondering if I could call you sometime," I asked.

"Um, I don't know if that's a good idea."

"Why?"

"I have a boyfriend, and booboo, you're not my type. I don't date Black guys. I like tall, light-skinned guys with dimples. You're not tall—"

"I'm taller than you."

"You're far from light-skinned, and you don't have dimples. Sorry, you're not my type."

In my head, a part of me was saying, "Fuck her." She was talking like I wasn't shit, but another part of me welcomed the challenge. If I could get her to fall for me with all the things she considered to be my flaws, then I knew I could get any woman to fall for me. If I could get her to break her rules of dating her type, then I'd be capable of anything.

"Get to know me. What do you have to lose?" I asked.

"Uh, all right, but don't stalk me. I hate to be stalked."

She grabbed my phone and typed in her number and email address. Then she punched me on the arm.

"All right, against my better judgment, I gave you my info. Fair warning, though. If you abuse it and smother me with texts and calls, I'll block you."

I laughed and said, "Duly noted."

"Good. You have a good rest of your night."

"You too."

I watched her walk to the door of her apartment building, and then I drove home. This was a game, and I play to win.

Over the next couple of weeks, I dedicated most of my free time to Ashley. We went to museums, movies, restaurants, amusement parks, and clubs. I cooked for her and her sister all the time. She was kissing me now. At first, it was only once in a while, and only in private. It evolved into her kissing me in public—even in front of our friends. I still hung out with Heather, Denise, and Kristen, but I found myself breaking plans with them—Heather mostly—and spending more time with Ashley. I used the excuse that studying for school and work had me tied up, but I was falling hard for this one.

I tried just to see her as a conquest. I wanted to tell myself I didn't like her, but the truth was she was everything I wanted. She was smart, witty, spontaneous, sexy, outgoing, and funny. I wasn't with her for just lust anymore. My plan was backfiring hard, and what made it worse was she still had a boyfriend. The ones I wanted always had fucking boyfriends.

Her boyfriend, Carlos, was Puerto Rican, six foot two, 26-years-old, and was always in and out of prison. He dropped out of school in the seventh grade, didn't have a job, and had a child with another girl. He stopped by Ashley's place about once every other month and only came around for some ass and to take whatever money he could get from her. Even with all those flaws, she still loved him. I saw her regularly, cuddled with her, and talked to her daily, but she still wanted him. Every time she told me he stopped by to see her, I would get jealous. Sometimes, I think she thought it was funny telling me about it.

"Hello," I answered.

"Hey, Kenny, can you get me some Advil?"

"Sure, what's wrong? Your head hurts?"

"No, my ass hurts. Carlos came over and pounded me in my ass."

"Well, since he's a pain in your ass literally and figuratively, he can get you the fucking Advil."

"He left already. Please, Kenny, can you get it for me?"

I should've said no. There was a CVS five minutes away from her house. She could've walked there herself, but like a pussy, I gave in.

She didn't even fuck me yet, but it wasn't a major priority for me because I wanted more than that. I wanted her.

Ashley and I were cuddling in her apartment, watching TV, when out of nowhere, she started crying.

"What's wrong?" I asked.

"I'm worried about Carlos. I don't know if he's locked up or dead, and I'm scared."

Hearing her cry over him reminded me of my mom always crying over my dad when he dogged her out. I figured this was the perfect time to convince her that she should be with me.

"Why do you want a guy who doesn't want you back?"

"You don't know what you're talking about, so just drop it. You don't even know him."

"You're right, I don't, but I bet I know you better than he does. When was the last time you've seen him, or he's called you? You see me or at least talk to me almost every day. When was the last time he took you out or bought you a gift? I'm more of a boyfriend to you than he is. Forget him. Give me a chance and be with me. Stop letting him use you. I know you can't be happy with him."

"I . . . I . . . It doesn't matter. You don't know him like I do, and who do you think you are talking shit about him like that? You come here, we cuddle, and I confide in you like you were one of my girlfriends, and that's all you are—just my friend. You're basically like having a gay guy around because no matter how touchy we get, I'm never going to fuck you. Here's a newsflash for you. I don't date Black guys. You can pretend we're together, but as I told you since day one, you have no chance with me. You're not my type. You talk all this shit about Carlos, but you work in a fucking bookstore. You drive a beat-up piece of shit Ford, and you're always so judgmental about Carlos not having shit when you don't have your shit together either. You tell me I should be with you, but what can you offer me that he can't? Nothing."

Her words cut me deeply. As kind and sweet as she could be, she could be equally as vindictive and cold. She knew how and what to say to hurt me. I told her about my past and the reasons I felt Bri left me, and she used that information against me as ammunition to throw in my face.

I felt like everything we did together was a waste of time. Again, I opened up my heart, and again, I got hurt.

"So, it's like that, huh?" I asked.

"Yup, it's like that."

I nodded, and I let myself out. I left her place with my mind reinforced that I'd never allow myself to think with my heart again. I didn't need to look for love. I needed to continue doing what worked—fucking girls without commitment or attachment—and for damn sure without catching feelings.

Chapter Seven

The Pursuit of Happiness

Three months passed, and I still hadn't talked to Ashley. My breakup with Bri had evolved me, but my last conversation with Ashley showed me I needed to grow even further and gave me the strength to do so.

My experiences so far taught me a woman doesn't want a man she pities. Women want strength. They want someone confident, strong, and financially stable.

My first act of evolution was changing my job. Since high school, I planned to open my own gym one day, which is why I double-majored in business management and exercise physiology. I decided to start learning the business, so I applied at Lifetime Fitness. I filled out several applications but didn't get any responses. I decided to dress up in my best suit and apply in person. The gym was packed when I walked in. A guy in his midthirties with a gray shirt was smiling and talking to some of the female members. His name tag read *Ron, Manager*. He was about six foot with a cedar complexion and medium build. I waited for him to finish his conversation, and then I made my move.

"Excuse me, sir, may I talk to you for a minute?" I asked.

"Sure, what's up?" Ron asked.

"I'm interested in working for this company."

"Yeah? That's cool. Fill out an application, and we'll get back to you."

I didn't come to fill out another application. I knew it was time to do something—it was now or never.

"I already filled out several applications, sir. I wanted to bring my résumé in and discuss it with you personally so that you can see why I'd be a good fit for this company."

Ron smiled. "Okay, kid, come to my office."

We walked to his office. I quickly glanced around it to learn more about him. I noticed he went to Howard University and graduated with a bachelor's degree in business management. I also noticed from his wall that he was a member of the fraternity Alpha Phi Alpha. All over his office and desk were pictures of him with celebrities and sales awards.

"Have a seat," he said. "So why should I hire you?"

"Well, sir—"

"Please call me Ron," he smiled. "You make me feel old when you call me 'sir.'"

"OK . . . Ron, I believe I can effectively and efficiently handle any responsibility that would be given to me here. I'm a fast learner, a hard worker, and I want a career where I can grow with the company. I think this company could be that career I'm looking for."

"Well, you're confident enough. I like that. Go on."

"I'm working on my bachelor's in both business management and exercise physiology. I'm on track to graduate this year with those degrees, and I plan on getting my master's in the same subjects so I can have the knowledge to rise in the ranks of this company. All I need is an opportunity to prove myself. I love challenges and believe if I put my mind to something, there is nothing I can't do."

"Wow. I'm impressed, but what type of job are you looking for?"

"Right now, I'm fine with almost anything you offer. If I can get my foot in the door, I have no problem working my way up and proving myself."

"I'm glad you said that because, to be honest, the most I can offer you with your qualifications is a job as the front-desk manager. I can also give you some hours working in the juice bar. I'd offer you sales, but with your class schedule, I think the front-desk manager position would be the best fit."

That was all I needed. I quit my other jobs and took the position he offered me, which, in reality, was a glorified secretarial position. In addition to working at the front desk, I worked in the juice bar. I made a killing in commissions selling supplements, and I was promoted quickly to the assistant manager for the juice bar, which meant no more front desk—and more money.

Ron became my mentor. He saw a lot of himself in me and took me under his wing. Like me, Ron started at the front desk before moving into sales. Once he got to sales, he was unstoppable and became one of the youngest managers in the company's history. He had the gift of gab and was a master salesman. Every gym the company sent him to went from shit to gold. Ron never slept and was into lots of legit businesses on the side.

What I admired about him more than anything was not only was he a ladies' man, he was street smart and book smart. He always read books and could fit into any social crowd. He knew a little bit of everything, and whenever I talked to him, he'd always give me a quote to help me with my problems. He never gave me a direct answer. He'd give me a quote related to the topic, and I'd used my interpretation of the quote to make my own decisions. When I asked him why he did that, he answered my question with another quote.

"Dr. Shad Helmstetter said, 'Choosing to live your life by your own choice is the greatest freedom you will ever have.'"

Things with the gym were good, but I needed more. It's funny how one interaction can change your life. While working in the juice bar, Joe, one of the personal trainers, walked in for a protein shake. He was a massive Italian bodybuilder who was very popular at the gym. We talked about sports and life working at the gym.

"You should be a trainer, man," Joe said.

"Nah, I don't know if I'd be good at that."

"You look like you're in decent shape. Do you train yourself?"

"Yeah."

"Don't you go to school for exercise physiology?"

"Yeah."

"Then you'd be perfect. All you have to do is get certified. Get these two national personal training certs, NASM and ACSM. Once you have those, you can pretty much get a job at any gym."

"Do trainers make good money?"

"You serious? Bro, is the pope Catholic? Of course. Trainers here make a minimum of thirty dollars an hour. I have specialty certifications on top of my regular training certification, so I can charge people more money to train with me. One guy I train pays me $100 an hour."

"What!"

"I'm telling you, bro, this shit is legit. Plus, you make your hours. You tell your clients the times you'll be here and set them up around your schedule."

"That'd be good for school. Shit, I'm sold. I'm in."

"Good. You're not limited to just training people here either. When you train on the side, you don't have to give the gym a cut of the money. Plus, if they pay you in cash, it's better when you file your taxes. With some of my clients, I either train them at their houses or train them at mine."

My mind was already made up. I'd use the little savings I had to get the certifications I needed to do this.

"Oh, I almost forgot to tell you the best part . . . the women. Most men have too much pride and won't admit when they need help with working out, so for the most part, your clients will mainly be women. Women will throw themselves at you, and the better you look physically, the more you'll attract, and the more money you'll make. Every trainer here either fucks or has fucked some of their clients—that goes for both male and female trainers."

I nodded. The perks only reinforced my decision.

I worked out more to make myself look more appealing for future clients and scheduled the tests for all of the certifications Joe said I should get. Since I went to school for exercise physiology, I aced all the exams without studying. Once all the certifications came in the mail, I told Ron I wanted to train. He was cool with it, and the minute I showed him the certificates, he had me start immediately. That was all I needed.

I was great at training. In my first month, I made the company $15,000 in sales. Ron looked like a genius for moving me into training, and I was making more money than I ever had. I wasn't satisfied, though. I wanted more. I changed my school schedule to only Tuesdays and Thursdays and scheduled clients on the other days. I gained more clients, and the money was pouring in. Ron saw this and talked me into opening up a bank account.

"Why do you waste your time and money going to a check-cashing place?" he asked.

I had no real answer to that question, so I just shrugged.

"We're going to my bank. I have a good guy that works at Citibank. Our goal today is to set up a checking and savings account for you."

"No doubt."

Once Ron had some free time, we went to the bank, and he introduced me to his friend, Jeff, who helped set up the accounts. Jeff also dealt with stocks, and he and I talked about different funds and shared stock market info.

"Your boy here is on point. He knows more stuff about the market than some of the guys we have working here," Jeff said.

"I see that," Ron replied. He faced me. "You're making money now. Instead of spending it on bullshit, why don't you follow your advice and start investing?"

He was right, and that was another turning point for me.

Since I hadn't bought anything extravagant with the money I was making, I had a few dollars saved. I invested in a lot of companies I researched and convinced Ron to do the same. He had nothing but faith in me and listened to all of my stock advice. My recommendations paid off. I made huge returns on mostly all of my investments, and between my training and the stock market, things were looking good for me. Ron invested way more money than I did, so he saw even greater returns from my advice.

Since I had my dream job and finally had some money in my pockets, I wanted to show off my success. I got rid of my old beat-up Ford Escort and bought a new S-Class Mercedes, a newer model than David had when I was dating Bri. I got vanity plates for it that read *"Kens Benz"* to further drive home the point to those who knew me back when I was struggling that I had made it.

I bought a whole new wardrobe of designer clothes and grew my hair out and got braids. My purpose for getting braids was to show my evolution and my strength. I wanted everyone to see that I changed. I wasn't that poor, weak boy anymore. Now, I was a strong, successful man.

The last change was moving out of my parents' house and getting a condo in Garden City in the Hampshire Development on Seventh Street, but I didn't decide to do that until Ron hooked me up with a side job training people for Def Jam Records.

"Ken."

"What's up, Ron?"

"A friend of mine told me about an opportunity to train employees for Def Jam Records. Would you be interested?"

"Hell yeah."

He laughed. "All right, call my friend Sonia."

He wrote her number on a notepad and handed it to me. "She'll be expecting your call. You have a chance to make some real money. Don't mess this up."

"I won't. You can trust me on that. How do you know these people?"

He smirked. "Having skill and talent is one thing, but networking is one of the best things you can ever do if you want to make it in life."

I nodded.

I went into the personal training office and pulled out my cell phone. I was a little skeptical that this job even existed, but Ron never gave me a reason to doubt him or not trust him, so I gave it a shot and dialed the number. A receptionist for Def Jam answered and transferred me to Sonia.

"Good afternoon. This is Sonia speaking."

"Good afternoon . . . My name is Kenneth Ferguson. Ron referred me—"

"Yes, Ron is a good friend of mine and told me you'd be a competent trainer for us. Did he explain what the job entails?"

"No, not exactly."

"Well, let me explain. The company needs a trainer to come to our Manhattan office about two to three times a week to train some of our higher-up employees and possibly one or two of our up-and-coming music groups we're working with. Does that sound like something you'd be interested in?"

"Yes, I'd be very interested in the position."

"Here's how this business works. If you're hired, once we set certain days that you'll be with us, you work around us. We don't work around you. We may call you at random hours to train employees. Are you OK with that?"

"I understand, yes."

"Good. I'm not going to sugarcoat it or make the job seem easy. Def Jam demands a lot and expects nothing but the best. If you get the job—and I'm saying *if*—I don't want you to think you're a lock-in for it—you have to go through an interview process. I don't know what senior management will ask, expect, or want. Can you handle that?"

"Yes, I can handle it."

"Good. Your interview is tonight at 11:00 p.m."

"Tonight?"

"Yup, tonight. Dress in gym attire, please, and if I were you, I'd get here significantly earlier than eleven. On time is late in the Def Jam world."

"OK. I'll be there earlier."

"Good. Ron has a lot of faith in you. Don't let him down."

"I won't."

"Confidence is good. Keep that. Good luck tonight."

She hung up before I could respond. I walked back to Ron's office. He was sitting at his desk playing Sudoku.

"So, how was it? When's your interview?"

"My interview is at 11:00 p.m. tonight. She sounds like she doesn't take shit from anyone."

Ron laughed. "I'd get there around ten twenty if I were you, and you're right. She doesn't take any shit. She's a pit bull in a dress, but she's a good woman."

"You sound like you know that from experience."

"I should. She's my son's mother."

"What?" I asked in both amazement and shock.

"Yup."

"How many children do you have?"

He smiled and said, "Four in total, three daughters and one son."

"Damn, no wonder you're always working."

We laughed.

I left the gym and got ready for my interview. When I got to the office, the receptionist told me to sit in the waiting area. A pretty woman wearing an expensive gray business suit walked up to me. She had a smooth caramel complexion, light brown hair and eyes, and thick thighs.

"Good evening, Ken, I'm Sonia. How are you? Are you ready for the interview?" She shook my hand. She had a firm business-type grip.

"I'm well, and, yes, I'm ready."

I felt underdressed like I should've worn a suit.

She took me to a room with sets of dumbbells and a few pieces of exercise equipment, but no actual workout machines. There were five people in the room—three men and two women.

"All right, Ken, put them through a thorough full-body workout using the equipment we have in this room."

I nodded. An hour later, I had them all exhausted and gasping for air. I wowed them with how effective I could be with limited equipment.

"You did an excellent job. You're hired," Sonia said.

"Thank you for the opportunity."

"All right, now that you work for us, we'll work out a schedule and tell you about the people you're going to train. Understand that we will use you on holidays. Def Jam is a twenty-four-hour, seven-days-a-week, 365-day-a-year gig. Again, before we go further, are you OK with that? We know we demand a lot."

"That's not a problem."

They offered me money that I couldn't refuse, and that's how I could afford my condo. I felt terrible leaving my mom with my asshole father, but I needed to be on my own. Part of the reason I lost Bri and why I couldn't get Ashley was because I wasn't ready. Everything I lacked before, I now had. This was my time.

Even though I had been working in the gym for a while, I was still adjusting. Everything was fast-paced, and there were so many different types of personalities to deal with. There was a lot of drama, and as Joe explained, lots of sex.

One morning, I was training my client, Linda, a beautiful Italian housewife trying to get in better shape for her husband. I figured she was trying to stay pretty so her husband wouldn't stray. She had a tight body, a gorgeous face, and was in her early 40s, but she could easily pass for late 20s.

Usually, during our training sessions, we made small talk—nothing too personal. She told me about her husband, Tony, his auto mechanic shop, and how his business was so successful she hadn't worked since they'd married fourteen years ago. On this particular day, our conversation got a lot more interesting.

We were in the back of the gym doing squats when Linda said, "I don't know how to ask you this, but do you have a girlfriend or someone special that you're seeing?"

"No . . . Why? What's up?"

I figured she was trying to hook me up with a friend.

"Well, I think you're handsome."

"Thanks . . . I think you're attractive too."

I was curious about where she was going with all of this.

"There is no easier way to ask you this, so I'll just be blunt. Would you be interested in fucking me?"

I was caught off guard. "Wow . . . I'd . . . I'd love to, but what about your husband?"

It was one thing to bed her, but her husband paid for her training. I couldn't risk losing out on money for a piece of ass.

"That's the thing. My husband would want to . . . um . . . watch. He likes to watch me get pleased by other men. It's a major turn-on for him. We have an agreement that I can 'play' with other men as long as we wear protection, and he gets to be there to watch."

I was curious to see if she was as athletic in the bedroom as she was in the gym. I had some suspicions, though.

"That sounds cool, and I'm interested, but is your husband going to want to touch you while we're doing our thing, or is he just watching?"

"No, he's just watching. He's very insecure about his dick size, so he wouldn't want to fuck me with you around."

"All right, sounds good. One more question, though. He isn't going to try to touch me, right?" I laughed nervously. "I wouldn't be cool with that."

She laughed too.

"No, of course not. He's straight. He just likes watching me get pleased."

"Cool. So when and where are we going to do this?"

"First, I have to talk to my husband, but since we are all in agreement, let's try to see if we can arrange a time as soon as possible. How does Friday night sound?"

I had some plans I'd need to move around, but I'd definitely change them for this.

"Friday night is good," I said.

The week couldn't end fast enough. Linda talked to her husband, and everything was set. I finished my clients at the gym and afterward, used the directions she gave me to find their house. Heather was disappointed I was canceling our plans, but I promised I'd make it up to her.

I got to Linda's house and parked in front. Before I left my place, and just in case these two were psychos and ended up killing me, I needed people I trusted to know where I was, so I let Ray and Lucy know just in case I didn't make it back.

I rang the doorbell, and a man who I assumed was her husband opened the door. I was caught a little off guard.

"You must be Ken. I'm Tony. How are you doing?"

He was calm and casual, which made me curious if he knew what I was there to do or if Linda lied to me about the whole thing.

"Hey, I'm good. How are you?" I said awkwardly.

"I'm good. I'm good. Linda is getting ready. Come in and make yourself at home."

I sized him up to see if I could take him if shit went south. He was about six foot two, 210 pounds. He didn't look like he worked out. He had slicked-back black hair and wore nerdy glasses.

"Would you like something to drink, Ken?" he asked.

"Nah, I'm cool. Thanks, though."

When dealing with people I'd just met, I never drank anything I didn't prepare myself. I didn't know them, so drinking anything in their house wasn't happening. I didn't trust them enough, and they could easily slip drugs into drinks.

I sat on the couch, and Tony sat on the other side. He turned on the TV.

"Is there anything you want to watch?" he asked.

"Nah, I'm pretty cool with watching anything."

"I like you," he laughed. "You're a very go-with-the-flow type of guy. That's good."

I didn't say anything to that.

We sat there and watched SportsCenter on ESPN. Linda walked down the steps wearing black and purple lingerie with thigh-high leggings. She had her makeup done to perfection. I looked at Tony to search his face for anger to warn me if this was a bad idea, but he seemed happy and excited.

"Hey, Ken. I see you found us easy enough. Do you need anything, or do you want to go straight to the bed-room?" Linda asked.

"Yeah, Ken, if you want, we can get started now," Tony said eagerly.

"Um . . . Sure, we can get started now," I said.

I was shocked at myself for actually being nervous. She grabbed her husband by the arm, and I followed them up the steps. They opened the door to their bedroom, and there was a massive bed in the center of the room. Right next to the bed was a club chair. Linda kissed me, then kissed her husband. Tony grabbed and hugged her.

"Have fun."

She kissed him deeply and went back to me. Linda led me to the bed. Nervousness had set in big time, and I wasn't hard yet. I had a million things on my mind. Was this guy going to seriously watch me fuck his wife? Was he going to try to touch me? Was he going to get mad and flip out when Linda and I were going at it? I had to stall and gain my composure. Linda gave me a condom, but I put it in my pocket.

"I want to please you completely," I whispered in her ear.

I pulled her panties down and lay her on her back. Then I kissed her neck and licked her from her neck down to her pussy. I put my hand on her ass and pulled her to my face. I licked her slowly and sucked on her clit, trying to gather my thoughts quickly. *I've done this a million times, and having her husband here shouldn't be any different. She came to me because she knew I could please her,* I kept telling myself.

Luckily, all of her loud moaning helped me get hard, but I wanted her to come. I slid the condom on. Her body was shaking. I licked two of my fingers and frantically worked them into her while I flicked my tongue swiftly over the top of her clit. She gripped the sheets. Her skin reddened, and her body bucked uncontrollably. Tony loved what he saw so far, leaned over in the chair, and kissed her forehead. I was glad he still had his clothes on.

I pulled her to me and placed her legs over my shoulders. She was turned on by the way I drew her roughly to me. She was incredibly tight when I entered her. She let out a loud moan and dug her fingernails into my back.

Tony looked concerned.

"Are you okay, honey?" he asked.

"Yes. Yes. I'm OK . . . It's fine," she said.

"Do you want him to stop or slow down?"

"No. I want it like this."

I was relentless, barreling my dick inside her and hearing her scream out in both pain and ecstasy. I could tell it hurt her a little, but she enjoyed it more and more as time went on. Tony's eyes were glued to the action. I laid Linda flat on her stomach and entered her from behind. My dick pulsated inside of her as I felt her pussy stretching to accommodate me. I stroked her swiftly. Tony leaned over and talked dirty to her.

"Do you like that black dick, baby? Do you like that big black dick inside you right now?"

"Yes . . . Yes, baby," she moaned.

I couldn't believe he enjoyed watching his wife like this.

"Do you like being fucked like a slut?" he asked.

"Yes, baby, I love it."

Linda's pussy tightened around my dick. Her body shook uncontrollably. I placed one of her legs on my right shoulder and kept the other to the side while I continued stroking her.

"Rub on your clit, honey. Tell me when you're going to come again. I want you to tell me. OK, baby?" Tony said.

"Yes . . . yes . . . babe."

She followed his instructions, and it wasn't long until she was letting him know she was there again.

"I'm . . . oh my God . . . I'm . . . coming."

She pushed me off and shook hard.

Tony kissed and held her.

"That was beautiful, honey. You looked so beautiful," he said.

Linda lay on the bed, weak and shaky from coming intensely.

She reached for my hardness, jerked, and sucked me until I lost all control and came on her face.

Tony gave her a towel, and she wiped herself off. She looked up at me and said, "That was incredible. Thank you so much for that. I loved it."

I smiled.

Linda put on her robe, and we all went downstairs.

"That was great, man. I love watching her come. Can you come back sometime so we can do this again?" Tony asked.

"Uh . . . Sure. I'm happy you both enjoyed it."

We sat around, talked, and laughed about the gym. Tony told me funny stories that happened at his shop. I shook hands with him, hugged Linda, and drove home, feeling proud of myself.

***

"Congratulations, Kenny," my mom yelled.

"I don't know why you guys are making such a big deal about this," I said. I wasn't overly excited because, even though I had accomplished a significant milestone by graduating with my BA degree, I would start classes for my master's in two days. I still had a long way to go before I felt I could celebrate.

"Oh, hush, and be happy. If you're not going to be excited about this accomplishment, don't spoil it for us," my mom said.

"We're so proud of you," Tiffani added.

"Yeah . . . We're proud of you," Heather said awkwardly.

I figured she didn't like Tiffani being there for my graduation and saw her as a threat. My mom and Tiffani were off to the side, looking at the camera when Heather walked up to me.

"Who's that girl, and why is she here?"

I laughed. "That's my friend, Tiffani. You have nothing to worry about. She has a boyfriend, and she's really good friends with my mom. She's like family. Besides her and my mother, you're the only special person in my life that I invited."

She smiled. That was a lie. I had four tickets. I invited Tiffani because she was special to me. My mom was a given. I invited my dad, who, as usual, disappointed me and was MIA. I asked Heather to make up for all the times I canceled on her. I wanted to keep her feeling like she was someone special because, even though she could be boring, she was a good woman, and the good ones were hard to find. This was a proud moment for me, and I needed a break from the hectic couple of months I'd been having.

Linda told her crew of fellow desperate housewives around the gym about our romp, and three of her friends wanted to do the same thing. It was fun at first, and I felt like "the man," but as time went on, I didn't like feeling like a novelty to them and like I was just being used to cross off fucking a Black man on their bucket lists.

I knew it was time to call it quits when I was at the home of Linda's friend, Caitlin. I was hammering Caitlin doggie style when I kept feeling like something was touching my ass. I ignored it and kept doing my thing. I turned my head and saw her husband Frank jerking off and trying to rub on my ass. He came, and it went all over my legs. I was furious and screamed at him. We almost had a fistfight.

"Calm down. So what you got a little come on your feet. Relax," Frank said.

"Fuck that. You knew the deal before we started this shit."

"Don't yell at me in my fucking house. Know your place, nigger."

That stopped me in my tracks, and that suspicion of being nothing more than a novelty instantly became a reality.

"What did you say?" I asked.

"You heard me."

I stomped toward him, about to knock off his fucking head.

"What? Are you going to hit me? If you *touch* me, your ass will be in jail. Get this straight—you're nothing special. A couple of my friends and I watch you fuck our wives because it's entertaining, but do you think we're threatened by you?"

"You should be. I'm giving your wives what you can't."

He laughed. "That's all you're good for. When we get bored with you, we'll find some other boy to take your place."

I looked at Caitlin. She looked uncomfortable but didn't confirm or deny what he was saying. I felt embarrassed and emasculated. I picked up my clothes, got dressed, and left. I met up with the other couples a few times, but I wasn't feeling it anymore after hearing what Frank said. Slowly, I cut them all off. Linda was disappointed, but she understood and continued to train with me.

I stopped dealing with couples, but my reputation around the gym was still strong. I had lots of one-night stands with members. I slept with some of them more than once, like my client Karen, but everything began to take its toll. I was exhausted all the time, and my grades were starting to slip. Between school, work, and juggling all of those women, it was becoming too time-consuming.

I wanted more. Being around Ray and Lucy and seeing other guys at the movies or mall with their girlfriends, I realized I wanted that again.

I wanted one girl that could give me everything. I organized my time better with work and school. I stopped having empty one-night stands and sleeping with members and clients and worked on seeing if it were possible to find what I was looking for in one of the women I already had.

Now that I had more money, the quality of the dates I took them on was better. Ron helped me a lot with that too.

"What? You got tickets for the Summer Jam concert?" I asked.

"Yeah, you want some?"

"Hell yeah. How much?"

If I didn't know Ron, I would've thought he was full of shit, but he *always* delivered.

"Give me fifty dollars," he said.

"Only fifty dollars a ticket?"

"Nah, fifty dollars total."

"Damn, thanks. Usually, those tickets cost a grip."

I took Denise to the concert, and Ron got me tickets for the BODIES exhibit for Heather. He also helped me to get Krissy a demo tape. I gave it to Sonia in hopes that she could get Krissy a record deal.

"It'll be awhile before I can check it out, but if she's as good as you say she is, I'll be in touch," Sonia said.

My schedule at Def Jam was sporadic and hectic, but it gave me the alibis I needed to juggle my three ladies. I made the bulk of my money working at Def Jam, so there was no way I was going to fuck that up. I didn't sleep with any of my clients there and kept things strictly business.

Things with my three women were good, but there was still something missing. Maybe it wasn't in the cards for me to be monogamous.

"All right, give me one more," I told my client, Karen, as she struggled to do the last rep of her lunges. Then I handed her a towel. Ron was giving a tour to a group of women. One of the women locked eyes with me. I didn't acknowledge her or wave, but I knew exactly who she was. I could never forget that long, red hair.

"Jesus, I'm gonna be sore tomorrow," Karen said.

I laughed and broke eye contact with the woman I was staring at. That woman was Ashley.

I walked with Karen to the PT office and scheduled our next appointment. When she left, I sat anxiously in the office. A million thoughts were going through my mind. What was she doing here? If we talked, would it be friendly or hostile? I wanted to hate her. I didn't mean shit to her because she never tried to reach out to me after that night I left.

A knock on the clear office door interrupted my thoughts. *Of course, it's Ashley,* I thought.

"Can I talk to you for a minute?" she asked.

"I can't talk long. I got a client coming in."

"I won't keep you. I just wanted to say I'm sorry. You were right. My ex, Carlos, was full of shit."

I nodded. I also realized she said, "ex."

"What happened with that?" I asked.

"Well, Carlos got locked up again. He fucked up big this time and got caught selling a shitload of heroin and ended up getting in a shootout with the cops before they caught him. I went to his trial with his family and saw a girl crying the day he got sentenced. I asked his sister, Yesenia, who the girl was and why she was crying. She told me, 'That's his girlfriend.' I looked at her like she had two fucking heads and said, 'But *I'm* his girlfriend.' She told me she didn't want me to find out like this, but he spent most of his time with her. I couldn't believe she kept me in the dark like that. I thought she was my friend, but I guess she put her brother first."

The last time we spoke, she flipped out when I poured my heart out to her and told her she should've been with me. I know I was petty, but I was glad she went through this shit. I didn't say anything, though. I just nodded and let her continue talking.

"When Carlos was taken away by the court officers, I walked up to the girl and asked her, 'Who are you to Carlos?' The girl looked me up and down and said, 'He's my man. Who are you?' I laughed at her and said, 'That's funny. He's been with me for five years.' The bitch laughed back at me and said, 'That's funny. He lived with me and slept in my bed every night. You must be the dumb bitch he said gave him money all the time.' That last part hurt. I left the courthouse feeling stupid and used."

I sighed, not caring that she got what was coming to her.

"I never apologized, and I'm sorry I said all that shit to you," Ashley said.

"It's cool. Everything you said woke me up and helped me realize I needed to do more with my life."

"I can see that. You look great. I only said those things to you out of anger. Everything you told me was the truth, but I didn't want to hear it then."

I nodded.

"I wanted to know if we could go back to the way things were."

In that second, I thought about the good times I had with her, and I remembered the bad. My mind told me to leave her alone, but my heart told me to see where things could take me. The heart wants what the heart wants, and sometimes, even though things aren't logical, our emotions can get the best of us.

"We can start slow and go from there, I guess," I said hesitantly.

"Cool. Slow is good."

Her friends knocked on the door and waved for her to come out. Ron was standing behind them.

"Your number is still the same, right?" Ashley asked.

"Yeah, it never changes."

"Good. I'll call you so we can meet up."

"Cool."

I wouldn't hold my breath for that call, but I was glad I had closure after our last spat.

She and her friends left.

"Hey, Ron?" I said.

"What's up?"

"That was that girl Ashley I told you about."

"I figured once she told me her name and kept asking questions about you. When I saw her come in here to talk to you, I knew she was trying to patch up things."

"What did she ask about me?"

"She asked how long you've been working here and if you were seeing anyone."

"What did you say?"

"I said you were one of my best trainers, and I didn't know about your love life, that she'd have to ask you."

"Yeah, we talked for a while. She said she wanted to try to go back to how things were."

"What did you say about that?"

"I said we could take things slow and see what happens. I still have feelings for her."

"Interesting."

"What do you think I should do?"

"You know I'll never tell you what decision you need to make, but I want you to think about this. According to Franklin P. Jones, 'Experience is that marvelous thing that enables you to recognize a mistake when you make it again.'"

"So, you think I shouldn't pursue things with her because it would be a mistake?"

He walked away as he said, "I don't know. You tell me."

I hated it when he never gave me a direct answer.

Weeks passed. Ashley and I started slow. At first, I only saw her at the gym. When I had some downtime, I trained her and her friends for free. Ron frowned on it. He never said anything, but I knew he felt she was using me. A part of me knew she was, but I couldn't understand why I didn't care. I just wanted to be around her, even if it didn't benefit me at all.

Things eventually progressed to us having dinner often. I spent time with her, but not as much as I did in the past. I kept Denise, Kristen, and Heather as my priorities.

As time went on, I felt those old feelings I had for her coming back. Before I knew it, I was falling for her again.

Ashley had a bitchiness about her that both attracted and infuriated me at the same time.

At times, she showed her loving side—a compassionate and caring side, but there were also times when she could be manipulative and cruel. When I was angry with her, she could look at me, give me a bullshit apology, and my mood would change in an instant. I didn't like that she had that type of power over me.

One day, I had plans to hang with Heather, but Ashley asked me to come over to her place at the last minute. I almost decided not to see her because getting some ass from Heather was guaranteed while getting some from Ashley was only a slim possibility.

The truth was I liked being around her. I called Heather.

"Hey, babe," I said.

"Hey, what's up?" she said, sounding excited to hear from me. "What are we doing tonight?"

"I know you're going to be disappointed, but I can't make it."

"Why?"

"I have to go to the city to train some of my clients. Their schedules opened up, and I have to work around them, so I'm pretty much their bitch when they call me. I gotta cancel our plans. I'm sorry."

"I hate your job. I know you make great money with it, but I feel like I never get to see you."

"I know. I promise I'll make it up to you."

That calmed her down.

I got to Ashley's. We talked and watched one of her favorite movies, *Labyrinth*. Then she got up and headed to her bedroom.

When she returned, she had her hand behind her back.

"Whatcha' got there?" I asked.

"Guess."

"I don't know. A present for me?"

She moved her hand from around her back and opened it. One gold Magnum condom was in her palm. I smiled.

"Are you serious?" I asked.

"Yup, I'm serious."

I didn't waste time. I stood from the couch, and she led me to the bedroom. We kissed excitedly and quickly took off all our clothes. She held my dick in her hands and put on the condom. I wanted her for so long, and now it was finally going to happen.

I climbed on top, eased into her, and slowly began my rhythm. She wrapped her arms around my back and matched my speed. After a short while in that position, Ashley climbed on top and rode me, controlling the depth and speed. She leaned over, and I sucked her nipples.

Ashley sped up, leaned back, then moved up and down and in circles. Her face had confidence written all over it like she knew she'd have me under her finger after she made me come. This was a game to her. She wanted control. My breathing was rough and erratic. My heart was beating out of my chest, my muscles tensed. I felt like I couldn't hold back much longer, but I adjusted. I slowed down my breathing and put my mind somewhere else because I didn't want to come yet.

I wanted *her* to be addicted to *me,* not the other way around, so I moved her off me. That bought me a few seconds to cool down. I positioned her for doggie style. Putting her in a different position helped me gain my composure. My balls slammed against her backside. I wanted her to be hooked.

Her pussy tightened. It felt heavenly, but I couldn't give in. I knew whoever held out the longest would have power over the other, and that was going to be me.

I kept stroking her, and when I felt like I was close to coming again in that position, I moved her on to her back. I spread her legs apart as far as they could go, held her by the waist, and stroked her mercilessly. She was wet beyond belief, her chest rose and fell, and I could feel the shivers ripple through her body. I licked my left thumb and massaged her clit. The stimulation drove her crazy. Her back arched, her hands clawed the sheets—and then it happened. Ashley finally gave in to her orgasm. *She was mine*. She broke first, so *I* had the power.

She put her hand on my chest and motioned for me to give her a minute. I wasn't satisfied yet. I wanted her to come again before I went once. I pulled out and immediately went down on her. I licked all around her lips, worked my tongue in and out of her, and sucked on the head of her clitoris. From the squeal she made, her orgasm must have snuck up on her. She slapped the bed hard, her pussy fluttered uncontrollably, and her legs trembled. She couldn't stop cursing. While she was still weak from the orgasm, I turned her around and hammered her from behind. I plunged into her quick and powerful.

"Shit," she cried out.

"Say my name."

She shook her head. I didn't know if she was overwhelmed with the intense feeling of our sex or if she was resisting giving in. However, I was unrelenting with my penetration.

"Say my name," I repeated.

Again, she wouldn't. While still in doggie style, I stood up for more leverage and pounded into her deeper.

"Ooooh, damn . . . my God," she screamed.

"Say it."

She swallowed hard. Her face was flushed.

"Say it," I demanded.

Her breathing was choppy again. Her vagina spasmed, telling me she was close to climaxing again.

"Ken!" she screamed out.

"Who are you with right now?"

"Ken!" she exclaimed.

I wanted to know she wasn't thinking about someone else. I wanted to know her feelings were for me. I wanted her to see the person that was making her feel this good was me.

"Who do you want right now?"

"Ken, Ken, Kennn . . . I'm coming!" she screamed.

Her body went limp, and she repeatedly jerked on the bed. I was happy she came numerous times, and I hadn't come once. I could see she was annoyed that she hadn't made me come yet. She went back to riding me. She placed her feet flat down and moved up and down rapidly on my length. My toes curled. I tried hard to hold back that feeling, but it was too late. I came hard and roared like a lion.

Soon, we lay on the bed panting. The rest of the night, we continued to try to outdo each other, trying to make each other come. Both of us wanted to feel like we were in control.

While I won the battle, I lost the war. Eventually, I went right back into cooking and spending most of my free time with her. Things were a little different now, though. She introduced me to her family. Her parents seemed to like me. We were having sex on the regular, and she was affectionate with me. That's the weird thing with sex. At first, I thought it was just a woman thing, but with sex came emotions, and she had me sprung.

Things weren't perfect. Whenever I hinted about us being exclusive, she brought up the fact that I still saw other girls. She insisted we were good the way we were. No commitment. No attachment. Just two people enjoying each other. I still kept Denise, Heather, and Kristen around and made sure to focus on one of them every week, so they didn't feel I was too inconsistent and leave me.

Whenever I needed to vent, I always turned to Tiffani.

"You're crazy. You know this, right?" Tiffani said.

"I know. I don't usually do stuff like that. I don't know what it is about her."

"Damn, is the sex that good that she has you sprung like that?"

"It's good. . . . I wouldn't say it's the sex that has me sprung, though, because I was feeling her way before we did anything physical."

"But from what you told me, it doesn't seem like she deserves to get those types of feelings, especially if she doesn't return them."

Tiffani looked and sounded jealous. Although we were friends, I knew she cared about me. Seeing her act that way made me appreciate her more.

"Thanks for caring," I said.

"You know I care. I just don't want you to reopen the same wound and get hurt all over again."

"I know, which is why I haven't told any of my boys about us reconnecting. If things with us don't work out, I don't want to hear it from them. I'll let them know if we ever become more than what we are."

"Just be careful."

I knew she was right, and I should be careful, but I also knew what I wanted. Ashley made me feel something Heather, Denise, and Kristen didn't. If it meant cutting them all off to be with her exclusively, I'd do that. I had doubts as I replayed the day we fought in my head, but many things had changed since then. I had a good job, a nice car, money, and my own place. We were having sex now, and I knew she was pleased. I told myself history wouldn't repeat itself this time.

It was New Year's Eve. I was in P. F. Chang's with Ashley and her dad, Daniel. He told me on numerous occasions he and her mom thought I was the best guy she'd ever dated. I liked that. I wanted this New Year to end what I'd been doing. I wanted to stop wasting time. I liked her. She liked me. Tonight was the night to start everything new. Tonight, I'd ask her to be my girl exclusively.

I had no problems cutting off the rest. I wanted Ashley. Kristen, Denise, and Heather all wanted to see me that night, but I told them I had other plans that involved working and networking. They were disappointed I wouldn't start the New Year with them, but I didn't care. If things worked out the way I wanted, I wouldn't have to make excuses about my job to avoid hanging out with them anymore. I'd be a one-woman man.

Ashley rolled her eyes as Daniel told me stories of how she was as a kid. We laughed and talked a little more before Daniel had to cut our lunch short because he had to fix an IT problem for one of the offices he worked at.

Ashley and I went back to her apartment. We had the apartment to ourselves. Her sister was out with her boyfriend and would be gone for the night. We were like honeymooners sexing each other all over the place, touching and pleasuring each other like we were newly-weds. When the sexing stopped, and we held each other in bed, I mustered up the courage to tell her how I felt.

"Ash, I'm really feeling you."

"I'm feeling you too."

"You know I care about you, and I never wanted this to be just another fuck. What I'm trying to say is I want you to be my girl exclusively. I don't want anyone else. I just want you."

"Ken, let's talk about this later. Let's just enjoy this right now."

I was annoyed. Was I being used again? Was she seeing someone else? Why wouldn't she want to be with me after I changed into everything she said I wasn't? I could've let it go, but I wanted answers. I rested my back against the headboard and sat up.

"It's a real simple answer, Ashley—yes or no. Either you want to be with me, or you don't."

"Why can't you just enjoy what we have? If it's not broken, don't fix it. I'm giving you what every man dreams of. I give you consistent ass regularly and no commitment. Why do you want to change all of that with a title?"

"You're not giving me what every man wants because this man wants you. I don't get it. It was so easy for you to commit to Carlos. You were so cool with that title. I do everything for you. I changed my life to be worthy of being with you, and it's never enough. Why can't you commit to me?"

"You changing your life was good for you. You did all of the things you were supposed to do. What do you want, a fucking cookie? I don't ask you for anything. I committed to my ex because I loved him. I don't love you. I can't force those feelings. I like you a lot, though. You take care of many of my needs, and I like that, but I don't have that spark with you."

That spark? I hated that fucking expression. That shit was mythological. Women always talked about finding the right man, but when he was right in front of their fucking faces, they couldn't even see it. I could easily manipulate other girls because they believed in this *spark* and felt they found it with me.

"I love you," I stated.

She laughed at me. I couldn't believe she did that. "What do you know about love?" she asked coldly.

"So, after all of this, the dinners, the fucking, the hanging out, you can't see yourself being with me?"

"Ken, to be honest, I don't see us ever being more than what we are right now. You take care of my needs, and I love you for that, but I don't love you."

The disappointment was all over my face. She returned to lying on my chest and fell asleep as if nothing happened. She was at peace while I was in hell. I lay there, staring at the ceiling. Inside my head, it killed me that the one I wanted so much didn't want me back.

When she finally woke up, she tried to be overly affectionate, hugging, kissing, and trying to compliment me on how sexy I was, but I was inconsolable and only let off a small grin here and there. I was distant and said very little the rest of the night, so she tried to talk a lot to mask the awkward silence.

It was about that time, and the ten-second countdown to the New Year was coming. Earlier that day, I was ready to stop sleeping around with all other girls for this one. I had felt this New Year would start with me being happy. Instead, I was sadder than ever.

The ball dropped. It was a new year, and nothing changed.

She kissed me, but I wasn't into it. I got up, gathered my stuff, and prepared to leave.

"Where are you going?" she asked.

"I got work early in the morning. I'm gonna head home."

She knew I could've easily spent the night with her, but I'd be in a funky mood all night, so she just let me be. I walked to the door, and she tried to give me a peck on the mouth, but I turned my face, and she kissed my cheek. She tried to hug me, but I wouldn't hug her back. She made me feel like I was nothing to her, so I acted as if she were nothing to me. I walked away, leaving her standing in the doorway, calling me to come back.

Chapter Eight

Darkness

The headboard banged loudly against the wall in my bedroom. Loud moans, heavy breathing, and sounds of the bed creaking echoed throughout the room. I was in a trance fucking Krissy from behind with my mind on Ashley the entire time. With each pump, I wanted to go through Krissy. I wanted her to feel the pain I felt inside, and with every thrust, I wanted to kill the weakness I felt and callous that soft spot in my heart that I still had for Ashley.

Krissy tried to turn her head to look at me, but I pulled her by her hair. I didn't want to be looked at. I couldn't even look at myself.

"Oh my God, Ken . . . oh my—"

Krissy's orgasm snuck up on her and caused her to curse loudly. I pumped away, harder and faster to get my rocks off. Then we lay in bed, panting.

"Ken?"

"Yeah."

"Are you OK?"

"I'm good . . . Why?"

"I . . . I worry about you. You scare me sometimes."

"Why?"

"I know there's something on your mind. You weren't with me. I mean, you were with me in the physical sense, but you weren't with me emotionally. What's going on?"

"I . . . I'm fine. I got a couple of things stressing me out, but nothing I can't handle. I'll be all right."

"Kenny, you know you can talk to me about anything, right?"

"I know."

"Well, I'm here for you. You can tell me anything."

I didn't doubt she'd listen to my problems and be that sympathetic ear for me, but I didn't want someone to vent to. I needed more. I needed to escape.

I slept with more women. Each gave me a sense of power and control and helped me forget about my insecurities, anger, and sadness. Even if it were only temporary, that feeling of euphoria I got from fucking them made me feel loved.

While I had the faux sense of love, it didn't fill the hole in my heart that Bri and Ashley left. It was getting bigger, and nothing was making it better.

I preyed on women who were pretty, gold-digging women because at least I knew what I was going into. They were using me, and I was using them. I'd go to bars and clubs, wear my Armani outfits, dangle my car keys, and watch as dumb, materialistic bitches flocked to me. I'd fuck some of them in the backseat of my car or in the bathroom stalls of the places I met them.

"Damn, that was good," the random girl I hooked up with said.

I met her at some hole-in-the-wall bar and brought her to my place for an easy fuck. I didn't even care to remember her name.

"Eh, it was all right. I've had better," I replied nonchalantly.

"What? Fuck you. You weren't all that either."

The nameless girl angrily gathered her clothes.

"Oh yeah? Let yourself out," I laughed.

"Fuck you. Why are you treating me like I'm some ho?"

"You fucked me on the first night after I bought you a few cheap drinks and flossed some cash. How'd you expect me to treat you?"

She looked angry and hurt, slamming the door behind her as she stormed out of my place. I didn't care about her or any of the other dumb bitches I had one-nighters with. I didn't care about anything anymore.

The next night, I had another similar experience.

"Do you like that?"

Some random girl I met in the bar was going down on me in the bathroom stall. She was terrible at it. I grabbed her head and shoved my dick deeper down her throat. She gagged, coughed, and pulled herself off me.

"I can't breathe when you do that."

I ignored her and pulled her back to me. She wanted to go back to sucking me off, but that bored me. I bent her over and banged her doggie style in the stall.

"It's too hard . . . oh my God . . . It hurts," she yelled.

I didn't give a fuck if it hurt. I kept pounding her. My rhythm was unrelenting.

"Oh God . . . Damn."

She placed her hand on my chest to try to slow me down. I pushed her hand away and continued. I pulled out of her, took the condom off, and came all over her ass. When I was done, I pushed her off me, and she fell to the floor. I adjusted my clothes and walked out of the bathroom. She followed behind me, struggling to adjust her clothes to look decent.

"Hey, what the fuck was that? You fuck me and treat me like I'm a piece shit?" she yelled.

"How'd you think I'd treat a skank I fucked in a stall?"

"Ooooh, I can't stand fucking men," she screamed.

Everyone was staring at us. She left the bar embarrassed and in tears. I walked to the bartender nonchalantly, paid the tab, and tipped him. Then I left the bar to go to a club in search of another conquest.

I told my friends about my late nights, and even though they all warned me to slow down, nothing they said made me feel better or made me want to stop doing what I'd been doing.

Tiffani came over to hang out with me briefly. We were lounging around in my apartment when she said, "Ken, something's off with you. You're not your usual self, and you don't look happy anymore."

"I'm good."

"If I weren't with Josh, I'd show you there *are* good women out there. I care about you, and I don't like seeing you like this."

I didn't doubt she could show me she was a great woman. I already knew that, but she had a man, and I wasn't him. Her compassion couldn't help me now. She knew whatever was bothering me had me acting out more than before.

"Thanks. I just need to get some things out of my system. I'll be fine."

I got a text from Donna that read, I just wanted you to know I'm thinking of you. I miss you, and I want to see you.

I wasn't in the mood to respond to her text.

A minute later, I got a call from an unknown number and ignored that too. First, I never answered numbers I didn't know. Second, when I was with Tiff, I didn't answer my phone to talk to other girls. I respected her too much for that.

We ordered pizza, watched *Love Jones,* and enjoyed each other's company. Tiff explained she and my mom planned a trip to go out to the Tanger Outlets in Pennsylvania. I was happy they had such a tight relationship.

"After the trip to PA with your mom, I think that next weekend, I'm going to surprise Josh and go home to Seattle."

"You want to spend all that money only to see him for two days? Why don't you wait until you have more time to spend with him?"

"I can't wait. The longer we're apart, the more we fight, and I miss him."

"I know you do, but that trip isn't cheap."

"It's not, but it's worth it. Plus, if I'm broke, I'll bug you to lend me some money."

I rolled my eyes and smiled. Tiff grabbed her purse to get going when my phone rang again with that same unfamiliar number.

"Damn, somebody sure wants to talk to you."

"If I don't know the number, they must not be that important."

We hugged. Tiffani kissed me on the cheek. "Take care, Kenny, and don't love them hoes."

"You know I don't."

She let herself out. Shortly afterward, my phone rang a third time. I finally decided it was time to see who was calling from this mystery number.

"Hey, Kenny . . ."

My jaw dropped when I heard the voice on the phone. I thought to myself that my mind had to be fucking with me. This *couldn't* be who I thought it was.

"Who's this?" I asked.

"Kenny . . . It's Bri."

All types of emotions were going through me. I'd moved on, but there was still something about hearing her voice that irritated me. I sighed and said, "What do you want?"

"I know you're still upset with me, and you have every right to be. I did and said a lot of fucked-up things to you."

"I haven't heard from you in almost two years, and *now* you spring up and tell me this shit? How did you expect I'd react? You think I can forget about everything and forgive you?"

"Ken . . . I know you can't forget what happened, but maybe you can forgive me someday. Maybe things can go back to the way they were."

"That's a lot of maybes. I've changed, and I'm sure you have too. Why are you even talking like this anyway? What happened with you and David?"

"That's over. He said I was just a challenge to him. He wanted to see if it would be easy to take me away from you, and once he did, the challenge was gone, and he got bored with me. I was hurt and realized how you must've felt. I thought since we had grown up together and I'd known him for so long that he looked at me as more than just some jump-off. I thought he cared about me, but I was nothing to him."

After hearing Bri say all that, I had no sympathy for her. I wasn't elated, but I still wanted to pay her back for what she did to me.

"Well, I'm sorry that happened, but I don't know if things with you and me can be the same again. Maybe we can try to be friends again. Do you have plans tonight?"

I had no intention of ever being friends with her again, and I didn't have plans with any of my other girls, so I had nothing but time.

"Sure, Kenny. What time?" She sounded excited.

"I'll pick you up at your house at six."

"I can't wait. I want to try to fix things between us."

"Me too," I said, but I was sure my way of fixing things was different from what she had in mind.

I pulled up to her house around 6:05 in my Mercedes and honked the horn. She came out wearing a lacy black dress that looked more like lingerie than anything else. I had to admit she looked good. Her mouth dropped open when she saw my car. She opened the door.

"Kenny, how did you get this car?"

"Everything is legal. I can afford stuff like this now. I'm doing big things at my new job. Like I told you before, a lot has changed."

"I can see that. You got huge. You've been working out hard, huh? Oh, and look at you—Armani? You must be doing it *really* big. What do you do now?"

"Remember when I told you I wanted to open my gym?"

"Yeah."

"Well, I'm a personal trainer now. I train people for Def Jam Records, and I work for Lifetime Fitness. I'm learning the business, so when I open my gym, my company will be bigger and better."

"Nice. So, where are we headed?"

"I figured we could go to Peter Luger for dinner and figure out what we're going to do afterward while we eat."

I could've taken her someplace more elegant, but she wasn't worth going all out for. When we got to the restaurant, I told her to order whatever she wanted, and she had no problem doing that. She ordered all types of drinks and got the most expensive things on the menu. I let her talk. She told me what she hated about David, what she loved about him, and how she was so hurt by what he did to her. The whole time, she never apologized or said shit about what she'd done to me or how she made *me* feel.

Whenever I tried to say anything about myself, she directed the conversation back to her. Just listening to her, I had no second thoughts about what I wanted to do.

The check came. She snuck a peek at how much it was. I pulled out my wallet. She didn't offer to contribute or leave a tip. I paid for it in cash, and she looked impressed when she saw me easily pay for everything. Those days of being broke were over. I wanted her to see that. I was mad at myself for never realizing she was this materialistic and money-grubbing. Was I too blind in the past to see this, or did she develop this when she was with David?

We left the restaurant.

"So, what do you want to do now?" I asked.

"Let's go back to my house and hang out like we used to."

"Sounds good to me."

We drove back to her place. Her parents were in Atlanta for vacation. Usually, she went with them. A curious look came across my face when I noticed boxes of clothes in the living room. I guess she saw it.

"Uh, I was living with David for a while. I just moved back home two days ago, which is why I didn't go to Atlanta with my parents. I didn't unpack everything yet," she explained quickly.

This showed me that she didn't come back to me because she missed me or had any remorse or feelings for me. Donna was right. Bri only saw me as a backup plan.

We went to her living room, and Bri put on the movie *Love & Basketball*. She knew exactly what she was doing. I loved that movie because the characters reminded me of us, and she was trying to play with my emotions, but what she didn't realize is that I had also mastered how to manipulate people with our time apart.

We sat on the couch, and she rubbed on my right leg. I started to rise in my jeans.

"You want to come upstairs?" she asked.

"Sure."

She held my hand and led me up the stairs. She was swishing her ass hard, trying to show me what I was missing—what she thought I still desired more than anything.

We got to her room, and she went to her nightstand and tossed me a condom. Bri quickly stepped out of her dress, bra, and panties. She pulled off my clothes and kissed all over my body.

"I missed you so much, Kenny. Just being with you today brought back all the good memories we had together. You were so good to me. You always took care of me, and I never had to worry about you hurting me."

This felt so familiar and comfortable, but I knew it was pure bullshit. I wasn't naïve like I was in the past. I knew what Bri was doing and why she was doing it.

"Damn, your body is slammin'," she said, rubbing her hands all over me.

I kissed her neck and stared into her eyes. She didn't have the look I saw whenever Heather, Kristen, or Denise stared me in the eyes, where I could clearly see they were into me. She had the face of a woman that felt she had me wrapped around her finger.

All the memories of her leaving me rushed into my head. I entered her fast. She gasped and wrapped her legs around me. She grimaced and moaned as I stroked her hard. There wasn't anything loving about what we were doing. It was rough and mean. She laid me down and rode me for a bit. I was determined not to let her make me come first. Like my first time with Ashley, this was all about who had the power. She put her hands on my shoulders, rocked, and swirled, trying her best to make me come quickly, but I had lots of experience now, so I knew how to hold back coming.

She broke first. I saw the beautiful sensation of ecstasy take over her. Her eyes rolled to the back of her head. Her body quivered, and she came all over me.

I pushed her off me and hammered her hard from the back. Every thrust was ruthless. The sound of my thighs pounding against her ass sounded like lightning striking.

She moaned louder. I pulled her hair with my left hand and smacked her ass hard with my right.

She winced from the pain. The entire time I was stroking her, I kept thinking of David fucking her the same way. She turned back and looked at me. Then she quickly buried her head in her pillow to muffle her moans. She didn't scream or complain. She knew precisely why it was this rough and took it.

I pulled out of her, took off the condom, yanked her by the hair, and jerked my dick until I came all over her face. She winced when some got in her eyes and mouth. She reached for her nightstand to get some tissues to clean herself off. Her eyes were glassy when she wiped her face.

"That was rough," she said.

I didn't say shit.

"At one point, I thought your dick was gonna come through my mouth. . . . You busted in my face too. You never used to do shit like that. It burned the hell out of my eyes. Now that you got all that anger out of your system, can we try to go back to the way we used to be?"

I laughed. "Nah, it was just a fuck. This doesn't change anything."

Then I repeated to her the same thing she said to me the night she hurt me. "Look, we're still cool. We'll still hang out and stuff as friends. It's not like I don't care about you, but I can't be in a relationship with you."

She looked truly hurt. She cried, looked at me, and said, "I'm sorry for what I did to you."

She sat naked on the edge of the bed and stared at the carpet. I got dressed, kissed her on the forehead, and said, "Goodbye, Bri."

She looked up at me but didn't say a word. She looked like a person defeated. She looked like how I did when she hurt me.

***

Between my experiences with Bri and Ashley, I was tired of feeling weak. I got a little payback on Bri, but I wasn't satisfied. To feel genuinely even, I needed to go a step further. Bri hurt me more than anyone could. She helped to create what I was turning into. I felt that she needed to suffer more.

I finally returned Donna's call. It was eight in the morning, but Donna always woke up early anyway, from what I remembered.

"Hey, Donna."

"Hey, Kenny. It's been a long time. How are you?"

"I'm good. A lot has changed—a new job, a new perspective on life—new everything."

"Well, that's good. I only got to talk to you here and there through text, but I never got to apologize. I'm sorry. I know I was messed up by not saying anything to Bri about that night we hung out. I haven't talked to her since, and I haven't seen you since that day either."

"It's cool. That's all in the past. Do you feel like hanging out today?"

"Hell yeah. It's been too long, and I've been bored hanging out around my house."

"All right, cool. I'll let you get ready, and I'll pick you up around noon."

"Good. I'll see you then."

"OK. See you soon."

I didn't tell her I saw Bri the day before. When she saw me last time, I was that nice guy that used to get stepped on. I was the guy who had compassion and couldn't sleep with her because I thought it wouldn't be right. That guy was dead. I wanted to collect what I missed out on back then. That was my intention for the day. To me, that would be the icing on the cake.

As soon as I left Bri's house, I knew I wanted to finish getting my payback by fucking Donna. I didn't care how it would make me look. I didn't care if Donna got hurt in the process. Bri and Ashley taught me that in the war of love, there were no feelings of remorse.

I pulled up to Donna's house and texted her to let her know I was outside. She came out and was confused because she didn't see my old car. I honked my horn, rolled my windows down, and waved to her. The expression on her face was priceless. I never got tired of seeing that look.

She got inside.

"Look at you, doing it big," she said.

I smiled. "I'm trying."

"You're succeeding," she laughed. "So, what's on the agenda for today?"

"For you, my dear, I'm going to be spontaneous and wing it. I don't know what we are going to do today. I have no real plan, but what I do know is that I would like nothing else than to spend this day with you."

She smiled. "That's what I love about you, Kenny. You're so sweet."

Everything I told her was bullshit. I always had a plan. We'd eat lunch, and I'd let her vent and talk about her problems. We'd see the Mets vs. Yankee game, which I already had tickets for at the will-call window. I'd take her out to dinner and have her for dessert.

Ron had connections with the Mets, so as soon as I left Bri's house, I set my plan up to fuck Donna. I had called Ron and asked him if he could get me tickets for the game. His friend, who worked at the stadium, only had field-level seats. I bought them in hopes Donna would say yes to hanging out. My backup plan was to bring either Heather or Krissy to the game if Donna couldn't make it. Either way, it was a win-win for me because I'd get some ass one way or another.

First things first, I told her we should hang out in the city. I parked my car at the Glen Cove train station, and we took the Long Island Rail Road into Manhattan. We walked around the city, looked in different stores, and talked about the fun we had when we regularly hung out. I liked having that conversation with her because I wanted her to feel safe with me and let her guard down.

We passed the American Girl doll store on Forty-Ninth and Fifth Avenue. I held her hand and walked her into the store. She loved all the dolls and was amazed at how much you could customize them.

"You should make a doll for yourself," I said.

"Nah, they're beautiful, but I can't afford one of these rights now."

"Don't sweat the price. I got you. Make the doll however you want it. You're one of my closest friends. It's on me. My treat."

"No, Kenny, it's OK. This doll is really expensive. You don't have to do that for me."

"I know I don't have to do it for you, but I want to do it for you. You're special to me."

Donna couldn't stop smiling. "You're too good to me."

"Only because you deserve it."

We picked out a doll and customized it to look like a little miniature version of her. She loved it.

I told her I knew of this nice Chinese restaurant on Columbus Avenue. We went there, and she enjoyed the food. After we ate, I said, "You know what would be cool?"

"What?"

"If we went to the Mets-Yankees game at Citi Field."

"Oh my God, I'd love that. I've never been to a Subway series game before, but those seats are probably all sold out."

I already knew that she's never been to a game.

"Don't worry, baby. I know people that know people. I'm sure I can get us seats."

"All right. Either way, I'm cool just being with you. I haven't had this much fun in a long time."

We looked to see what time the game was starting on our cell phones, even though I already knew and had tickets. I took her to Modell's on Forty-Second Street.

"Are you getting something from here, Kenny?"

"Yeah, I'm getting something for both of us. If we're going to this game, we have to go in style."

I bought us authentic Yankee jerseys and fitted hats for the game. She was ecstatic. Then we took the seven train to Citi Field. One of the locals had a dog named "Coffee" that was always decked out in Mets gear with a pipe in his mouth. The owner used the dog for panhandling, and the dog became famous. Donna wanted to take a picture with Coffee, so I told her to hang out there while I worked my magic.

I picked up our tickets from the will-call window and held her hand as we walked into the stadium. Donna's eyes were all over the place in amazement.

"I can't believe we're here," she said.

"I'm happy that you're happy."

She smiled.

We went up the escalator one flight, and I handed her the field-level ticket.

"No fucking way. Come on, Kenny, be honest. You had this planned."

"OK . . . OK . . . Maybe this part, but only because I know you've always wanted to go to a game, especially to see a Subway series."

"You're the best."

"I never get tired of hearing that," I laughed.

She playfully punched me in the arm.

We enjoyed the game and cheered our hearts out for the Yankees, who won. When the game was over, I asked her if she wanted to come over to my new condo. She agreed, and we began our trip back home.

We got to my car, and Donna couldn't stop talking about how much fun she had. We walked to my condo, holding hands. I opened the door, and Donna's eyes looked all over my place.

"Damn, Kenny, you've come a long way. I remember when you were a skinny, bigheaded boy who had that beat-up old Ford Escort. Now, you got a Mercedes, a condo, and you're all cut up and sexy. I'm happy for you."

"Thanks. I needed to grow up, and that's what I'm trying to do now. Let me give you a tour of the place."

We laughed as I showed her around the condo. I saved my bedroom for last. Once we got there, Donna lay down on my bed.

"Your bed is so big. I'd never leave my house if I had this."

"Be careful. You're looking sexy lying on my bed like that. I might join you."

I walked up to the bed. Donna crawled up to me and met me on the edge. We stared at each other long and hard. I slowly pulled her to me, and we kissed long and deep. We held each other. I never took my eyes off her as I slowly undressed her.

At first, she looked a little hesitant, but she had a naughty smile on her face. She slowly undressed me as I got into bed with her. We hugged, kissed, and she pushed me on my back. She licked my neck, chest, and stomach before putting my dick in her mouth. I put my hand on top of her hair and worked her head up and down the length of my dick while her thick lips worked their magic on me. It wasn't enough to get head from her. I wanted to fuck her. I needed to seal the deal on what I was too much of a pussy to do in the past.

I held the sides of her face and kissed her. I licked around her areolas, sucked on her nipples, and gently blew on them. I slowly rubbed on her clit and felt her getting extremely wet.

I went down on her, licking all over her clit and lips.
I sucked, slurped, and worked my fingers until she was
screaming, cursing, and coming all over the place. Donna
couldn't take it anymore.

"I need you inside me. Hurry up," she said.

I ran to my dresser drawer and put on a condom. When
I came back to the bed, Donna straddled me. She grabbed
my dick and gradually eased herself down on it, rocking
slowly. I placed my hands on her butt and moved my hips
some to get in sync with her. We had a nice rhythm going,
and our eye contact was on point with every movement.
We switched positions. I told her to lie on her stomach. I
lay on top of her and entered her from behind. We held
hands as she moaned. In this position, I could feel every
nook and cranny of her pussy.

"You feel so . . . so . . . good . . . oh my God," she said.

"You do too."

We continued to move in all types of positions and
pleased each other for the rest of the night.

I woke up the next morning and stared at Donna's
beautiful bronze body lying on my bed naked. I grabbed
my cell phone, took a picture of her in her birthday suit,
and sent it to Bri with the caption: Someone loved your
sloppy seconds.

I laughed to myself, put my phone on my nightstand,
and went to take a shower. The water felt good on me.
The shower was always a place where I could think. I
thought about what I had just done. Wasn't what I did
to Bri the other day enough? Did I have to go this far?
Even with those thoughts, I felt justified. Bri hurt me and
didn't care. Donna used me when it was convenient for
her payback, so why should I feel guilty getting mine?

I got out of the shower, dried off, and walked back into
my bedroom only to see Donna dressed and holding my
cell phone.

"You used me, Ken," she said.

That caught me off guard. My first mistake was that I didn't have a password on my phone. My next was that I had my cell phone away from me in the first place.

"I . . . I . . . didn't mean to . . ." I cleared my throat and adjusted my attitude.

"Everyone uses everyone. That's life. You used me too. Remember the last time we hung out? You made your comment to get her jealous, and who did she take her anger out on? Me. So now it was my turn."

"Your turn?"

"Yup. You shouldn't have been on my phone anyway."

"Your phone kept alerting you that you had a text message. I went to shut it off to go back to sleep, but I saw it was from Bri. I thought maybe she was trying to apologize, but I read what she wrote to you, and I saw what you sent to her.

"She texted me after that and said, 'You had to shit on me too? Thanks a lot. I know I fucked up. I didn't need both of you to rub it in my face.'

"I texted her back. She said you fucked her the other day, busted on her face, and made her feel like a fucking ho. Is that what you think of her? Is that how you feel about me?"

"She got what she deserved. Nothing I do to hurt her will ever compare to the shit she put me through. How I feel about her has nothing to do with how I feel about you."

"That was wrong, Ken. You've changed. You don't care about anyone anymore."

"I care about the only person that has been there for me—me. When it was convenient for you to fuck me out of spite, it was OK, but now that I did it, *I'm* the bad guy? Don't throw this double standard bullshit at me. I did the same thing you wanted to do back then, but I wasn't a pussy and went through with it this time. I don't care how bad she's hurting. I don't care if you think I'm fucked up for doing it. Now she knows what it feels like to be played."

Donna stared at me. "Just take me home, Ken."

"Gladly."

The whole ride, we didn't say one word to each other. I pulled up to her house, and she said, "I thought you were one of the few good guys out there, but you're just like all the other fucked-up guys I've met. I never want to see you again. Seeing you was one of the biggest mistakes I've ever made."

She slammed my door and ran into her house. I got out of my car, opened the trunk, and grabbed all of the bags from our date the previous day. I put the bags on her doorstep, took one last look at Donna's house, and walked back to my car. I couldn't deny I felt bad for hurting her, but she was a casualty in my love war. At least this time, *I* was the last one standing.

"Adam, seriously, you need to stop acting irrational right now," I said.

"No, she needs to understand I'm a martial artist, and I have to dedicate a lot of time to practice. I'm trying to be successful with this and my acting, and that's going to mean time apart from her."

"I get that, but you have to learn to balance. You can't decide you're not going to call her for days and think she's going to be OK with that," I explained.

"Why not? She can call me too."

I ignored his stupid statement.

"I don't know why you're even talking to this fool. He ain't gonna listen to you anyway," Perry added.

We were on our way to pick up Jessie and Denise at their houses to go to my father's open mic night performance at Nakisaki's in Hempstead. Nakisaki's was a nice little Jamaican/Chinese restaurant that had a bit of everything. They had a decent band that provided the music for the performers.

"Brotha, you can't accept gifts from her on holidays and your anniversary and not get her gifts too," I said.

"I don't work much. Gigs haven't been steady, and after paying for school, bills, and my martial arts school, I don't have much money left. Plus, if she got me a gift expecting something in return, that's not a gift. That's a trade."

We chuckled.

We picked Jessie up first. Perry and Jessie hugged and kissed.

"Tell me something sweet and romantic," Jessie said, staring Perry lovingly in his eyes.

Perry looked deep in thought at first but then smiled. "Baby, you remind me of my pinky toe."

Jessie looked confused. "Your pinky toe?"

"Yeah, because I know eventually I'm going to bang you on a table."

We all laughed. She playfully slapped him upside his head.

"You're so fresh."

"Like my daddy always said, if it ain't fresh, it ain't no damn good."

Jessie's smile faded when she saw me. She greeted Adam and said a quick hi to me. We got back inside the car.

"Where are we headed now?" she asked.

"We're going to pick up Ken's friend Denise, and then we're going to Nakisaki's. His father is singing at the open mic there."

"Wait, he's bringing a date there? Today is Thursday, right?" Jessie asked.

"Yeah, he's bringing a friend. Today is Thursday. Why?"

Jessie just smirked. "I guess you're not bringing Kristen tonight, huh?" she asked.

I looked out the window and said, "Not tonight."

"Remember this . . . Players always get caught."

"You remember this . . . I'm not tied down to no one, so I can't get caught if I don't belong to anyone."

"Both of you knock it off. We came out to have fun, not to have a debate. Damn," Perry said.

Adam had to add his two cents in. "Yeah, Ken, you shouldn't be talking disrespectfully to a Black queen like that anyway."

"Shut up," I yelled.

"No, he's right. You should have respect when talking to me." She rolled her eyes at me and then smiled at him.

"How are things going with you and my girl, Lilly?"

Now was my chance to mess with him. "Yeah, Adam, how's Lilly?" I asked sarcastically.

Adam signaled for me to shut up and told Jessie that everything was perfect. I decided not to push the issue.

We got to Denise's house. I texted her that we were out front and met her at the front door. She gave me a warm kiss.

"I've been thinking about you all day," Denise said.

I kissed her again. "I thought about you all day too."

We held hands and walked to Perry's car. I introduced Denise to Jessie. Of course, Jessie was her usual bitchy self and gave Denise a fake smile and a curt hello. Denise sensed the tension but ignored it and squeezed in the backseat with Adam and me.

On the way to Nakisaki's, we joked and listened to the radio. When we got there, the place was packed. I saw my mom and my aunt Carol sitting at a table. They waved.

Perry, Adam, and I waved back. I quickly walked Denise over and introduced her to my mother. Denise was ecstatic to meet her finally. My mom wasn't so enthused because she knew I saw other girls. She smiled, and she and my aunt were cordial with Denise.

We went back to our seats and ordered food and drinks. The first couple of singers were terrible, but everyone was respectful and cheered for them anyway. The host for the open mic came on the floor and presented the next singer.

"This next performer I'm about to introduce has been a big attraction for the restaurant. Put your hands together for my girl Kristen Dos Santos."

My mouth fell open when I saw Krissy come on the stage. Our eyes locked. She stared directly at me. Sadness was on her face. She didn't take her eyes off me. She froze for a minute and then turned to the band. She talked to them briefly and faced the crowd again.

"Hey, everyone . . . I . . . I'm going to do a different song than what I originally planned on singing tonight. I'm sure you guys have heard it on the radio. I'm just going to warn you, guys, I sing from my soul and get emotional, so if I cry, I'm just in my zone with the song."

The crowd nodded. I shifted in my chair. Denise sat, unaware Krissy was another girl I was seeing. I looked at Jessie. She smirked and winked at me. I was sloppy. I knew Krissy sang at open mics all the time. It didn't cross my mind that she would possibly be here tonight.

Jessie's face relished the fact I was uncomfortable with the whole situation. Now it made sense why she asked if today was Thursday. She knew Krissy would be here.

Krissy sang "Ex-Factor" by Lauryn Hill. With tears trickling down her face, she sang the song so passionately she had everyone else crying too. She looked at me constantly during her performance. I could feel her pain, wondering how I could bring another girl to her performance, knowing how much she cared for me. I felt uncomfortable, and Jessie loved every minute of it.

When the song was over, there was a roar of applause from the crowd. Krissy took a bow. Everyone cheered and begged her for an encore. The host pleaded with her to do another song. Krissy had an undecided look on her face but agreed to sing one more song. She walked over to one of the band members and asked if she could use the piano. He smiled at her and said, "Anytime."

Krissy sat down at the piano and adjusted the microphone so she could sing while she played.

"This next song I'm going to sing is deep, and I'm sure every woman in here has gone through this and will appreciate it."

Krissy sang "Fallin'" by Alicia Keys. The room was silent and in awe of her playing and singing. She looked at me while she sang. The expression on her face and the lyrics to the song gave me a feeling that I could fix this setback even though it would be hard. All I had to do was talk to her and explain that Denise was nothing to me.

She finished to another thunderous applause. Jessie got up and walked away from the table. I figured she was going to see how Krissy was doing. The host returned to the stage, thanked Krissy for her performance, and introduced my dad.

"This next singer is here to bring some of that smooth, old-school R&B flavor. Let's give it up for one of our regulars, James Ferguson."

My father talked to the band and headed to the microphone. "This song goes out to my beautiful wife, who is in the audience tonight. I know I'm not always a good man, but I want you to know I love you."

All the women in the audience said, "Awww."

The band played R. Kelly's "When a Woman Loves." My mom couldn't stop smiling. Aunt Carol was stone-faced because she knew my father was full of shit. My dad sang, and all the women in the audience were captivated by his song. I saw on my mom's face that she could never leave him. She loved him too much, and he knew what he had to do to keep her around. It was similar to what I'd do later to keep Krissy around. I didn't like that I was acting in the same way that he did.

My dad finished the song to loud applause. He waved, blew kisses to my mom, and left the stage. Jessie came back to the table with Krissy. I was pissed but tried to keep my composure. If I acted emotionally, I was bound to make a stupid mistake.

"Hey. It's Denise, right? I noticed you enjoyed my girl Krissy's performance, so I thought I should introduce you to her since she is such good friends with Kenny and me," Jessie said.

Perry shook his head at me and gave Jessie a look. However, she disregarded his look and watched to see how things would unfold.

"I didn't know you knew Krissy. Why didn't you say something?" Denise asked.

I stayed silent, tried to keep my face emotionless.

Seeing I was going to stay quiet, Jessie spoke for me. "Yeah, girl, Krissy and Ken go way back—"

Krissy interrupted. "Hi, thanks for coming out."

"I rarely get to hang out with Ken like this, so this was definitely a treat," Denise said.

Since her answer was so vague, I could easily play the "she's just my friend" card, but Krissy decided to go deeper with the conversation.

"So . . . you and Ken are . . .?"

"We're friends," I said.

Denise looked shocked and annoyed.

"Oh, I see," Krissy replied.

Perry tried to end the awkward moment by saying that my father had just walked to my mother's table.

"Well, I'll talk to you soon. I want to congratulate my dad real quick. You were great tonight."

"Thanks," Krissy said.

I grabbed Denise by the hand and brought her over to my mom's table to say hi to my dad. My dad quickly looked Denise up and down, smiled, and patted me on the back. I didn't like that. I didn't want his approval or for him to feel I was anything like him. I introduced him to Denise, and they shook hands.

"You were great up there, Mr. Ferguson," Denise said.

"Thank you, my dear, and please call me James."

She smiled. My mother didn't.

We talked a little more with my family.

Perry signaled for us to come on because Jessie was ready to head out. We walked to the car, and Perry and Adam tried to talk about different topics, but there was still tension the whole car ride. Perry decided that it would be best to drop Denise off first since Jessie lived closer to the rest of us, and Denise was the furthest out.

I walked Denise to her door. I could see the anger all over her face.

"What was all that tonight, Ken?"

"All of what?"

"Don't play dumb with me. You told your friend that we're just friends. What was that about? Are you with her? Are you fucking her?"

"Stop all that noise. I'm not with anyone. You know I care about you. When I decide to be in a relationship, it's going to be with you, but right now, I still have to learn how to trust again. I need time."

Her face softened. I pulled her closer to me, and just like that, all of her anger melted away.

"I know you care about me. I just get impatient. You're not sleeping with her, right?"

"No. At one point, we thought something was there, but we realized we're just friends. Nothing more."

"Did you ever sleep with her? Before you answer, I saw the look on her face when she saw you. It looked like she had feelings for you. Don't lie to me, please."

"OK. We were intimate in the past, but that was the past. I'm not doing anything with her currently."

"I don't like that you slept with her. I feel like there's a lot about you, I don't know. I feel like I'm only partially in your life. I want to be more involved. I want to hang out with you and your friends."

"I promise you will. We'll make plans soon, and you can meet Ray and Lucy. This Friday, we'll have a date night, just the two of us."

Damn. I realized I had plans with Heather that night. Oh well, I'd cancel our plans and try to see her after I hung out with Denise.

"Cool. You're always talking about them, so it'll be good to meet finally."

I pulled her tight to me. We kissed and hugged. Jessie was in the car, yelling something to Perry. Adam was looking at me, shaking his head.

"I had a good time tonight," Denise said.

"I did too. I always have a good time with you."

"Well, my monthly visitor is here now, so I won't invite you in, but Friday, it's on."

"All right, you got it. I'll call you tomorrow."

"Bye, sexy."

We waved goodbye to each other, and I walked back to the car.

"Ugh. I can't fucking stand you," Jessie said.

"Right back at you."

"Go to hell, you fucking dog."

"Don't you know all dogs go to heaven?"

"You think you're slick. You're a manipulating dick-head."

"Yo, Perry, check your girl."

She rolled her eyes at me and turned to him.

"Perry, they say birds of a feather flock together. I hope you're not some wannabe playa like your boy here."

"Look, don't wrap me up in y'all's beef. I only want and need you."

When he said that, her demeanor softened.

"Ken's a good dude. He's just going through shit right now. He'll straighten out. Not every guy can be as good as me, you know."

She shook her head and smiled. "Oh God, can your head get any bigger?"

"Wait 'til tonight, and I'll show you how big my head can get."

"Oh my God, you're so nasty," she said, giggling.

"And you love that shit."

"I think I just threw up in my mouth," Adam said.

"Shut up, hater," Perry said.

"I'm going to stay over at your place tonight, baby, so can you stop by Krissy's for a bit?" Jessie asked.

"That's cool with me. Yo, Adam, you in a rush to get home?"

"Nah, I'm good. That's fine."

We got to Krissy's. She opened the door. She hugged Jessie and kissed me. Jessie looked irritated by that and grabbed her arm.

"Let's talk, girl," she said.

Jessie pulled her into Krissy's bedroom.

"Yo, you seriously need to check your girl," I said to Perry.

"Everything is cool here. You need to make your game tighter."

"Got 'em," Adam instigated.

"Well, I'm going to listen in on what shit your girl is saying about me now, so I can patch it up when she's finished badmouthing me."

"Do your thing, playa," Perry laughed.

I walked to Krissy's room. The door was open, so I listened closely to their conversation.

"Fuck him. That asshole had the nerve to bring another bitch to your fucking open mic night. You don't need him. He ain't shit. You deserve better than him," Jessie snarled.

"I know. He tells me all the time I can see other guys. I know I'm not the only girl he sees, but he makes me so happy. He always uplifts me and takes me out, and when I'm with him, he treats me as if there are no other women in his life, and I love that. I hate to say it, but I love him."

"Do you love being played? Do you love it when he cancels plans with you? Do you love knowing when he cancels with you that he's probably fucking someone else?"

"No."

"Good, because he's an asshole. I talk to Liza all the time, and he still sees that girl Heather. Her dumb ass feels the same way about him as you do. He's playing you both. Is the dick that good?"

Krissy laughed. "Yes. The sex is amazing. He's smart, funny, and treats me like a queen. He may not be entirely mine, but he's better than the usual guys I meet."

When she said that part, I knew I had her. It didn't matter what Jessie said. I knew I'd get Krissy to forgive me.

"All right, girl. I don't see it, but as long as you're happy, I'll be happy for you."

"Thank you."

"Well, let me get back to my man before Ken contaminates him," Jessie joked.

"You're too much," Krissy laughed.

I stepped away from the door. Jessie walked past me.

"Asshole."

"Love you too," I said sarcastically.

I walked into Krissy's room.

"Hey, can we talk?" I asked.

"Sure."

"I'm sorry about tonight."

"It's OK. I know you see other girls. I just needed to know she wasn't your girlfriend. That would've crushed me. I always wanted you to come out to hear me sing, but I gotta be honest, seeing you there with her hurt me."

"I'd never do anything to hurt you purposely. You know that, right? I care about you. I'm not going to lie and say I don't go on a date here and there, but she has nothing on you. I don't value her the way I value you."

Krissy hugged and kissed me. "I believe you."

Krissy made a late-night dinner for all of us. We were stuffed and satisfied. Lilly came over after her shift at the hospital and had some of the leftover food. I had to admit her ass was looking great, even in hospital scrubs.

We sat in Krissy's living room, watching *Chappelle's Show* episodes. Lilly was always flirty with me whenever I saw her. Often, she'd touch me, rub on me, and I wondered if Adam ever got uncomfortable with it. He never said anything, and I never brought it up. I just let it be.

"All right, I'm about to head out," Perry announced around 2:30 a.m.

"Lilly's going to drop me off," Adam said.

"Can you spend the night with me? I'll take you to your car in the morning," Krissy asked.

If she were Denise or Heather, I would've said no. As a precautionary measure, I never let any of them know

I had my own place. I figured if they knew, it would be too convenient for them to stop by unannounced, which would be bad, so I told them I still lived at my mother's house.

"Of course," I smiled at her.

"Yo, Perry. I'm just going to stay here for the night," I said, holding Krissy tight to me.

"Really, Kristen? After everything that happened tonight, you're going to let him spend the night?" Jessie asked with an attitude.

Lilly looked confused. "What happened tonight?" she asked.

"Girl, I'll tell you later. Anyway, we're out of here."

We all said goodbye, and I spent the rest of the night sexing Krissy into forgiveness.

Chapter Nine

All Falls Down

"Adam, calm down."

"Nah, I can't believe she broke up with me. Why can't she get that I love her, but I got things I want to accomplish in life?"

"It's fine to have things you want to do, but you have to learn how to balance. I work, go to school, and do my thing with all these girls. You only saw her when it was convenient for you."

"I know I should've worked on that, but I want to make it with my acting."

Since Adam was like my brother, I let it slide that we were having this conversation at five in the morning. He crashed on my couch after fighting with Lilly.

We were lounging in my living room. I had plans to meet up with my girls, so I was getting ready for my long day of seeing all of them. He vented because Lilly finally said enough was enough and broke up with him. She was tired of him not calling her and rarely seeing her. At first, he tried to act like he was okay, but as he continued to talk to me, I could tell it bothered him.

Despite knowing my plans for the day, he wanted to tag along with me to see how I balanced all of these women.

The first on my list was Denise. I knew she had class at one, so I could keep our meeting short and sweet. We met her at IHOP. We had breakfast and then went back to her house. Adam sat on the couch while I went to her bedroom to have her as a snack. I quickly undressed her. My eyes looked at her hungrily—her eyes shared the same wanting. She jumped into my arms. I held her and brought her to the bed, where I put on a condom and went to work on her. I pushed her legs back and teased her with my dick—moving my hips in circles. I stroked her fast and so deep until we couldn't tell where she ended, and I began.

Her moans echoed off the walls. She knew Adam could hear us, and she didn't give a shit. She wanted the whole world to know she was coming. She jerked violently. I knew that position always got her off quickly because, in it, I always touched that special spot that sent her over the edge.

I continued to stroke her as she held her legs way over her head. I loved that she was so flexible. The speed of my thrusting and deep penetration made her body shiver, and her pussy pulsated around me. Seeing her enjoying it so much got me worked up, and we ended up coming together.

We lay there, panting and smiling. I quickly jumped in her shower, and once I cleaned up, we dressed each other, and I kissed her goodbye.

"I wish you didn't have to go to class," I lied.

"I know, babe, but I can't miss too many, or my professors will fail me."

"I know. I'll call you later tonight."

She kissed me and said, "You better."

It was on to the next one—Heather. I knew it'd be easy to keep things short with her. I called her and told her Adam's girl left him, and I had to be there for him, but I wanted to make sure I saw her today.

We got to her place. She was a little annoyed that I brought him with me, but she was still excited to see me.

Again, Adam sat on the couch, and again, he had to suffer and hear me wearing Heather out.

As soon as we got to her bedroom, I slid my hands over her leggings and panties and pushed them down. I watched as she seductively stepped out of them. I dropped my pants, groped her breasts, and tongue kissed her into bliss. I ripped the condom wrapper with my teeth and put it on. She wrapped her arms around my neck, and I grabbed her ass. I lifted her against the wall, and she wrapped her legs around my thighs, then pulled me into her. I moved inside her as she rocked her hips to match my rhythm. Our movements became erratic and primitive. I could feel her heart beating through her chest as she held me tighter when I increased the speed of my strokes. Her juices trickled down my thighs, and I relished in the sight of her face being so expressive.

After we were both satisfied with orgasms, I told her I had to go. I hopped into her shower and washed up. She was disappointed I couldn't stay, but she thought it was nice I was there for my friend. I kissed her goodbye.

Adam and I walked to my car, headed to Kristen's this time.

"How do you do that?" he asked.

I knew what he meant, but I played along.

"Do what?"

"How do you have relationships with all these girls and feel . . . and feel nothing?"

I didn't know how to answer that. I never realized it, but I guess I had become desensitized to the whole thing. "I just stopped caring," I said.

"How can you be intimate with a woman and not care?"

"Feelings get in the way. Having feelings can get you hurt. I still haven't gotten over being hurt by Bri, and that's why it's so easy for me not to care now."

"No offense, but I hope I never get like that."

"We have two different outlooks on life. I don't think you could be like me, and trust me, you don't want to."

"Why do you say that?"

"I don't trust women anymore. I don't even know if I can or if I ever will again. With that being said, doing what I'm doing now is comfortable for me. I don't give too much of my heart to them. If I lost one of them, I wouldn't be devastated."

"It sounds like you've given up. I can't do that. I'll find my queen someday."

"I hope you do."

We pulled up to Kristen's house. I rang her doorbell. She was a little surprised to see Adam with me and gave me a confused look.

"Hey, guys," she said.

"Hey. Adam is hanging out with me for the day. He's been a little down."

She nodded.

We walked into her house. Adam nudged me and frowned. He didn't want to seem like a punk in front of one of Lilly's friends.

"Yeah, I'm sorry things didn't work out with you guys," she said.

"It's fine," he replied.

He didn't say anything more about the topic.

Kristen walked Adam to the living room and turned on the TV. "You want anything to drink, Adam?" she asked.

"Nah, I'm cool."

Kristen held my hand, and we walked to her bedroom. When she walked into her room, I playfully slapped her ass as she closed the door behind us. She pushed me down on her bed and pulled her T-shirt over her head. She wore no bra. She took off my boots, then tugged on my jeans and underwear, pulling them completely off. After she put a condom on me, she started riding me.

She put her hands on my chest and rolled her hips up and down my length with her clit rubbing softly on my pubic bone. I grabbed both of her tits and played with her nipples. The speed of her riding increased. She came and screamed out.

We lay in her bed, sweating. I didn't come yet, but I had come so much today, I knew it would take a lot for me to do it again. Krissy stood up to get a bottle of water from her desk. When she reached for it, I bent her over the desk and took her from behind. She gasped. I stroked her mercilessly and pulled her hair so she could watch our movements in the mirror. I felt her orgasm rush through her. Seeing her big, firm ass pressed up against me and watching her expressions in the mirror turned me on, and I had an intense orgasm of my own.

I lay on top of her, both of us breathing heavy. When I pulled out of her, I almost had a heart attack. The condom we used was broken! The only thing left of it was the ring on the bottom.

"Shit," I yelled.

"What?" she asked, sounding concerned.

"The condom broke. I just came inside you."

She sighed. "Is that such a bad thing?"

"Hell yeah, it's a bad thing. I don't want any kids any-time soon."

"Is it that you don't want kids soon, or you just don't want a kid with me?"

"Don't start that shit right now. Kids are no joke. I'm not ready to be a father right now."

"I doubt anything will happen. I'm sure one slipup won't do anything."

We calmed down and showered together. When that was over, we dressed. I kissed her and told her I'd call her the next day. Adam and I left and headed back to my house.

"I'm just going to head out," he said.

"You sure? I just texted Ray about getting dinner."

"Yeah, I'm just gonna chill out at my place and practice my Kung Fu forms for my auditions. I need to distract myself from Lilly."

"I understand, brother. Do what you need to do."

Adam left, and I headed over to Ray's house.

"Yo, what's up? You guys ready to go?" I asked Ray.

"It's just you and me. Lucy had to stay late at work."

We ordered Chinese and watched TV. I told him all about my eventful day.

"Damn, man. I don't even know how you're standing right now. If I did that many women in one day, I'd need a power nap."

We laughed.

"You know there's a part of you that wishes you could do this too."

"That's where you're wrong, man. I love Lucy, and she's everything I need. I don't want other women."

"I remember when I used to feel that way, but all of us can't find one girl and live happily ever after."

"Our relationship is nowhere near perfect. We have our problems and fight all the time like any other couple, but the one thing that never changes is that we love each other."

We discussed relationships and strolled down memory lane about high school. I wished times could be simple like those days again.

"Uh, I hate when you wear those jeans. They make your package look like a division sign in them. They're too damn tight," Jessie said.

"Yup, *long* division, girl," Perry replied.

They chuckled amongst themselves.

Perry invited me out to dinner at Houston's, a steak restaurant next to Roosevelt Field Mall. He said Lilly insisted I come along. As we waited for her to get to the restaurant, Jessie excused herself and went to the bathroom.

"So why did Lilly want me to come along?" I asked Perry.

"I don't know, bro, but I think she's feeling you. She's bad and all, but I don't think you should fuck this one. Adam is still hung up on her."

"I know. He was moping around all day yesterday when I was with him."

"Yeah, while he was moping, Lilly kept telling Jessie how you're so hot and shit, and how we should all hang out."

"What?"

I always suspected she was feeling me, but I guess that confirmed it.

"Yeah, I reminded her that you're fucking her best friend, Krissy, but she didn't seem to care. If Jessie acts more bitchy than usual, it's because she knows Lilly is feeling you, and Jessie thinks you're going to be fucking both of her friends and hurt Kristen."

We didn't know it, but Jessie was right behind us.

"That's right. You're a dog, and I don't want you preying on my friends."

"I'm not a dog. I'm a single guy that's living life to the fullest."

"Yeah, you're full of shit. You like to mess with girls' heads, which makes you a dog. I don't know what these girls see in you anyway. You ain't shit."

Hearing her say I wasn't shit reminded me of how Bri and Ashley made me feel. It was one thing to attack me fucking around a lot, but attacking me personally, I had a *big* problem with that.

"They see a man who's smart and powerful."

"You might be book smart, but you're just a weak lit-tle boy. You must not be that powerful if that girl Ashley played your ass. I'm sorry, how many times? Oh, yeah . . . twice."

I was fuming.

"Before this night is over, I'm going to show you how powerful I am," I said.

"Whatever."

She was attacking my pride. I could've just ignored her, but I wanted to shut her know-it-all mouth up. A couple of minutes later, Lilly got to the restaurant and sat with us at the table.

"Sorry I'm late. I had to get dropped off here by one of my coworkers. My car is acting up, and I got a ride in to work today."

"It's all good, girl. Don't sweat it. We'll give you a ride home later," Jessie said.

"Hey, Ken, you're looking good."

"You're looking pretty good yourself."

"All right, enough with the bullshit. Let's eat," Jessie said.

As always, she never liked to see me happy.

We ordered and talked about all types of things, but we didn't mention Adam or the breakup. Lilly kept flirting with me at dinner. She constantly touched me, winked, and made raunchy jokes to me.

In my head, I knew I shouldn't even be here with her. She was Adam's ex and off-limits—at least until he gave me the OK. Jessie was getting angrier by the second watching us talk together, and I enjoyed seeing her irritation.

After dinner, we decided to see the new Tyler Perry movie. Since it was a Tuesday night, the theater was pretty empty. Besides us, there was only one other couple there. Perry sat at the end of the row, Jessie sat next to him, Lilly sat next to her, and I sat next to Lilly. During the movie, Lilly rested her hand on my lap and rubbed my leg. My dick started to rise, and she rubbed my hardness. Jessie watched Lilly rubbing me and looked at me in disgust. I loved that.

"Damn, girl. That shit feels good as hell," I whispered to Lilly.

"Yeah, it does."

"Put it in your mouth," I said. I put on a serious face, so she knew I wasn't joking.

"Here?"

"Please. I'll return the favor after the movie. I promise."

She had a naughty look on her face, licked her lips, and unzipped my pants. She pulled my dick out and held it in her hands like she wasn't sure if she should do it.

"Hey, it's not going to suck itself," I said.

She kissed it and went down on me while the movie played.

"Oh, hell no. What the fuck is wrong with you, Lilly?" Jessie yelled.

Perry turned his head, saw what Lilly was doing, and said, "Oh shit. Ken, what the hell are you doing?"

The other couple, six rows in front of us, didn't see what Lilly was doing and shushed Jessie and Perry. Lilly didn't miss a beat. She kept taking me deeper and deeper into her mouth. I put my hand on the top of her head and kept working it on my hardness. She wrapped her hands around it, her tongue rolling over the head of my dick as she sucked and stroked me at the same time. I held her head down on it and made sure she swallowed every drop when I came. She licked the sides of my dick. Jessie was seething.

"I can't believe you just sucked Adam's best friend's dick in the damn movie theater."

"That relationship is dead and gone and was never real anyway. Adam only called me and fucked me when it was convenient for him."

Perry had a worried look on his face.

When the movie was over, the girls went to the bathroom, and Perry talked to me in the lobby.

"Yo, what the fuck was that, Ken?"

"I know, I know. I wasn't thinking."

"Come on, man. You should've never let her suck you off. There's no coming back from this now." Perry looked deeply concerned. "I hope Adam never finds out about this shit."

"He won't. I'm not saying shit. Can you make sure Jessie doesn't mention it?"

"Brother, you know I can't make that woman do anything. I'll seriously try, but once she gets mad, her mouth gets reckless, and there's no cooling her off. She's seriously pissed at you right now, but I don't think she'd be crazy enough to say anything to Adam about it. That would cause too much beef with Kristen and Lilly."

Lilly and Jessie came out of the bathroom.

"All right, let's get out of here," Jessie said.

"Do you mind taking me home, Ken?" Lilly asked.

"Are you serious right now? What did we just talk about? Why do you want him to take you home, Lilly?"

"Relax. I'm a big girl. I can take care of myself," Lilly said.

Jessie shook her head. "I can't believe you right now."

She grabbed Perry by the arm, pulled him toward the exit, and said, "Come on. I'm done with both of them."

They left the theater.

"So, now that the drama is over, can I come over to your place?" Lilly asked.

"Sure," I said hesitantly.

Driving to my place, I was at war with myself. I knew damn well I shouldn't be fucking around with Lilly. I let Jessie's dumb-ass comments and my pride get the best of me. This was a mistake. Lilly broke my thoughts.

"I hope you know I plan on you reciprocating the 'special treatment' I gave you in the movie."

I grinned uncomfortably and nodded. We pulled up to my place. I opened the door, and we walked in.

"Do you want anything to drink?" I asked.

"Nope. I just want you to give me what you owe me."

I wanted to say no. Doing anything more with her would only make things worse, but I didn't want to be an asshole and tell her I wasn't gonna return the favor.

We walked to my bedroom, and she undressed. Her body was beautiful. We kissed, and my hands went all over her smooth, dark skin. She lay on my bed and spread her legs. My mind went numb. I pushed all my cares aside and just lived in the moment. I stepped out of my clothes, put on a condom, and began eating her out. I made circles with my tongue, darted my tongue in and out of her, and sucked on her clit until it was swollen and throbbing.

"Look at me. I want you to watch me eat you," I said.

"Oh my God, you're going to fucking make me burst."

She lifted her head and saw her clit between my thick lips, sucking and licking on it like it was the greatest thing I'd ever tasted. I curled my fingers, gently rubbing the top of her pussy. Lilly threw her head left and right, her back arched, and she bucked wildly as she came intensely all over me. While she was still twitching from me eating her, I grabbed her by her thighs, spread her legs, and quickly entered her, thrusting hard.

"Oh my God," she screamed.

I kept stroking away. Another orgasm got hold of her. Lilly's erratic breathing was turning me on. I turned her on her side and entered her from that angle, thrusting rapidly in and out of her. This is what she wanted. She didn't want love from me. There would be no feelings for each other after tonight. She just wanted to be fucked. Her victory would come from being satisfied by the best friend of the man she felt didn't care for her. The only thing she was to me was another notch on my belt.

As the night went on, I continued to give her what she wanted.

When it was over, she lay in my bed naked. I stared out the window as she slept. I felt like shit. I felt heartless. I'd slept with a lot of women, but I had never gone so far as to sleep with my friend's girl. She slept contentedly while I was up, regretting my actions.

I had drifted off to sleep, but a loud banging on my front door woke me. I rushed to my living room, wondering who lost their damn mind banging on my door like that. I looked out my peephole—it was Adam. He looked furious. I sighed and opened the door.

"Ken . . . Did you do it?" Adam asked, staring at the floor.

I tried to play dumb. I didn't know what he knew, and I didn't want to incriminate myself. "Do what?"

"Did you go out with Perry, Jessie, and Lilly? Did you let Lilly suck you off in the fucking theater? Tell me you didn't, and I'll believe it. Tell me you and Perry didn't go out with my ex-girlfriend when we were fresh off a breakup."

I couldn't say anything. Adam stared me in my eyes and started crying.

"Tell me Jessie is lying. You and Perry wouldn't do that to me, right? Perry wouldn't invite you out on a double date with Lilly, right?"

When he said that, Lilly walked out of my bedroom wearing only her panties.

"They didn't do anything to you. *You* did this to you," Lilly stated.

Adam's mouth dropped open. He looked at me and looked back at her. He put his head down, huffed, and asked, "Why?"

I didn't know if he was talking to me, to her, or just in general.

"Why did I do it?" Lilly asked. "I did it because I was tired of you not appreciating me. Everything was always on your terms. You didn't give a shit about me. All I was to you was a wet hole when you were horny. You only bothered to see me when you wanted some ass. I wanted attention. I wanted someone to return the favor when I went down on him."

Adam's head went up when she said that. She continued her rant.

"Oh, did *that* get your attention? Last week, after three weeks of not seeing you, you finally invited me to come over to your place. You asked me to suck your dick, and when I did and asked you to return the favor, you told me you're trying to be a 'good Christian' and didn't do it. That hurt me."

Tears streamed down his face as she went on, telling him about the flaws in their relationship.

"You treated me like I was a ho. You didn't value me. Everything else had a priority over me, and all you cared about was your career and martial arts. It took me fucking your friend for you even to show any indication that you cared."

Adam turned to me. "Why did you do it? How could you do this to me?"

"I swear I wasn't trying to hurt you. I wasn't thinking, and I—"

"You and Perry are dead to me. We're no longer friends."

"Wait, Adam, . . . let me explain—"

"There is nothing to explain. We're not friends anymore. For you to even think about doing this shows you have no respect for me. Stay away from me. Tell Perry to do the same."

"Wait. Perry had nothing to do with this. If you're going to be mad, be mad at me, but he tried to talk me out of it."

"Jessie told me he knew Lilly was feeling you. She said she told him not to invite Lilly out with you guys, but he did it anyway. He's a coconspirator, so he gets the same treatment. I'm cutting you both out of my life."

Lilly got dressed and headed for the door. "You and I have to talk some more," she said to him.

"I don't talk to hoes," he replied.

They argued in the hallway until the elevator came and continued on their way out. I called Perry. I knew Jessie would be there, and I was sure he knew nothing about her talking to Adam.

"Dude, what the fuck? It's crazy early. Somebody better be dead," Perry said.

"Your fucking girl told Adam everything."

"What?"

"Yeah, he just came to my house. I'm not going to lie. I fucked up and slept with Lilly. He came over while she was still here, and we had a big argument. He said Jessie told him everything, and now he's done with both of us."

"Nah, that can't be. Jessie doesn't have his number."

"He *specifically* said it was her."

Perry woke Jessie up, and I could hear them arguing over the phone.

"Jessie, wake up. Baby, did you tell Adam about tonight?"

"You're damn right I did," she replied defiantly.

"What the fuck? Why would you do that? He just went over to Ken's house, and now he's mad at him *and* me. How'd you even have his number anyway?"

"Oh well, he needed to know, and I got the number from your phone when you were sleeping. I had a little chat with him and let him know what was going on behind his back."

Perry came back to the conversation with me. "Yo, let me call you back. I got to deal with this here first."

"All right. Take care of that."

We hung up.

Perry and Jessie had a big fight that almost led to them breaking up, but they decided to work it out. Jessie admitted she was wrong for what she did and even apologized to me, but the damage was done. Adam wouldn't talk to Perry or me.

Perry and I tried to apologize, but he wouldn't listen. Because of Jessie's big mouth, Krissy found out. Krissy and Lilly argued and cut each other off. I almost lost Krissy during this whole disaster, but after a lot of begging, apologizing, and gifts, she eventually forgave me. I couldn't stand myself at that point. I lost one of my best friends because of my stupid pride.

It was Saturday night. I seriously didn't feel like being around any of the girls I dealt with. The drama with Adam, Perry, and I was eating me up inside. To cut off all ties with us, Adam even stopped talking to Ray. He explained everything to Ray and told him he wasn't mad at him, but he would be distant because we all ran in the same circle.

I needed some time away from the madness that had been my life. I went to my parents' house, sat in the living room, and watched TV. My mom was at church, and who knows where my dad was. Ray was at work, and Perry was out with Jessie. I took out my braids, washed my hair, and took a nice long shower. After I dried my hair and got dressed, I did some cleaning around the house. Now that I had moved out, I knew all the chores were on Mom, so I tried to help her out. When I was throwing the trash outside, I saw Kim across the street.

"Hey, Kenny, what are you doing tonight?" she asked.

"Nothing really. What about you?"

"Nothing. I'm bored. Lucy had to work late, and none of my friends have any money. Damn, why you got your hair out like that?"

"I'm getting it done in the morning. Did you eat yet? If you want, I'll treat you to dinner."

"You aren't going anywhere with me looking like that. Come here, and I'll braid your hair. Then you can repay me by taking me out to dinner."

I went over to Ray's house. His grandmother had gone to Georgia to visit family, so the place was empty. Kim grabbed the combs and the grease and started to braid my hair. We laughed and joked about the past.

"You know, Kenny, I'm still mad at you for missing my thirteenth birthday. We changed all of the dinner arrangements for you to come—and you missed it. I had to go to shitty-ass Sizzler. It was disgusting."

"I apologized for that a million times. My mother forced me to go to church with her. There was nothing I could do."

"I hope you know when you take me out that I'm ordering everything I can think of."

She was a good girl who was street smart and book smart. In life, those are two essential qualities.

"I'll tell you what. To make up for it, we'll go anywhere and do anything you want."

"Really? I'm going to hold you to that."

"Seriously, whatever you want."

She finished braiding my hair and then got ready. She was dressed to kill. She had on a nice, form-fitting, black dress that showed off her busty cleavage. It was hard not to look at her. She had seriously grown-up. She wasn't the same little girl who followed Ray and me around when we were kids. She was a woman now. I pushed those thoughts to the side. I cared for her. She was like family.

I drove us into Manhattan, and we went to Studio Mars on Fifty-Second Street. She stayed true to her word and ordered the most expensive thing she could find on the menu. I didn't mind, though. She deserved it. Over the years, I'd seen her pick the wrong type of guys, mostly losers who didn't have ambition and just hung out in the streets. I watched them all hurt her and take whatever they could from her. Their example of a date night was treating her to McDonald's and letting her get a value meal. I wanted her to feel like a queen.

We ate, and she told me about the classes she had to take to become a nurse. When dinner was over, I took her on a horse and carriage ride to the comedy club on Forty-Second Street. The comedians were hilarious. We were both laughing our asses off the whole time. My cell phone went off a couple of times during dinner and at the comedy club, but I didn't feel like being bothered. I was content hanging out with Kim.

When the comedy club was over, we held hands, got ice cream, and walked around the city.

"I'm loving this night. I'm not ready to go home yet. . . . You know, I've never seen your new condo. Can we hang out there?"

"Sure."

I had work in the morning, but I didn't care. She was good company. We got to my place and watched the replay of the Knicks game. Kim rested her head on my shoulder with her feet up on my couch.

"So, did I make up for your thirteenth birthday? Are we even now?"

"Not yet. You said we could do anything and everything I wanted tonight, right?"

"Yeah."

"There is only one thing I want to conclude the night, and then we'll be even, and my night will be perfect."

"What's that?"

"You."

I knew *exactly* what she meant, but I wasn't trying to go there. I played dumb. "What do you mean by that?"

"If you want me to say it bluntly, I want you to fuck me."

"Come on, Kim. You know we can't do that. I care for you too much to make you a statistic, and you know we can't be together."

"I know that, and I don't care. I don't want to be in a relationship. I just want to fuck. I've liked you since I was a little girl, and even if we only spend one night together, I'd be happy with that."

We kissed. This felt wrong. I didn't want to take advantage of her. I honestly cared about her, and I didn't want to betray Ray. My conscience was already bothering me with Lilly and Adam. I didn't need more drama. Our hands felt all over each other. She took off her skirt, and she was just in her bra and panties. Our eyes met.

"Kim, we can't do this."

"This is what I want. You promised."

We continued to kiss. She pushed me down on the couch and took off her bra and panties. The fact that she was so aggressive was turning me on. She pulled off my shirt, pants, and underwear. She went to go down on me, but I stopped her. As much as I would've loved that, what we were about to do was bad enough.

She went in her purse and pulled out a condom, smiled, and put it on me. She positioned herself on top of me and eased my dick inside of her. Then she started a slow rhythm on top of me while my hands were all over her breasts. She grabbed the sofa and used it for leverage as she increased her rhythm. Soon, she let out a loud moan and came on top of me. She got off me and wanted me to take her from behind. I grabbed her waist and entered her.

"Give it to me hard," she moaned.

I grabbed her waist with one hand and pulled her hair. She loved it. I couldn't enjoy it thoroughly because I was too busy thinking about how wrong it was. I didn't know how I could look Ray in his eyes after tonight. I already fucked up with Adam, and now I was making the same mistake by betraying Ray.

Guilt was all over me as I kept pumping away. Kim pushed back, and it felt heavenly. Finally, I couldn't hold it anymore, and I came intensely. We both lay on my living room floor, gasping. I stood up from the floor and got bottles of water for us. Then I got back on the floor. Kim lay on top of me and fell asleep. I didn't sleep well. I kept thinking about what I had done. I didn't want her to be a statistic. She meant more to me than that. Ray always talked to me about settling down and not sleeping with so many women. He was one of my best friends, but he'd never forgive me if he found out about this.

The next morning, my two earliest appointments from Def Jam rescheduled for later on in the day, which was perfect because it gave me time to make breakfast for Kim and talk to her.

"Damn, you give me the best night ever and now, the best morning. I'm really happy."

"Kim, I enjoyed last night too, but you know we can never do this again, right?"

"We still can, Kenny. I know you're worried about my feelings, but it's all good. We can take care of each other's needs and stay friends."

"We can't. You know if Ray ever found out about this, he'd kill both of us."

"He never has to know. I'm not going to tell him anything, and besides, I'm a grown woman. I make my own decisions."

"I know, but don't you feel a little guilty about the whole thing?"

"No. I told you I wanted you since I was a little girl, and doing this felt so right to me. I know we're never going to get married or be in a relationship, but a part of me is just happy you wanted me as much as I wanted you."

"I'm very attracted to you, but this can't happen again. Don't tell anyone, including Lucy."

"I'm not going to tell anyone. It'll just be our little secret, but you have to promise me one thing."

"What's that?"

"That you'll consider doing this with me again. If you can't consider it, then no dice."

"OK, OK, I'll consider it."

"Good."

Before I knew it, we were at it again in my bedroom, screwing each other's brains out.

I drove her back to her house, and she had the look of victory on her face.

"Why are you smiling?" I asked.

"Because I finally got what I wanted, and I know that as long as you consider it, I can have more when I need it."

"Wow, somebody got cocky all of a sudden."

"No, I just like getting what I want."

I dropped her off in front of her house. Ray saw her get out of my car.

"Where were—" he was about to ask where she was with me, but Kim interrupted him.

"I was hanging out in the city and got drunk. I didn't want you to flip out on me, so I called Ken to pick me up, so I didn't have to hear your mouth."

"Jesus, Kim, you got that drunk that you needed some-one to come rescue you? I hope you didn't make any stupid decisions."

She snickered. "Nope. I was fully conscious of every decision I made yesterday, and I'm glad I made them. On top of that, I'm grown."

She winked at me. I frowned at her.

"Get your grown ass in the house," Ray playfully said to her as he chased her.

"Bye, Ken. Thanks for everything," Kim said.

"Bye, Kim."

"Yo, sorry about that, man. I hope she didn't mess up any of your plans."

"Nah, it's cool. . . . She's like family."

"You doing anything tonight?"

"Probably taking Denise out. What's up?"

"Well, I know you promised her we'd hang out. Do you want to do that tonight?"

"Yeah, that sounds good. We'll hang out later."

We exchanged ideas, and I went back to my place, feeling guiltier than ever.

I was still stressed out with the whole Adam and Kim situations. Denise and I were at Ray's house, waiting for them to get ready. Lucy introduced herself to Denise.

"Hey, it's Denise, right? Kenny speaks so highly of you," Lucy said.

"Aw, thank you. He's always talking about you guys too. It's nice to meet you finally. His Def Jam schedule always messes up everything with planning stuff."

"Yeah, I know that's rough. Well, let me finish getting ready and let the men figure out where we're going tonight."

"Sounds good to me, right, honey?"

"Yup," I said.

I had no idea what we were going to do. We'd probably get dinner and go to a club—anything fun. Denise was thrilled when I told her we were hanging out with Ray and Lucy because she never felt like she got to meet my friends. Little did she know, I meant for it to be that way. I didn't need Jessie saying shit in front of her again, but I didn't have to worry about Lucy or Ray telling her about the other girls because they were loyal to me.

We went to this Italian restaurant on Route 110 called Bertucci's. We laughed and talked about relationships. Ray got up to go to the bathroom while Denise and Lucy were discussing cheating.

"Only selfish assholes cheat. If you're not feeling the person you're with, then you should do that person a favor and have the common decency to break it off with them. Why cheat? You aren't happy anyway, so leave them," Denise said with firm conviction.

"I used to think like you, but I realized that anyone could cheat. It all depends on the circumstances. Sometimes, people don't cheat because of the physical act of it. Sometimes, they cheat because they need an emotional release from the person they love," Lucy responded.

"If that's the case, if they feel they need a release from that person, then they should *release themselves* from that person. Cheating only hurts people."

"Maybe the person cheating doesn't want to lose what they have. Maybe the person knows what they're doing is wrong and wants to correct it, but doesn't know how to do that without losing the person they love. Sometimes people want to have their cake and eat it too."

"Well, I hate people like that. People like that don't deserve to be with anyone. Better yet, they deserve to find someone like them, so they can know how it feels," Denise countered.

They both continued with their debate, but Lucy's words didn't sit right with me at all. Lucy was a firm believer in honesty in relationships. What could've possibly changed her mind about cheating? I was very suspicious about everything she was saying.

Ray came back and kissed her on the cheek. She winked at him and looked at me as if to tell me not to bring up anything she said. I nodded, and she returned the nod.

We changed subjects. We decided to go out dancing and went to the Crazy Donkey in Farmingdale. We had a good time, but I was concerned about Lucy and Ray. On the dance floor, they kissed, danced, and stared into each other's eyes like soul mates, but I wondered if something was going on.

After hanging out at the club, I told Denise I had work early in the morning so that I couldn't stay at her place. She was disappointed, but she was happy she got to hang out with my friends. She exchanged numbers with Lucy, hugged Ray goodbye, and we drove to her place. I made sure she got her rocks off before I went home. I didn't worry about getting mine. I had way too much on my mind.

Tiffani called me distraught and crying. The clock on my nightstand said it was four in the morning.

"Kenny, can you please pick me up from the airport," Tiffani asked.

"Sure, what time?" I asked groggily.

"Can you come now? I'm at JFK. I need you."

I cared about Tiffani, so regardless of what time it was, early or late, I'd be there for her. She wouldn't get into details over the phone on what happened, but she said things with her and Josh were over for good.

Inside, I had a small victory. On the one hand, she wasn't with him anymore, so I had a shot. On the other hand, she loved him. I'm sure she would grieve, and no one could predict how long it would take for someone to heal from a breakup, especially if it was a bad one.

I picked her up from the JetBlue terminal. When I got there, she was standing outside in the rain. She wasn't even under the awnings. She just stood out there soaked with the look of a person that was exhausted and defeated.

I parked my car in front of where she was standing.

"Hey, you can't park your car here. Move your vehicle immediately," one of the security guards yelled at me.

I ignored him and hugged her. I opened the door for her, grabbed her bags, and quickly put them in my trunk so the security guard would get off my back. Then I pulled off.

"Tiff, what's wrong? What happened?"

"Josh cheated on me. . . . I don't know how long this has been going on. I feel so fucking stupid," she sobbed.

I felt her pain. Guys had been trying to get in her pants since she stepped on campus, and she was faithful to Josh this whole time. Right now, I didn't care about my feelings for her. I only wanted to help her and make sure she was okay.

"Pull over," Tiffani said.

I pulled over on the side of the Van Wyck and held her as she cried. While she lay against me, she explained what happened.

"I came home to surprise him because I wasn't there for his birthday. I wanted to be there, but I had an important game and couldn't miss it. I thought I'd surprise him with a weekend visit, spoil him for at least two days, and enjoy being with him since we rarely got to see each other.

"When I got to Seattle, I caught a cab and went straight to his house. When I got there, I saw his car was parked, so I knew he was home. I knocked on his door—no answer. I called his house and cell phone—no answer. I thought maybe he was taking a nap. Since his room was on the first floor and on the backside of the house, I opened the fence and went into his backyard. His big German shepherd barked at first, but once the dog realized it was me, he stopped. I climbed in his window like I had done countless times when we were growing up . . . only to see Josh fucking Deborah Owens, a girl we went to high school with."

"Shit," I said.

"Oh, it gets better. I screamed, and Josh kept saying it's 'not what I think.' Deborah looked at me like she didn't give a shit. Josh asked what I was doing home, and I explained I was there to surprise him for his birthday, but the surprise was on me. He gave me some lame excuse about being 'lonely' and needing someone to 'take care of his needs.' He said he didn't have feelings for Deborah. It was just sex. I told him none of that shit mattered. My entire time here in New York, I never touched any other guys. I have needs too, but I loved him enough to endure."

I nodded, and she went on.

"After saying all of that, I let him know we were over and told Deborah she could have him. Josh didn't argue with me. He didn't fight for us. He just said maybe that was for the best and offered to take me back to the airport, but after seeing how he didn't give a shit about us breaking up—after all the years we've been together, and all the memories and times we've had—I told him no and just called a cab to go back to the airport. He said he was sorry it had to end this way and went back into the house with Deborah. He didn't even wait outside with me for the cab to come.

I didn't see my parents. I took the red-eye flight back to New York and cried the whole trip back. I had to explain to everyone on the flight that I just had a bad breakup to stop people from thinking I was crazy. I called you as soon as I landed."

"Tiff, I'm here for you. Do you want to go to a diner somewhere or something?"

"No, not right now, Kenny. I need time to think. Can you take me to my place?"

"No problem." I held her hand and rubbed it.

I understood. I drove Tiff to her place, and she invited me in. She was still depressed and didn't want to be alone. While she had friends on the team, she didn't have anyone to talk to about her problems like me.

We walked inside. Rachel and Kelly saw me step in with Tiff. They waved and looked at each other. I waved back and walked up the stairs with Tiff. We got to her room. Tiffani's roommate rarely was ever there. Most of the time, she stayed with her boyfriend on the base-ball team, which was good because Tiff had the room to vent and mourn. We sat in her room for about two hours. I told my clients from the gym that I had a family emer-gency and wouldn't be in so that I could be there for Tiff.

I held her.

"Thanks for always being there for me and taking care of me whenever life kicks my ass."

We kissed.

My mind had a million thoughts running through it. While I wanted to feel that warmth, was this the right time? She was hurting. Would doing this with her knowing that her mind wasn't clear be taking advantage? A dark part of me didn't care. I didn't pull away. I kept kissing her. She started to undress. A part of me wanted to stop her. I wanted her more than anything, but not like this. I wanted our first time being intimate to be special—not out of revenge or vulnerability—but that dark part of me wanted to do the deed now because nothing was ever promised tomorrow. This was the moment of truth.

Tiff was completely naked, lying on her back, looking at me with eyes that said she wanted me to help her escape reality. I put on a condom, and in my head, I knew no matter what happened, our relationship would be different.

I kissed her thighs. She opened her legs, showing me that beautiful treasure she had between them. I kissed that special part of her that made her a woman. I gave her long, soft strokes with my tongue, licking her from top to bottom, and gently sucked on her clit. She placed her hand on my head. Her moaning let me know she was enjoying this release of tension. I spread her pussy open with two fingers—fingering in tune with me sucking on her clitoris. She held my face in her treasure and came intensely. My face glistened as I lapped up all her juices. Then I got on top of her and entered her slowly. She shuddered and held on to me tightly as I moved inside her. Her legs rested on my shoulders as I pushed deep in her. This felt so right because I genuinely cared for her. I laid her on her stomach and entered her from behind. We held hands as I pushed deeper into her.

When it was over, I knew I could be with her forever.

"Damn," Tiff said.

"I've wanted you for a long time."

"I know. I wanted you too. . . . Ken, I don't want us to become just this."

"I know, me neither."

"I don't want to rush into anything, but I can see myself being with you."

"I want that too."

"Good, in the meantime, since you want to wear me out, can you go downstairs and get me something to drink?"

"Of course."

Tiffani slapped my ass as I went to put on my boxers and sweatpants. I walked down the steps to go to the kitchen. Owen and Antoine were in the living room with Rachel and Kelly.

"Yo, I can't believe you fucking did it, bro. I knew you were going to hit that," Antoine said.

I stood there, smiling awkwardly.

"You're the fucking man. I had to bring Antoine here as proof, so no one can lie and say it didn't happen when I collect my money. Don't worry. I'ma give you a cut," Owen said.

"Nah, I'm good. I don't need anything."

"When Rachel called me and told me you were over here with Tiffani, I knew you were going to hit that today. Where is she now?"

"Upstairs, lying down."

"Damn, you wore her out like that? Yo, we're going to have to start calling you the pussy whisperer," he laughed.

Rachel and Kelly had smirks on their faces but didn't comment.

"Was it good?" Owen asked.

". . . It was great."

"Really, Ken?"

My heart jumped out of my chest. Tiffani was behind me. I didn't know how much she heard.

"Uh-oh . . . busted," Rachel said.

"So, all I was, was a game for you, Ken?"

She started to shake. Tears welled in her eyes instantly. "I . . . I . . . thought I meant more to you. I thought you cared about me, but I was just a game to you, just another notch on your belt."

"Tiffani, it's not like that. Let me explain—"

"What's there to explain? You got what you wanted, right? You made me feel like we could've had more, but you never planned on that, did you?"

"I meant everything I said." I reached for her.

"Don't fucking touch me. Get away from me," she yelled.

"Can you *please* listen to me?"

"No. *You* listen to me. I *never* want to see you again. Don't call me. Don't look at me. Tell your momma I'm sorry, but I can't hang out with her anymore. Her son is a douche bag."

"Hey, at least you got to meet his mom. Me and Rachel fucked him, and all we got was bowling and cheap pizza," Kelly interjected.

"Shut up," I screamed.

Tiffani ran up the stairs, and I ran after her. There was laughter downstairs. She ran into her room, slammed, and locked the door.

"Tiffani, please open the door and talk to me. I didn't make the stupid bet. You mean more to me than any of those skanks downstairs."

"I used to believe that, but I don't anymore."

"I'm serious. I wouldn't hurt you."

"Answer this question. If you knew about the bet, why didn't you ever say anything to me about it? We talk about everything, Ken. Why wouldn't you bring it up unless you were in on it too?"

"I swear on my life I wasn't in on it. Please, believe me."

"Ken, just leave me alone. I'm done. Leave, or I'm calling the coach, and I mean it."

My body felt heavy with regret. My conscience was hurting. I couldn't get Tiff to listen to me. I felt so out of control with myself lately. I betrayed Adam and lost him. I betrayed Ray, and now I hurt the only girl in my life I truly cared about. I didn't want to lose her. My shoulders heaved up and down. I felt defeated. I walked down the steps with my head down and eyes watering.

"Now she knows how we all felt when you were done with us," Rachel said smugly with her arms folded.

"That was fucked-up," I said.

"Why should she think she's any different than the rest of us? She shouldn't feel special."

"No, *you* shouldn't feel special. I *cared* about her," I shouted.

"Well, boo hoo. Now you know how it feels *not* to be special. She's *done* with you."

I walked out without responding.

For the next couple of weeks, I tried everything to get Tiffani to talk to me. She wasn't trying to hear anything I was telling her. I apologized to her a million times. I tried explaining what happened, but she wanted nothing to do with me. The hardest part was seeing how this affected my mom. I stopped by my mom's house to visit. She was sitting in the living room by herself, reading the Bible.

"Kenny, what happened with you and Tiffani?"

I didn't know how to answer that question. I didn't want my mom to know there was a bet that I could get Tiffani in bed.

"It's just a big misunderstanding, Ma."

"Tiffani said that you hurt her badly, Kenny. She said that she loves hanging out with me, and she's going to miss me, but she can't now because of things with you and her." Her eyes watered.

"She said she'll always cherish the times we spent together, and I was like her mother here in New York, but . . . Who am I going to talk to now?" she asked, sobbing.

I held my mom, and she cried in my arms. I didn't realize how important Tiffani was to her.

I felt even guiltier. I tried to be persistent with Tiffani. I called her daily. She changed her number. I emailed her every day. She blocked me. Whenever I saw her at school, she wouldn't look at me. I thought in time, things would pass, but I found out Tiffani was transferring schools. She received a partial scholarship to play softball for Syracuse. Now I had lost Adam and Tiffani. Once again, I lost someone I cared about. I felt like the world was crashing down around me.

Chapter Ten

Ray's and Mom's Life Shattered

I had a long week of working at the gym, Def Jam, and going to school. Between training people and writing papers, I was exhausted and mentally drained. I was looking forward to the weekend and relaxing at home without any female companionship for a change. My cell phone rang. I saw it was Ray, but I decided I'd talk to him later. I let the call go to voicemail. Ray kept calling me. I started to get worried because he would never call me continuously like that unless it were important. I answered the phone to hear him crying.

"Ray, what's wrong?"

"She doesn't love me anymore, man. Lucy doesn't want to be with me. You . . . You gotta help me. She'll listen to you."

"What? What happened?"

"Right in the middle of us having sex, she started crying. She pushed me off and said she couldn't do this anymore. She didn't love me anymore."

Ray sobbed. I understood his pain. As soon as he told me the story, I immediately figured she was cheating on him. I felt guilty. I suspected something was up, but I never said anything.

On top of that, he was one of my best friends—the only one of my friends that truly understood me—and I secretly slept with his sister. All of those thoughts were going through my head. Tired or not, busy or not, I had to be there for him. I owed him that and more.

"I'm so sorry, man. What did she say when you asked her what's wrong? Is there another guy?"

"She said she was bored—bored with me, bored with her life, and bored with being in a relationship. She said she's felt like this for a while now, and she couldn't handle being in a relationship with me anymore. She said there wasn't anyone else, but she needed to go out and experience life without me. You have to help me. She'll listen to you. You have to make her see we belong together."

I heard the desperation in his voice. He honestly believed I could single-handedly save his relationship. While it was an honor to see he had so much faith in me, I felt a lot of pressure because I knew it was hard to change someone's mind once they made it up. She might've told Ray there was no one else, but I didn't believe that shit for a second. I figured she said that to protect him from the truth, but I kept my negative thoughts to myself.

I promised him that as soon as I finished training my last client, I'd meet up with him, and we'd talk more about how to handle his situation.

Ray kept texting and calling me. He couldn't wait. I canceled my last client and drove out to meet him. When we were kids and needed something to do, we would build something. I decided to build a new computer for myself, so I told him to meet me at Micro Center in East Meadow. Ray stepped out of his car, and I could see the pain all in his face. He loved Lucy. She was his life. I didn't just want to help him because it was the right thing to do. I wanted to help him because I didn't want him to become like me deep down. His relationship with Lucy was the only thing I believed could one day stop me from fucking around and finally get me to settle down.

While being with different women had its appeal, a big part of me wanted something real. I wanted to find a girl that loved me just as much as I loved her. I wanted that genuine feeling of being in love, not the relationships I had mistaken for it. I wanted what I felt Ray and Lucy had.

We gave each other a quick bro-hug and walked into the store. Ray told me everything all over again while we picked out parts for the computer.

"Are you sure there is no one else?" I asked.

"Nah, man, there is no one else. Lucy said she's just been with me for so long that she doesn't have the same feelings for me anymore."

"I'm not going to sugarcoat it, man. You don't just lose feelings for someone overnight. Something had to happen for such a drastic change like this."

"I don't know. Maybe she doesn't think I pay enough attention to her or appreciate her. Maybe I need to compliment her more or take her out more."

"Look, I got four courtside tickets for the Knicks game tomorrow that I got from one of my clients at Def Jam. I wasn't planning on going, but maybe we can go to that. I'll bring one of my girls, you bring Lucy, and we can all have a good time. At least, that's a start."

"See, that's what I'm talking about. If we take little trips here and there, she'll remember all the fun we had over the years. I knew you could help me. Thanks, man. Can you do me a favor, though?"

"What's up?"

"Can you talk to her tonight? I told her you know everything, and she wasn't mad about it. She wants to keep this between the three of us, though. We haven't said anything to Kim yet."

When he said Kim's name, it sent a shiver down my spine. I felt guilty again.

"Yo, what exactly do you want me to say?" I asked.

"You'll work it out. You're good at talking to women."

I took a deep breath and said, "All right."

We finished getting all the parts for the computer and made our way back to his house. I parked my car in his driveway and noticed my dad's car was parked across the street at my mom's house. That pissed me off a little, but I had another problem to deal with now. We brought all of the bags and boxes into his house and put them on the dining room table. Kim wasn't home. Lucy was upstairs in their bedroom watching TV.

"Lucy, Ken is here," Ray yelled upstairs.

"OK. Send him up here," she said.

Hope was all over his face. I knew I couldn't let him down. It would be a miracle, but I had to try to fix this. I walked up the steps and went into their bedroom. Lucy was wearing a purple NYU sweatshirt, flannel pants, and had her hair in a ponytail. We hugged.

"Hey, Kenny."

"Hey, we know why I'm here. I seriously don't like to be in your business like this, but what's going on?"

"Kenny, I love Ray. You know I do, but I can't do this anymore. Most of the time you come around here, we're home. We don't go anywhere. We don't do anything. He sits at home after work and watches TV or plays his video games. He has no ambition to better himself or to make our lives happier. I'm not a goddess, but I try to stay in good shape for the most part. I go to the gym five days a week to stay healthy and appealing to him, but he let himself go. He doesn't work out, and he does nothing to keep me physically attracted to him anymore. He doesn't care.

"For years, I tried to talk to him and tell him how I felt. He always said he was going to change. He'd change for like a week, maybe two, and then things would go right back to how they are now. I'm sick of it, Ken. I don't even know if I'm happy being with him or if I'm just with him because he's all I know. I've been with him since the third grade, Ken."

When she said the part about him being all she knew, it made me believe someone else was involved. While her argument was strong, her body language was calm. It didn't seem tense like a person would be if they were bothered by something.

I'd known Lucy for a long time, and I had seen her when she was mad about something she was passionate about. This wasn't how she usually acted.

"You said you don't know if you're truly happy. Do you know how many women wish they could find the type of relationship you guys have? Do you know how many of the girls I fuck with wish I could be to them what Ray is to you? It's true, you guys haven't dated anyone else, but the reason you've lasted this long is that you're right for each other. You complement each other, and that's hard to find. Be straight with me. . . . Is there someone else?"

"No, there's no one else. I'm just tired of being in a relationship that's going nowhere. I wanted us to have our own place. He's content with just staying here at his grandmother's. I ask him to go places with me. He always wants to stay at home and watch TV. I don't want to feel like an old married couple when I'm still in my prime. I want to go out. I want to have fun and see the world. I want to feel pretty. I want Ray to tell me I'm beautiful and mean it, without it feeling like it's forced."

I understood her frustration. Everything she told me made sense, but I needed to help Ray. I had to put up more of a fight to help save his relationship. My only strategy was to play on her insecurities. She was a smart girl, but she didn't have much experience dating. This would be advantageous for me because she had seen me with lots of women. I knew I had to play on her fear of meeting someone like me.

"I know it seems that these are major problems, but all of these things can be fixed. People our age aren't looking for relationships. They're looking to fuck and run."

"Kind of like you?"

"Yup, exactly like me."

When I said that, she shifted in her chair. She was getting uncomfortable, and that's what I wanted. It meant she'd be more likely to listen to reason.

"Look at me. Do you think I want a relationship right now? Hell no. Eventually, we all know we have to settle down, but that isn't in the cards right now. You have someone that truly loves you and would do anything for you. Do you want to throw that away and risk getting hurt by guys like me? What if you leave Ray and realize later you made a mistake? What do you do then? Do you risk losing something that so many women are trying to find for simple problems that can be fixed?"

Lucy started to tear. I held her.

"I don't know what I should do. I don't know if I should leave now or leave later and waste more of each other's time. I do love Ray, I really do. I just want to be happy," she said.

I felt terrible to be in this situation. I didn't like seeing Lucy hurt, but I needed her to understand that they were meant for each other. After about an hour of talking, I told her I would get Ray so they could speak in private. I went downstairs, and Ray had started working on my computer.

"Hey, sorry I started without you. I didn't know how long you two would be up there, and I needed to do something to get my mind off things. How did it go?"

"She loves you, man, but there are some things you two need to work on. Go upstairs and talk to her alone. Listen to her and apply what she tells you. Whether you do it will determine if you guys stay together long-term or not. You have to convince her you're going to change, and not just saying things to please her right now."

"So you think I still have a shot?"

"I do, but you're on thin ice. Remember what I just told you."

"Cool. I'll call you to come up when we're finished talking."

"All right."

Ray ran up the stairs and opened the door. All types of different emotional sounds came from the room. There was yelling, crying, and at some points, laughter. I felt that things could work out with them. They had a strong relationship and history.

Another hour passed, and I had just about finished putting my computer together. Ray and Lucy called me up, and we talked together. They concluded that they'd try to work it out and stay together, and I was happy I could help them stay together. We all hugged. I loved them like they were family, and helping them gave me a sense of accomplishment.

I left Ray's and went across the street to my parents' house. My dad's car wasn't there anymore. I entered to the sound of my mom crying.

"Ma, what's wrong?"

"Your father is leaving me."

"What?"

"For the past two months, whenever I'd call the house during the day, he wouldn't answer the house or his cell phone. I got suspicious and confronted him about it."

"What did he say? Was it other women?"

She sucked her teeth and stared off into space.

"Your father explained to me that on one of the rare days he went to work, he met a woman that gets him, and they'd been spending a lot of time together. He explained that while I loved him, I wasn't in love with him, and he needed to feel loved. He told me he was leaving for good this time, so I told him if he left, the other heifer would have to put him on her insurance and pay for his cell phone, car, student loan, and every other expense I paid for every month."

I shook my head.

"I told him that if he was going to leave me for the other woman, he couldn't stay in the house that I pay for by myself."

Between Ray's drama and my own, my head was spinning. My mom was devastated. I cursed my father.

"You see, you have to let him go. After all you've done for him, *this* is how he repays?" I yelled.

"I know, I know, but I love him. I don't want him to leave me. I don't want to be alone," she sobbed.

That last part hit me because I knew what it felt like not to want to be alone. My mother was an old-fashioned woman. She wasn't the type to go out with many men or even go to places to meet them.

"This is unforgivable, Ma. You can't take him back after this."

"I don't think he is going to come back. I shouldn't have been so hard on him. . . . I—"

"Are you listening to yourself right now? You're justifying him leaving you after all you do for him."

She cried harder. I talked to her until I thought she was stable enough to leave, and then I headed to my place. I needed this fucking day to end.

My stress with my parents bothered me all night. I didn't sleep well. I knew I needed to take someone who was stable to the game and to help me relax and take my mind off things, so I decided to take Heather with me. She hadn't seen or heard from me in two weeks, and I figured this was an excellent way to make it up to her. Having my friends around made her feel special, and I knew they wouldn't say anything negative to her.

Heather and I knocked on Ray's door, and he opened it quickly. His eyes looked teary. I pulled him close.

"What's wrong?" I asked.

Ray sobbed openly. "She's still gonna leave me, man."

We talked in the kitchen.

"This morning, I saw Lucy was up early. She told me she couldn't sleep because she realized it was over, and she couldn't be with me anymore."

"We should still go out. Let's have a good time hanging out in the city, and when we come back, I'll talk to Lucy again."

He was reluctant but agreed. I called up to her, and Lucy walked downstairs. She seemed unaffected.

"Hey, Ken. I'll be ready in a minute."

"What happened after I left?"

"I thought about everything, and I just don't want to be with him anymore." She said it without any remorse or hesitation. She didn't seem saddened or disappointed. She looked relieved and happy.

"Lucy, let's go tonight and have a good time, but can we please talk again later?"

"Sure, Ken, but I'm not going to change my mind. I'm sticking with my decision."

Lucy went back upstairs to get ready while Ray went into the bathroom to shave. I quickly gave Heather a condensed version of what was going on. She felt a little awkward being in this situation, but she understood. I had a feeling this wouldn't be a good outing.

We rode in my car to the train station and took the Long Island Rail Road to Madison Square Garden. Heather and Lucy were dressed to kill. Ray and I just looked like two huge Knick fans. We both had on jerseys, jackets, and hats. We walked in and took our seats. Heather and Lucy were excited. Will Ferrell, Spike Lee, and other celebrities were at the game and seated close to us. None of it fazed Ray. Lucy didn't even sit next to him. She sat next to Heather.

Ray stared at the court in a daze. The game started, and Lucy was having the time of her life, laughing with Heather and high-fiving other fans around us. Ray was looking more miserable as time went on. The ultimate killer of the night was when one of the guys behind Lucy started to talk to her and asked for her number. Ray lost it and started crying. I tried to talk to him, calm him down, and save him from this public embarrassment, but he didn't care. He was hurting, and even I couldn't reach him. Lucy saw him crying and looked emotionless. She just told the guy she wasn't interested and went back to enjoying the game.

Ray was inconsolable. He was crying so hard that the people around us were staring and pointing. I took him out into the lobby area.

"You see, man, she doesn't give a fuck about me. She's having the time of her fucking life, and I'm the one out here crying like a bitch."

I couldn't say anything to that, but I tried to calm him down. "She cares, man. She's just confused. I'll talk to her again. Try to keep it together."

"I've been with her my entire life. She's all I know. I never cheated or treated her wrong, and *this* is the thanks I get? If she leaves me, then I feel like I've wasted my life."

I knew he loved her, how hurt being in this situation felt, but I couldn't stand back and say nothing. "Hold up. Regardless of whether you're with her, your life still has purpose and meaning. It doesn't matter how long you've been with her. Remember this, 'Never allow someone to be your priority while allowing yourself to be their option,'" I said, using a quote he and I learned in our high school English class.

"Please don't quote Mark Twain to me."

"It's true. Anyway, if worse comes to worst and you guys end up splitting, you have to realize there is life without her. Sometimes shit happens, and we don't get what we want. We fall, but we have to pick ourselves up again and learn from our mistakes."

He started to tear up again.

"I don't want to be with anyone else. I want her."

I felt that. What he was saying was all too familiar to me. I calmed him down enough to return to our seats and finish the game.

The train ride home was awkward. Lucy mostly talked to Heather and didn't even acknowledge Ray. We got off the train, and I dropped Heather off at her house. She wasn't happy that Ray and Lucy's drama cut into her time with me, but she understood.

I drove to Ray's house.

"Lucy, can we talk alone?" I asked her.

She sighed, rolled her eyes, and said, "Yeah, c'mon."

Ray sat down on the couch next to Kim and watched TV. He didn't say a word.

"Is everything all right? What's going on?" Kim asked.

No one answered. Lucy and I walked into the bedroom. She sat down on the bed.

"What's up?" she said, sighing.

"What happened tonight? You looked like you didn't even care that your man—the guy you live with and say you love—had been crying over you in public."

"Ken, save it. Nobody sees when I'm crying over feeling stagnant in my life with him. Nobody sees that I'm unhappy. People only see the happy couple that has been together since they were kids. I'm tired of pretending to be happy."

"I get that, but I didn't think your frustrations with him would cause you to completely not care to see him crying in public. I'm not buying that. Lucy, be honest with me, *is* there someone else?"

Lucy started to tear. She looked up at me. "Fine. You want the truth? You're right. Are you happy now?"

I didn't want to believe it. "What exactly am I right about?" I asked.

"I'm seeing someone else, Ken."

My mouth fell open. I suspected it, but I never thought it could be true. They were the couple I wanted to emulate eventually, and now, I felt it was all a façade. The only word I could muster up was "Explain."

"I've been seeing this guy, John, at my accounting firm for about three months now. It started innocently. We talked and started hanging out to vent and escape our relationships. We had a lot in common, and we enjoyed each other's company."

"Is that when you were supposed to be working late?"

"Yes. I needed time for myself. Anyway, I feel things for John that I've never felt for Ray. Lately, I've stopped feeling guilty about sneaking off with him and found myself feeling progressively detached from Ray. Every day I spend here, I feel trapped. I'm grateful to Ray for a lot of things, but I'm not in love with him anymore."

I didn't know what I should do.

"Those feelings you think you feel are the newness of the relationship. Every time I meet a new woman, I think I see something in them that all the others are missing, but it still doesn't make me commit. The truth is that the problem is with me, not them. Are you seriously going to leave Ray?"

"Yes. I found a small condo in Long Beach, and I'm using my savings to put a down payment on it. I've thought long and hard about this, and I'm sticking with my decision. Please don't tell Ray about John, though."

"Are you kidding? There is no way I'd tell him. If he found out you were with another guy, it would kill him."

"Good. I know you're good with keeping secrets."

She had this look in her eye like she knew something. Rather than blurt anything out, I asked, "What do you mean by that?"

"I know, Ken. You don't have to play dumb with me. Kim is my best friend. She tells me everything."

I was shocked and pissed, but I still didn't know what and how much Kim told her. "Told you everything about what?"

"I know you and Kim fucked. She told me all the details. But don't worry. Our secrets will be safe with each other." She smirked at me.

Damn, she was good. She knew I wouldn't say anything now because there was a risk she would tell Ray about Kim and me.

"Look, I'll take care of Ray. Do me a favor, though. Once you leave him, stay away. It's going to take him a long time to recover from this, and I don't want him to see you around all the time and reopen the same wound."

Lucy looked hurt but agreed. "I understand," she said.

We hugged, promised to take both of our secrets to the grave, and opened the room door. Kim ran up the stairs, crying.

"Lucy, please talk to me," Kim said.

Kim looked up to Lucy like an older sister. Breaking up with Ray would be like leaving her as well. Lucy's eyes welled up with tears. They both cried and went into the room together. I walked downstairs, and Ray was still watching TV.

"Hey, do you want to go out for a drive with me?"

"Nah, I get it. She's leaving me. I just want to be alone right now."

I felt terrible for my friend. I talked to him for a bit, told him I'd always be there for him, and I'd help him through this. He cried, and I helped to calm him down. He decided to sleep on the couch until she moved out, and I agreed that would be for the best.

I was exhausted too.

We said our goodbyes, and I went home. I felt bad not telling him about Lucy cheating on him, but I felt ignorance was bliss in this case.

My family life had gotten even worse. My dad left my mom and found an apartment with the other woman. My mom was so devastated by it that she called me at Def Jam sounding suicidal one day. I left work and went to see her as fast as possible to make sure she didn't do anything crazy.

My dad was the usual dickhead he always was. He stopped by the house periodically to get his things. My mom told me about one particular time when he stopped by and asked her if she wanted to go to a concert at the Nassau Coliseum with him. Since it was a Sunday, and my mom never missed church for anything, she passed. He told her he was still going to go but would take a nap at the house first. He put his cell phone in the living room to charge and napped in their old bed. While he was sleeping, his phone rang, and for some reason, my mom felt she needed to hear the woman's voice that stole her husband. She wasn't even sure if the person calling was her, but she needed to know who was calling, so she answered his phone.

"Hello?" she said.

"Um, can I . . . um, talk to James?" the woman asked.

"Who is this, and what do you need to say to my husband?"

"Um, I'm a friend. Is James there?"

Frustrated, my mom knew this was the woman. This is who destroyed her world and caused her husband to leave. She went into their bedroom, where so many memories were shared, and threw the phone at him.

"James, your bitch is on the phone."

He quickly grabbed the phone and talked to the unknown woman.

"Yeah . . . Don't worry about that. . . . Of course, we're still going. . . . I just stopped by to get some stuff. . . . All right . . . cool . . . I'm on my way to pick you up. . . . See you in a few."

"James, who was that?"

"It doesn't matter who she is."

"*Really*, James? After everything I've done for you? After everything you've put me through? You're gonna do me like this?"

"Look, it is what it is. Deal with it."

He gathered his things and walked out the door. The rest of the day, my mom sat in the house, wishing God would help her. Help her to stop the love she had for my dad. Help her to move on from this hell he was putting her through.

After that day, she started to lose faith. She was tired of everything and prayed that God would end her life, so she didn't have to deal with my dad's bullshit anymore. When her depression became too much, she called me.

"I can't take it anymore, Kenny. I can't live without him."

"Stop talking like that. You don't need him. He's the one slowing you down. You have a doctorate. You have so many good qualities, and he's the cancer that is killing you. Cut him off."

"I can't."

"You can't, or you won't?"

She didn't say anything. I needed her to understand she was better than this. My cell phone vibrated, letting me know I had a text message. It was from Ray, but I didn't read it. A minute later, I got another one and another after that. While my mom was sitting there with her head in her hands, I quickly glanced to see what the first text message said.

Oh my God, this bitch cheated on me.

I was nervous now, and my fears were correct.

And she told me you knew this whole time.

Guilt and worry were all over my face. I didn't know why Lucy told him I knew, and worst of all, I didn't know if she told him I had slept with Kim. The last message was just one word.

Why?

I didn't have time to respond to that message. My mom needed me, and while that was its own little drama, it had to wait.

I talked to my mom for about a good hour and a half. She decided she was going to go to church. I felt sorry for her because besides having my aunt and me to talk to, she would've had Tiffani, but I fucked that up.

My mom got ready and left for church. She let me know that after church, she was going to sleep over at my aunt's. As soon as she left, I quickly ran across the street to Ray's house. I knocked on the door. He yelled for me to come in. I braced myself for the worst.

"Why? Why didn't you tell me?" he asked.

"Look, man, you were so hurt about the whole situation with her leaving I didn't want to make things worse."

"Fine. I'm still pissed you didn't tell me, but I get it."

I felt a little better. He didn't mention anything about Kim, so I guess Lucy didn't say anything about that.

"I'm done with her. She took the last of her stuff today. My bedroom and parts of this house look bare and empty, and that's how I feel right now—bare and empty. She's not coming back. My life will never be the same."

"Don't say that. You'll get over her. Look at it this way. Now you can finally be my wingman."

I tried to joke, but he didn't find it funny. I wasn't serious, though. Ray was a good guy. He didn't need to be emotionally detached like I was.

"I tried to have one more intimate moment with Lucy, hoping she'd realize she was making a mistake and convince her not to leave, but we ended up arguing, and she slipped up and told me she was cheating on me."

"Brother, again, I'm sorry about that. I was only trying to protect you."

"I know."

While we were talking, Kim came home. We stared at each other for a few seconds. Kim looked concerned. She ran and hugged Ray.

"I need to be by myself for a minute. I'll be back. I'm just gonna go for a drive to clear my head," Ray said, looking defeated.

I nodded.

"Okay," Kim said, rubbing his arm. She walked into the kitchen. Ray put on his black Columbia jacket and walked out the front door.

When I walked into the kitchen, Kim was sitting on top of the kitchen counter, staring at the floor.

"I can't believe Lucy did this to him. She was like a sister to me. If something was wrong, she should've told me. I would've said something to Ray before this all got out of hand," Kim said.

"I know you feel like you could've helped, but you couldn't have made this any better. This was between him and her. She had been feeling this way for a while. This is something they have to go through on their own."

"I know, but he's hurting so bad, and there's nothing I can do to help him."

"Be there for him when he needs it. I'm going to take him out a lot to keep him busy."

Kim looked at me, hopped off the counter, and hugged me. Then she kissed me sensually on the lips.

"Come upstairs for a little."

"Come on, Kim, this is not the time or place for this. On top of that, why the hell did you tell Lucy about our time together?"

"It was just girl talk. She wouldn't say anything."

"She can't say anything. Do you know how Ray would feel if he found out that on top of everything, I fucked his sister? I'm not going to make his life any worse than it is now."

"OK, OK, I'm sorry. I wasn't thinking. I've known Lucy for years. She wouldn't say anything."

While I wanted to believe her, I couldn't. I never thought Lucy would cheat on Ray, but she did. I never thought she'd ever leave him, but it happened. I prayed Kim was right. I talked to her a bit longer, then went back to my parents' house. I had an extreme migraine dealing with all this shit. I sat in the living room and watched random things on cable. Soon, Heather called me.

"What's up?" I answered.

"Why haven't you called me? The last time I heard from you, you were helping your friend out. What about me? Maybe for once, *I* need you. Maybe I want you to care for me and be there for me like you're always there for them."

I was already aggravated. I didn't need more stress today.

"Look, save the theatrics. I got a lot of shit going on in my life, and I don't need this shit right now. If you can't deal with it, then you can fucking step. I'm tired of this shit. Leave me the fuck alone."

Her voice sounded shaky. "Do you *really* mean that, Kenny?"

"Yeah, I mean it. If you want to talk to me, call me when you're in a better mood or lose my fucking number. I don't have time for this shit right now."

"Kenny, I'm—"

I ended the call. I massaged my temples as I sat on the couch, irritated, and continued to watch TV.

My phone rang again. I saw it was Kristen this time. I needed to hear a positive voice with all the shit I was going through right now, so I picked up.

"What's up, sweetie?" I said.

"Hey . . . Kenny. Um, can I ask you for a favor?"

I was a little curious about what she could be asking for. Her voice sounded as if she was nervous or scared.

"Sure. Anything, sweetie, what's up?"

"Um, I need to have surgery tomorrow, and I need to ask if you can take me to the doctor's office for the, um, procedure."

"Is everything OK?"

"Yeah, it's just a minor surgery that I need to take care of. I won't be able to drive afterward, though. Can I come over to your house and hang out a little bit after the surgery?"

Her voice had a desperate tone to it. She didn't turn to her friends or her family. She turned to me. Although I had work the next day, I felt that I owed it to her to help her out with everything I put her through.

"Of course, sweetie. You know I'm here for you."

"Thanks, it means a lot to me. I'll pick you up at around 8:00 a.m. tomorrow. I need you to drive back. I'll hang out with you a little bit afterward, and then I'll drive home."

"OK. I'm staying at my mom's, so come there. Are you sure you'll be OK to drive afterward?"

"Yeah . . . I'll see you in the morning. See you tomorrow, Ken."

"Okay."

I stopped by my place, packed a bag, and headed back to my parents' home. I knew my mom was with Aunt Carol, so the house would be empty. I doubted my dad would be showing up.

The next day Kristen came at 8:00 a.m. sharp. She parked her black Honda Civic in the driveway and honked the horn. I came out of the house. She got out of the car, hugged, and kissed me. Her hugs always felt genuine and warm. She asked if I could drive. I agreed. She had on a gray Baby Phat jumpsuit.

She looked nervous, stressed, and tired.

"You good?" I asked.

"Yeah, I'm cool. This is just something I need to take care of ASAP."

Krissy didn't look sick or hurt, so I was curious about what type of surgery she was having.

"What kind of surgery are you getting?"

"It's nothing major—minor surgery. I don't want to talk about it. I should be fine in a couple of hours after the procedure."

She was vague with her answer, so I left it at that. She entered an address in her GPS for a place in Smithtown. Then she turned on the radio, and Ashanti's song, "Foolish," was on. She sang along with the radio, which reminded me of the time she sang at the open mic night. Every time I heard her sing, I was moved. Her voice was so powerful and soulful. She sang the song and started crying while she was singing.

"You sure you're OK, Krissy?"

She wiped her face and smiled at me. "I'm fine. That song always makes me emotional."

I rubbed on her hand, and we continued to drive. She looked like she had a lot on her mind. I had my own stress dealing with my family and Ray's situation.

We got to the address on the GPS. I wasn't sure if this was the right place. It didn't look like a hospital. It was just a plain tan building. Kristen froze for a second.

"Are you sure this is the building?" I asked.

"Yeah . . . I'm positive," she said sadly.

"What's wrong?"

"I . . . I . . . I don't like going to this doctor. Come on, let's hurry up and get this over with."

Kristen's pace was fast and determined. We walked in, and she talked to the receptionist. I sat down in the TV area. I looked over at her, and the receptionist rolled her eyes at me. The doctor's office was filled with women, and they all seemed to have an attitude, so I figured this had to be her gynecologist.

Finally, she sat next to me and held my hand. The TV in the waiting area was on Saturday-morning cartoons, so we had to entertain ourselves with that or read the magazines on the coffee table. The nurse called her name, and Kristen kissed me on the cheek and went to her.

All the women in the office saw that and sucked their teeth.

Kristen was in the office for about two hours. Between watching the Saturday cartoons and playing games on my cell phone, I was bored as hell. She came out looking pale and weak. I held her arm and helped her out of the office to the car.

The whole ride back to my parents' house, Kristen was quiet. She just stared out the window in a daze. I didn't know what I should do or say. She didn't seem like she wanted to talk. Finally, we got back to my mother's house, and I pulled up in the driveway.

"Hey, do you want me to order us lunch? What are you in the mood for?" I asked.

"Ken, I think I'm just going to drive home."

"But you said you were going to hang out with me for a while. You said you'd be too weak to drive."

"I don't think us hanging out right now will make me feel any better."

"OK, what's the deal? Why were you so quiet on the way back? Why do you think hanging out with me wouldn't help you feel better?"

"You seriously don't know, Kenny?"

"Know what?"

"You really didn't know where we were, Ken? Ken, we were at an abortion clinic."

My mouth dropped open. Then it hit me. No wonder the receptionist rolled her eyes at me. No wonder all the women there were giving me an attitude. No wonder there was nothing but women there. They were all there for the same thing—to have an abortion. It all added up. I remembered the last time we had sex, and the condom broke. It was possible I could've knocked her up.

"What . . . Who's—"

"It was yours, Ken. I haven't been sleeping with anyone but you. I knew you wouldn't want to keep it. I knew you didn't want to have a family with me. I didn't want to fuck up your life, so I figured I'd get the procedure done and not tell you about it. But it's killing me that I went through with it. I had a life inside of me, and I got rid of our child for you because I love you. It hurts because you don't love me the same way."

Kristen sobbed. I felt like shit. I wasn't ready to be a father, that's for sure, but a part of me wished she would've told me earlier. I reached over to console her and put my arms around her, but she pushed me away and held her face in her hands.

"Krissy, come inside. Let's talk in the house."

"No, Ken. I'm going home."

She unloosened her seat belt and opened the passenger-side door. She closed it and slowly made her way to my side. I got out and tried to reason with her.

"Look, Krissy, I feel horrible. I didn't know what was going on, and I didn't mean for you to go through this. I want to talk about it."

"I can't talk to you right now, Ken. Just looking at you makes me feel so stupid and sad. I need time to be alone. Goodbye, Ken."

Kristen pushed me aside and slowly eased herself into the driver's seat. I tried to convince her to come inside the house, but she wouldn't listen. Krissy put on her sunglasses and pulled off. She left me standing there, talking to myself. I seriously felt like a villain. I felt like my father.

Slowly but surely, my world was crumbling before me. My mom was an emotional wreck when my father left. Adam and Tiffani were no longer friends with me and wouldn't talk to me. Ray was inconsolable. Perry was so in love with Jessie that we rarely hung out anymore, and my relationships were all collapsing around me.

The first was Heather. I was at the gym training my clients when I got a call from her, but I didn't answer and sent it to voicemail. She called me repeatedly, and out of spite, I kept sending her to voicemail.

After my last client, I called her back to see what was so important that she needed to blow up my phone with calls.

"Hello," I said.

"Ken, this is Mrs. Nolan, Heather's mother. Heather is in the hospital right now. She's in critical condition after she tried to commit suicide today. She left a note explaining if she couldn't be with you, she didn't want to live anymore and drove her car into oncoming traffic and got into a horrible accident."

I was speechless. There was nothing I could say to make this right. I felt guilty and responsible.

"I'm so sorry. . . . I—"

"Look, do me a favor and stay the fuck away from my daughter. This is *your* fault."

"I never meant to do anything that would drive her to do something like that."

"Yes, you did, Ken. Yes, you did. Every time you made plans with her and broke them, every time you didn't call her and left her hanging by the phone, every time you gave her false hope that you were going to one day be with her completely—all of those things drove her to this. To her, you were her world, but to you, she was just a piece of ass, and you manipulated her. *You're a fucking monster!*"

Her words hurt because she was right. I was guilty of all of those things. Hearing them from Heather's mom made me see the impact my actions had. I tried to apologize again.

"Mrs. Nolan, seriously, I'm sorry and—"

"Save your bullshit for someone else, Ken. Do my daughter a favor and stay the fuck out of her life. Don't call her, don't text her, write her, email her—nothing. I'll help her get over you so she can go back to her normal life before she met you. Stay away from her."

She ended the call, and I felt horrible. As badly as I wanted to talk to Heather and apologize for all the bullshit I put her through, I respected her mom's wishes and left her alone. I erased all methods of reaching her so I wouldn't be tempted to get back in contact with her.

My next loss was Denise. We were at the food court in Sunrise Mall when she brought up the topic of being in a relationship.

"Kenny, we need to talk."

"About?"

"What are we doing? I like you; you like me. We have great chemistry together. We have fun together. We have lots in common. Why are we not in a relationship?"

"Why do you feel we need a title? We're good the way we are. We live in the moment without the labels."

As soon as I said that, I felt like an asshole because at one point in my life, Ashely said similar bullshit to me, and I remembered how it made me feel.

"That's the problem. There's *no* attachment. I want to know that you're mine and that I'm not sharing you with a million other girls. I know I'm not the only one you're seeing. I don't stress you out about it, but it does bother me. I want to be with you. We mesh. It makes sense. We have a history together."

"We do have a good time together. We do have history, but it's not you. It's me. I'm not into being in relationships."

When all else fails, I always used my past to try to get me out of the relationship talk.

"I know you still have some issues because of your ex, but I'm not her. I wouldn't do that to you. You can trust me. You can be in a relationship with me and let go of the bad memories of that bitch."

Damn, it isn't working. She was persistent about this whole relationship thing. She kept giving me reasons why we should be in a relationship, and I kept shooting them down.

We left the mall with her cursing me out and telling me I wasn't shit. She said she hated me, and she was going to find a man that would appreciate her.

The next morning, I got a disturbing phone call from her.

"Hey," I answered.

"I'm in the fucking hospital, Ken."

"What? Why?"

"I heard about a party off-campus at some house a bunch of guys rented and decided to go to it with my friends. We got shit-faced drunk, and I met a guy at the party. I was drunk and wanted to move on from you, so when he took me to one of the bedrooms in the house, I didn't care that I was fucking him on the first night."

That stung, but I shrugged it off. "Did he hit you or something?"

"Let me finish. You owe me that much."

She never snapped at me like that before, so I knew this had to be serious.

"Anyway, he bent me over, and I noticed he kept holding my head down and only wanted to fuck me from behind. His hands and dick kept feeling different as we kept going, and I was having a hard time breathing with him holding my head down. I screamed at him to let me go and struggled to lift my head when I realized there were *six* other guys in the room, all with their pants down and dicks out. The guy that was fucking me wasn't the same guy I came in the room with.

"I screamed for him to stop, but he ignored me and kept pumping away. The other guys took their turns on me too and ignored me. I repeatedly screamed for them to stop. When they were done fucking me in every hole, they laughed, high-fived each other, and left."

She was crying. I was speechless. Finally, she composed herself and went on.

"When I got out of the bedroom and told some people I knew from school what happened, they called the police. I found out the guys at the party crashed it and didn't even go to my school. They had all raped me without protection, and I couldn't give a good description of the guys because I had my head down most of the time. This is all *your* fucking fault. If you would've just been with me and stopped stringing me along like a fucking kite, I wouldn't have been at that fucking party. Now I've been raped, and I don't know if any of them gave me a disease or got me pregnant. I don't believe in abortion, so what would I do if one of them knocked me up? If I had listened to my gut and stopped dealing with you the second you told me you didn't want a relationship with me, this shit would've never happened."

I felt a lot of emotions. Angry, sad, but most of all, guilty. She was right. This was my fault. I could try to think of reasons why it wasn't, but I knew I was responsible in my heart and soul. If I would've stopped playing games with her, she would've never been at that party.

"You can't blame all this shit on me. I would never wish this on anyone. I—"

"Stay the fuck away from me. Get out of my life. I never want to see you again."

"Denise, I—"

"I don't want to hear it. You're the worst thing that ever happened to me." She hung up.

Her words cut me deeper than any knife could. Again, my actions led to someone else getting hurt. Between Heather and Denise, I needed someone to uplift me. I wanted to feel a connection. I called Kristen. I didn't want sex. I just wanted someone to pick up my tanked self-esteem.

"Yes, Ken?"

"Hey . . . How are you?"

"I'm fine."

"What are you doing right now?"

"Ken, it's been about three weeks since I've seen or heard from you. I can't do this anymore. You know I love you. I'd do anything for you, but this is killing me inside. I got rid of our child because I knew you didn't want that life with me. I know you don't want me. It hurts, but it's the truth. I don't want anyone else but you, but I'll never have you. I'm not strong enough to let you go, so I'm asking you to let me go. Let me go, so I can find someone that wants to be with me and love me the way I deserve to be loved. Someone that'll give me what you'll never give me."

I was emotional. After everything that had been going on, I truly felt like a *monster*. Krissy was right. I liked her, but I never wanted a relationship. I put her through so much, and now she was asking me to have the decency to let her go.

"Krissy, I'm sorry I've put you through so much shit. You've always been there for me when I needed someone, and I haven't been fair to you. I get that now. If you feel that me letting go of you will help—as much as I'll miss you, and I know I'm gonna regret this—I'll let you go and not hold you back any longer from finding what you're looking for."

"I know. I'm gonna regret it too, but I can't do this to myself anymore. You'll always have a place in my heart. You're not a bad guy, but you have a lot of emotional stuff you need to work on. You never let me in. Promise me the next woman you meet that you'll let her in and trust her. That's the only way you'll be able to be in a relationship, Ken."

With tears streaming down my face, I said, "I will. You take care of yourself. I'll respect your wishes and let go. I won't contact you anymore. You're a good girl, and you deserve someone that'll appreciate you and treat you better than me."

I could hear that she was crying too.

"Thank you . . . goodbye, Kenny."

"Goodbye, Krissy."

We hung up, and I had finally hit rock bottom. I needed someone to talk to. I felt horrible and alone, so I drove to Ray's house. I figured he'd be home and would help me through my world that was crashing down around me. I pulled up in front of his house and looked across the street to see if my mom was home. Her car wasn't there. I walked up to his front door and rang the doorbell.

The door flew open. Ray rushed me.

"You motherfucker. You fucked my sister."

Shock and terror were all over my face. Ray punched me in the face with all his strength. I was dazed and off balance. He tackled me and continuously punched me in the face. Finally, he got off me and spat in my face.

"You're a fucking asshole. You were supposed to be my best friend, and you fucked my sister. I listened to you for the longest talk about all the girls you preyed on, and I never thought you would do that to my sister. I didn't care about the other girls, but this is my family, and I can't believe you used my sister like that. You know, you're always talking about how you spend your life trying not to be like your father. Well, guess what? You're *exactly* like him. *You're a fucking monster*. No one can love you. How could they? You don't have a soul to love. From now on, you don't exist to me. Don't ever talk to me again. Stay away from my family and out of my life."

I was dazed by all the punches but tried to reason with him. "Ray, listen, I never meant to—"

"Shut the fuck up," he screamed. "You're always making excuses and trying to make yourself seem like a good guy, but you're not. You're the villain. Forget you know me. Forget we were ever fucking friends. If you see me in the street, keep walking, and if you ever come near my fucking sister again, I swear to God I'll kill you."

I knew there was no reaching him, so I got up and walked to my car, defeated—mentally and physically.

Chapter Eleven

Amendment

The words "you're a fucking monster" . . . "no one could love you" kept replaying in my head. This was the second time in a month that I was called a monster. I sat on my black leather couch and reflected on life and my past. I had come a long way from the boy that dated Bri, but what type of man had I become?

I hadn't left my apartment, gone to work, or talked to anyone on the phone in a week. I just sat home and reflected. When Bri dumped me, I started acting heartless not to hurt anymore. Now, I was hurting people regularly. The hard fact was no one ever believes they're the bad guy. In everyone's mind, they're the protagonist, but Ray helped me realize I was the villain. I became what I hated—a clone of my father.

I walked into my bathroom and took a long, hot shower. Taking that shower reminded me of my childhood when I used to wish the hot water would make my skin lighter. Now, I wished it could erase the evil deeds I'd done. I got out, dried off, and stared at my reflection in the mirror. My physical appearance had changed a lot. I was thinner, in better shape, my hair was braided, and my eyes were different. My eyes didn't have that same innocence they used to. I didn't recognize the man staring back at me. I didn't recognize who I'd become. I changed too much.

My actions not only hurt good people but cost me my friends. I was alone. How could I expect anyone to love me with my heart being so ugly?

I changed once, and now I needed to evolve again—not into the same naïve boy I was before or the hard monster I was now—but a medium, a gray, someone who wouldn't be walked over like I had in the past, but wouldn't purposely hunt and hurt women like I did now. To become this new person, I had to change a lot of things.

I started with the small stuff first. I decided to cut my hair as my first step to letting go of this life and starting fresh. When I first started growing it, my hair represented my newfound strength, but now, it reminded me of the times when I was at my cruelest.

Next, I quit Lifetime Fitness and got a new personal trainer job with Synergy Fitness in Baldwin. I had too much negative history at Lifetime. I made a lot of money with the company, but I wanted a clean slate—a place where I hadn't slept with any members. I went to see Ron before I quit and explained everything.

"So, you're going to leave this place, huh?" he asked.

"Yeah, it's time."

"Good choice. I'm going to miss you here, so don't be a stranger."

"I won't."

"Awhile back, I told you a quote about finding the truth for yourself. Now, I'm going to tell you a quote about your decision that I want you to follow. 'The art of living does not consist in preserving and clinging to a particular mode of happiness, but in allowing happiness to change its form without being disappointed by the change; happiness, like a child, must be allowed to grow up.' Charles L. Morgan said that. You've had tons of experiences, and it has gotten old to you. Now, it's time to grow up from this. There is nothing wrong with growing and wanting more out of your life. I wish you well and take care of yourself."

"Thanks for everything," I said.

We hugged, and I left.

I still had the Def Jam job. I had enough money saved to pay my bills and hold me over for a while as I started fresh at a new gym. I added another class to my school schedule. I wanted to finish my goal of getting my master's degree. The heavy demands of papers and research kept me busy and not thinking of dating.

Next, I traded in my car. I didn't want to have the memories of the things I had done in that car. I didn't need a vehicle to measure my success anymore. I wanted something more modest, so I bought a Lincoln Continental. It was big enough to hold my exercise equipment and was luxurious, but it wasn't too flashy. I also decided to move. My condo was beautiful, but it was also expensive. I thought about all the mistakes and one-night stands I had while living there, and I wanted a fresh start. I wanted to escape my past and be closer to my mom, so I got a condo in Freeport near the Nautical Mile.

Eight months passed. I hadn't slept with one girl. I hadn't even gone on any dates. I only went to work, kept my head in the books, and focused on becoming a better person. I didn't want to rush to meet someone and relapse back to my old self. I did what Lucy and Adam told me to do earlier. I took the time to heal.

I worked at a new gym. It was nowhere near as busy as my old one, but it kept money in my pocket. I kept things strictly professional with all of my clients.

I came home from the gym one day and got a call from Perry. We still hung out here and there and spoke from time to time, but it wasn't like it was in the past. We didn't have Ray or Adam around anymore. It was just the two of us, and since Jessie didn't like me, we hung out less.

"What's up, brother? How you doing?" Perry asked.

"I'm good, man. Long time no see or hear."

"I know. . . . I've been crazy busy, which is sort of the reason why I called you."

"What's up?"

"I'm getting married, man, and I want you to be my best man."

"What? The person who said marriage was for suckers?"

"I told you before if I find a woman that legitimately loves me for me, without all that materialistic nonsense, I'd marry her. I found that with Jessie. Now to make it perfect, I need you to agree to be my best man."

"Does Jessie know you're asking me?"

"Yeah, she knows."

"What did she say?"

"It doesn't matter what she said. She knows it would make me happy, and it's what I want, so she's cool."

"Did you ask Ray and Adam to be in the wedding?"

"Ray isn't answering anyone's calls, and Adam told me a flat-out no. He isn't even coming to the wedding. That hurt a lot. He's still mad about Lilly."

"I'll talk to him. It'd be nice to have at least the three of us together again. What has he been up to anyway?"

"He's on this off-Broadway show called *Soul of Shaolin*. I hear he's pretty good in it."

"Nice. Well, I accept. I'll be your best man, and I'll try to talk to Adam to get him to be in the wedding too."

"Cool. Thanks, man. Talk to you soon."

"No doubt. Talk to you later."

We hung up.

I wanted to see Adam again to apologize to him and try to let him see I'd changed. I bought tickets to his performance. He was in full costume. Since he's Black and 99 percent of the cast was Asian, it was easy to find him even in costume. He had gotten better. The fluidity in his movements showed that not only did he spend a lot of time perfecting those moves, but he was also passionate about what he was doing. I was proud of my friend.

When the show ended, I waited by the front entrance where the performers were exiting.

As always, Adam was last.

"Yo, Adam."

Adam turned around in excitement at first—until he saw it was me. He frowned and turned away.

Coldly he said, "What do you want?"

"I saw your performance. You're living your dream, and I'm happy for you, man. I just wanted to apologize. I've changed, and I—"

He cut me off. "You've changed? You've *changed?* When did this happen? After you fucked my girl?"

"I know I messed up. I had a lot of things wrong with me back then, and I did a lot of stupid shit. I'm honestly sorry."

"Ken, you're never going to change. Nothing you say will make me forget what you did."

"You always told me God forgives those who are truly sorry, and you always wanted to follow his instruction. Follow it now. Forgive me. I know I was wrong. I know I hurt people. I'm not that guy anymore."

"I forgave you a long time ago. I won't forget what you did, though, and I won't put myself in a position where you can let me down again."

"I can't make you do anything you don't want to do, but do me this favor. Perry is getting married. He wants us to be in the wedding party. Do you think you can do that?"

"I won't be in his wedding party. He was a coconspirator with the whole Lilly situation. Tell him I'll go to his wedding as a guest and wish him well."

"Thank you."

"Ken, after the wedding, don't look for me again. We'll always have history. I'll always cherish our good times together, but you're toxic, and I don't need your negativity around me anymore."

I looked at my old friend—a man who I felt was as close to me as family, a person who was like a brother to me. I put my head down, walked away, and said, "Okay."

Maybe he was right. Maybe I was toxic.

Six months passed, and it was finally Perry's wedding day. I never thought I'd see the day. With Perry's father-in-law and father combining their efforts, they created one of the grandest weddings ever.

Perry did everything in style and had his wedding at the Oheka Castle in Huntington. The place was amazing, and the view was incredible. Inside the castle, every person at the wedding received their own bottle of wine. Perry had doves released at the end of the ceremony, and he and Jessie rode away by horse and carriage.

The reception was beautiful. He had every type of hors d'oeuvres imaginable. There was an open bar, and the entrees were delicious. Everyone had their choice of filet mignon, baked salmon, or chicken Parmesan. I had the filet mignon. For dessert, Perry had tables that seemed endless with desserts. There was even a fondue fountain. He had both a live band and a DJ. He also had a videographer and a photographer.

Lilly and Kristen were at the wedding, but they didn't approach or talk to Adam or me the whole time. Since the fallout with Lilly and Kristen, Jessie thought it best to have her family in her bridal party and used her sisters and cousins. Kristen looked at me, gave me a slight smile, and waved. Lilly winked at me. They congratulated Jessie separately and then left separately after talking to her.

It was finally time for me to give my best man speech. I thanked Perry for the honor and made jokes about our memories in high school. I told the audience a polished version of what Perry said would make him get married and how Jessie met those requirements. I told them how Perry was like a brother to me, and now that they were married, this made Jessie my sister, and I valued that. I got loud applause. Jessie hugged me and said she appreciated the speech. Perry looked so happy with her. They looked complete, and I wanted that. I finally realized I'd always truly wanted that.

After dinner, Adam walked over to Perry. He gave him a quick hug and congratulated him. He kissed Jessie, handed her a card, and told them he was leaving. I walked outside to say goodbye to him.

"Adam, hold up."

"Yeah?"

"Thanks for coming."

"OK. Take care of yourself, and I hope you find what you're looking for. I'm going to be traveling with the show, so I guess I won't see you guys around."

"Good luck with everything. You worked hard, man, and you deserve nothing but success."

"Thanks."

We shook hands, hugged, and I took another long look at my friend as he walked away. I was sure this was it, and I'd never see him again.

I stood outside and admired the view. The wind was blowing, and the sky was a beautiful mix of day and night. I was happy for Perry because he finally found his perfect woman, but I was sad because I was alone.

Even though I had so many women in my life to prevent me from feeling this way, in the end, it didn't help because I was still alone. I felt depressed. Someone touched my shoulder, which broke my train of thought. I quickly turned around. It was Perry.

"You all right?" he asked.

"I'm good, man. Don't worry about me. You should be in there having fun with your wife and enjoying your day. I'm fine."

"I know you and Jessie don't get along, but I'm hoping that'll change."

"Yeah, me too. I finally get it now. I want what you have."

"It takes time, man. I never thought I'd be here, but everything comes into perspective when you find that one. The only woman I want in this world is Jessie. You'll find yours one day. Trust me."

We gave each other a brotherly hug and went back inside to the reception.

Two months had passed since Perry's wedding. With him being married, I saw him even less than before.

It was a Saturday night. I had just finished all of my clients and had no plans for the rest of the night. I didn't have school work to do because the semester had already ended. I walked out of the personal training office and collided with this woman holding a shake.

"I'm so sorry. Let me buy you a new one," I said.

"Is this your way of taking me on a cheap date?" she joked.

I smiled at her. "Let me get you a new shake. What did you have?"

"I had the Peanut Butter Madness."

"No problem. I'll get you another one."

The front desk guy was busy scanning people in and handling payments. The salespeople were all busy showing people the gym floor, so I made the shake for her myself.

While making it, I checked her out a bit when she was looking at her cell phone. She had flawless fair skin. She looked mixed, but I couldn't tell with what. She had a soft angelic face with gray eyes, toned yet feminine arms and legs, and a tiny waist with a hearty booty. She was wearing a tight Nike running suit.

She looked up from her cell phone and caught me checking her out. I quickly looked away and finished making her shake. I couldn't believe this. For the first time in a long time, I was acting shy. I handed her the shake.

"Wow, the first date, and you're already making me meals? You're a keeper."

We shared smiles.

"I'm Ken."

"I'm Lynn. Nice to meet you."

"Again, I'm sorry I spilled your shake."

"It's no problem. Thanks for the new one." She smiled and winked at me.

We walked out of the gym and went our separate ways.

Since I had nothing to do, I decided to head to Barnes & Noble and spend my Saturday reading the stock market and exercise books.

I headed to the magazine section first. All of the exercise magazines were on the middle shelf. I reached to grab one, took a step back, and bumped into someone. I turned around, and it was Lynn from the gym.

I stood there with an embarrassed and confused look on my face. "Hi . . . I keep bumping into you."

"I see that. Are you trying to get a cheap feel?" she joked.

"Nah, I'm bored, so I decided to hang out here at the bookstore tonight. What about you?"

"Yeah, I had no plans, so I just decided to work on my lesson plans for next week and get some ideas for new lessons."

"Ah, so you're a teacher."

"Yeah, I teach kindergarten. You gotta keep those little guys active."

"I feel that. I'm pretty much doing the same thing. I'm just looking for new ideas and workouts to try with clients to keep them motivated and fit. I'm also reading a few stock books too to keep me current with the market."

"Nice, what are your other plans for the night? Is your girlfriend meeting you here?"

"Nah, no girlfriend for me."

"No boyfriend, right?"

"No, no, just single. I'm not into guys."

She winked at me again.

"Just making sure. Anyway, since you're not doing anything, and I'm not doing anything, do you want to get dinner together?" Lynn asked.

She was direct and to the point. I liked that, but I didn't know if I was ready to date yet, but it was just dinner, though. I decided what the hell. It's not that serious.

We went to Red Robin for dinner. We talked and got to know each other.

"There are a lot of things I want to know about you, but for now, where do you see yourself in five years?" I asked.

"Damn. You're putting me on the spot like that," she joked. "Well, I hope to be engaged or married. I want to get my second master's in Educational Leadership and pass both school building leadership tests to become a principal. I want to complete the New York City Marathon—oh, and I want to be a season ticket holder for the Knicks."

"What do you know about the Knicks? That's my team."

"I'm a die-hard Knicks fan. I've been watching them since I came out of the womb. You don't look like you can play ball."

"What! You're talking trash?"

"I can back up my talk," she said confidently.

"OK, so we have to play one-on-one soon so that I can show you what a *real* ballplayer looks like."

"Oh, please. I'll destroy you. I played ball in high school, and I got a scholarship to play at Sacred Heart. I have a killer jump shot."

"Damn, that's pretty good. You played in college and got a scholarship? That must've been a big help financially with paying for school."

"Yeah, that helped pay for my undergrad degree. Too bad it can't help me with my master's now."

"I hear you on that. What made you want to be a teacher?"

"I love being a kindergarten teacher. I enjoy working with young kids. When they're young, I get to deal with them before they're older and get bad," she laughed. "But seriously, I feel like the earlier years are when they can truly be reached. I think right now, I'm the first step in molding their young minds."

She was smart and driven, and I liked that. She was also funny and spontaneous—I *really* liked that. We exchanged numbers and agreed we should hang out again.

When I got home, I was happy I met Lynn but wondered if I really wanted to get to know her or if I was just horny, and my old habits were trying to form again. I decided I wouldn't call her. I wasn't ready to date yet.

The next day I saw Lynn at the gym again. We chatted a little about different workouts and new equipment we'd like to see in the gym.

"Ken, let's have dinner together tonight," she said.

I figured that the first part of fixing myself would be to learn self-control, so I agreed.

We met up for dinner at the Grand Lux Café in Garden City. She got there first and waited for me in the parking lot. When I pulled in, there was a spot close to her car.

"Hey," she said, kissing me on the cheek.

"You look beautiful."

We walked in and were immediately seated.

We started with generic date questions: "What's your favorite movie? What color do you like? Do you have a dog?" Somehow ended up with us talking about our families.

"I'm sorry for staring, but your eyes are gorgeous," I said.

She smiled back at me. "Thanks. I've been told my mom had them too."

"*Had* them? Did your mom pass? If she did, I'm sorry. I didn't mean to bring her up."

"I don't know if she's dead or alive. I've never met her."

She went on to tell me about her family and how she was raised primarily by her dad. She explained that her mom was an Italian woman married to a man who wasn't her father. Her mom was having an affair with Lynn's dad, Nick, who was Black. Her mom got pregnant, and since she wasn't sleeping with her husband, she knew Nick had to be the father. She kept the pregnancy hidden. Because of that, Lynn was born prematurely. Out of fear that she could lose her well-kept lifestyle, she left Lynn with Nick and had him promise that he'd raise her entirely on his own. As time went by and after a paternity test, there was no doubt Nick was her father, and he gladly accepted the responsibility.

Lynn spoke highly of her dad. He was a machinist and had his own business making parts for different companies. She explained how she hated her mom and promised herself that she would be a way better mother than hers when she had kids. I could relate to her feelings because I felt the same way when it came to my father.

The way she was so passionate with her words drew me to her. I ended up telling her all about my dad.

"I knew my dad, but it was like I didn't. He always cheated on my mom and left us for days, weeks, and sometimes even months."

Lynn touched my hand, and we smiled at each other. Then she told me about her past relationships.

"I feel like a lot of the mistakes I've made in life were because I didn't have my mom to guide me," I said.

"What mistakes?"

"My choices in men. I haven't had the best of luck when it comes to dating."

"Trust me, I hear you on that."

Lynn told me about her relationships with guys who used to abuse her, both physically and verbally. She poured her heart out to me, telling me all about how they broke her heart and how she made many stupid mistakes due to a lack of experience with dating.

"My high school first love took my virginity and dumped me right before prom. My first boyfriend in college beat the shit out of me and verbally put me down, and my ex-boyfriend, Sean . . . Well, I thought he was the one. I thought I would marry him and live happily ever after, but things didn't work out. We're still friends to this day, but we'll never date again."

"So, you still talk to your ex?" I asked.

"Yeah. We're close."

I sat back in my chair. She still talked to Sean, which made me question if I could ever have a serious relationship with her. I didn't need another repeat of my relationship with Bri.

"You look bothered by that. Is something wrong?" she asked.

"Nah, I'm good. If you don't mind me asking, what caused you and your ex to break up?"

"I'm still not comfortable getting into it, but let's just say, I thought he was the right one for me, but I wasn't the right person for him."

A ton of questions whirled through my head, but I could tell whatever happened was a sensitive issue to her. I left it alone. I figured when she was ready, she'd tell me.

I didn't want to hurt Lynn eventually, so I decided to tell her important things about me.

"Since you're so honest with me, I have to tell you the truth about my past," I said.

I told her about Bri. I told her about Ashley. I told her about all of the women I had hurt and how I regretted it now. I told her about the friends I lost and how I was trying to change and be a better man right now. I could see it was rough for her to listen to my story by her facial expressions and how she looked at me. She didn't say anything. She just listened. I knew it was too early to tell her about *all* the skeletons in my closet, but if I did plan on eventually going further with this girl, I wanted to be completely honest with her and not waste her time. I was done with wasting people's time.

When I finished telling her everything, I felt like a massive weight was lifted off my shoulders.

There was an awkward silence for a while, and she didn't look me in the eyes at all. I started to regret telling her everything immediately. We finished eating.

"I gotta call it a night. I'm taking the kids on a field trip tomorrow, so I have to wake up early," she said.

I took that as her saying she wanted to go home. "I understand."

I paid the bill. We went to the parking lot and gave each other a brief hug.

"Thanks for dinner. I'll see you around the gym," Lynn said.

"You're welcome. I enjoyed your company. I'll see you around."

We said goodbye, and she drove off. I was disappointed because I liked her, but I know I saved her from falling for a monster like me by being honest with her.

Two days passed, and I hadn't heard from Lynn. I hadn't even seen her at the gym. I guess I scared her off. The fear that I'd be alone forever was in the back of my mind.

One day, I sat in my living room in a tank top and shorts, watching TV. I was depressed. I tried to call Perry, but the call went to voicemail. I was watching an old Knicks game when I got a call on my cell phone. I picked it up without checking because I figured it was Perry. I needed to vent.

"Hello," I said.

"Hey."

"Lynn?"

"Yeah . . . I'm sorry I've been avoiding you. . . . Everything you told me caught me off guard."

I regretted telling her the truth. Maybe what nobody knows won't hurt them, but I was glad she called me.

"Yeah, I'm sorry about that. I just really like you. I didn't want to scare you off, but I wanted you to know the truth. I'm not perfect. I have flaws, but I'm trying to change."

"I know, and that's the only reason why I decided to talk to you again. You could've not told me anything and kept me in the dark, but the fact that you told me makes me believe you genuinely want to change."

"So where do we go from here?"

"We become better friends. Look, I'm not in a rush to be in anything either. You need to heal from your past, and I definitely need to heal from mine. Let's be friends and see where that takes us. Maybe we can help each other heal."

"That sounds good to me."

Chapter Twelve

Redemption

"Is that all you got?" Lynn asked.

"You're trash-talking me, and I'm winning?" I laughed.

I can't lie; it wasn't easy. Lynn was tougher on the basketball court than most men I'd played with. She always came at me hard and forced me to play with my full effort. I loved that. I loved that she brought out the best in me.

Over five months, we had seen Knicks games together and gone to countless movies, museums, and Broadway shows.

Lynn was really into running and got me to do 5K and 10K races with her. I wasn't much of a runner, but it was the togetherness that I loved the most. I was falling for her fast. Lynn stayed at my place two times a week and even had clothes there. She introduced me to her dad, who was cool as hell, and her best friends, Erica, Kelly, and Jackie. They gave me their approval, and we hung out together on the regular.

It was still early in our . . . whatever it is we were doing, but I introduced her to my mom. My mom loved her. They hung out all the time. It hurt my heart when my mom made me promise I wouldn't hurt this one. It reminded me of things with Tiffani, and I regretted how that ended.

"All right, two more baskets, and I win. Don't forget to give me my reward when this is over," I laughed.

"The game isn't over yet, and you're not winning this. *I* am."

"I love that confidence, even though it's in vain because you're taking an L."

We still hadn't had sex yet despite being with each other every day for five months. Believe me, I wanted to. We'd been naked together countless times and got each other so worked up that we both felt like we'd explode, but I cared about her, and I wanted more than a fuck.

Lynn also told me she wasn't sharing herself with a guy again until they were in a relationship, and she knew she loved him. We had a mutual understanding when it came to going any further. We were both dealing with our problems the best way we knew how, so we settled for kisses and massages.

I scored another basket. "One more point," I said.

"Shuddup," she said while she jokingly pushed me.

I scored again.

"You just got lucky," she said as she rolled her eyes.

"Aw, don't be mad. Just give me my reward."

Her pout turned into a smile as she kissed me passionately on the lips.

"I love you, Ken."

I didn't know if it was too early or even if I felt the same way yet.

"I—"

"It's OK, Ken. You don't have to say it back right now. I want you to say it when you mean it."

I nodded, hugged her tight, and kissed her again.

"Let's go back to my place, and I'll give you a loser's backwash."

"Ha-ha."

We went back to my place, showered together, and I made us dinner.

"Why lasagna?" she asked.

"I wanted to make you food that starts with the letter L, so you can remember the *loss* you had today."

Again, Lynn playfully punched me in the arm, then got serious for a moment and asked, "Ken, where do we go from here?"

I knew this day was coming, and I understood what she was asking. We'd been acting like we were in a relationship, but we never gave ourselves a title.

"Where do you want it to go?"

"You know I want more than this. I told you today that I love you. I'm in love with you, but if I'm going to feel this way, I want more from you than just a friendship."

"I do too, so I guess we are together then."

"What? That's not how you ask me," she laughed.

I smiled. "What do you mean? You said you wanted more. I said I wanted more, so that means we're together, right?"

"Nope. Ask me."

I sighed playfully.

"Lynn Sian Johnson, would you give me the honor and the privilege of being in a committed relationship with me?"

"I guess," she joked. Lynn smiled, nodded her head, and said, "Yes, of course."

We hugged and kissed. She grabbed her cell phone and headed for the bedroom. "I have to tell my girls about this," she exclaimed.

She was so excited and happy, and I was too, but I'll admit I was a little scared—scared I would be opening myself up to getting hurt again and scared I may eventually hurt her. But I pushed those thoughts away and enjoyed the moment. I finally found someone that made me happy. I called Perry.

"Yo, what's up, brother?" Perry answered.

"I'm good, man. Yo, you won't believe this. I found someone."

"What do you mean? You all right? I don't think I heard you correctly. You sure it's just one?" he joked.

"Yeah, just one. She's smart, outgoing, funny, ambitious, and sexy as hell."

"She got a booty?"

"Her ass is ridiculous, but she's the total package."

"I gotta get a glimpse of this chick."

I didn't realize it, but Lynn was standing right behind me. She hugged me.

"I'm glad you're excited about us being together too," she whispered.

I kissed her.

"Yeah, we need to meet up soon."

He agreed, and we promised we'd get together over the weekend.

It was late. Lynn spent what seemed like an eternity in the bathroom, but she looked stunning when she came out. She had on knee-high lace stockings with matching panties and bra.

She took out her hair tie and let her wavy hair flow down. She looked amazing. She lit candles all over my bedroom and turned off the lights. The candles made her body look like it was glowing, and I couldn't wait to have her finally.

I thought about how strongly I felt connected to her. It was more than a physical attraction. I loved all of the little things that made Lynn, Lynn. I loved her ambition and all her strengths. I loved how she brought out the best in me and pushed me to strive for more in life. I loved how she accepted my past and didn't judge me or look down on me.

Most importantly, I couldn't picture her not being in my life. I realized that this was different than with the other girls in the past. I loved her.

She lay on the bed, and we kissed long and deep, looking at each other with desire and wanting. Our hands roamed over each other excitedly. I loosened her bra, my mouth all over her neck and breasts. My hands explored every inch of her body.

Lynn took off my tank top and pulled down my boxers. She licked her lips, touched, and rubbed that part of me that made me a man. I laid her down on her back and took off her thong. She opened her thighs, showing the beautiful part of her that made her a woman. She held the top of my bald head as my face moved inside of her vagina with my tongue leading the way. I was licking, sucking, and fingering her until her eyes rolled back. She was in complete nirvana.

After a few moments, I took a condom out of my nightstand, and she held my butt with one hand and guided me inside her with the other. She shuddered, wrapped her legs around my back, and clung to me as I pushed inside her. Our bodies were in tune with each other. She felt heavenly. Her moans echoed off of my walls.

We switched positions. She rode me, controlling the penetration and speed. Then she moved faster. She shook her head quickly, praising the Lord and telling me how good I was making her feel. I felt her walls fluttering. Her breathing was heavy. Her legs trembled, and then that beautiful spasm when you know a woman reaches her peak of satisfaction—when her entire body is paralyzed by complete ecstasy. She collapsed on my chest. I could feel her orgasm run through her body like a wave.

We went to bed that night, satisfied. I was so in love with her. At that moment, I felt like this was my first time truly making love.

***

The next morning, Lynn had to be at work early, so she left before me. I got dressed, set the timer on my camera, and took a picture of myself with my arms extended as far as they could go.

I printed out the picture and went to the florist in Freeport off Guy Lombardo and ordered roses to be sent to her school. I put the picture I took in a card and wrote: *I love you this much.*

Then I went to work. During some downtime between clients, I drove to the school where she worked. I went to the main office to get permission to stop by her classroom and ran into the principal, Mrs. James.

"So you must be Ken. Lynn has told everyone about you. She thinks the world of you. You had everyone jealous when we saw your roses and card today. They were beautiful."

"Thanks. Is there any way I can stop by her classroom for one second to tell her something important?"

"We don't let visitors walk around the school. Is it urgent?"

"Yes, very."

"Is everything OK?" she said, looking concerned.

"Everything is fine. I just have to tell Lynn that I love her. I didn't tell her yesterday, and I wanted to tell her in person, not just by a card. I want to tell her as soon as possible."

"Oh my God, you're perfect. Lynn is in room 103 with her class." Mrs. James gave me a pass. I rushed over to Lynn's classroom.

I looked in the window and saw the roses and card on her desk. Lynn was drawing with her students. I knocked on the door. Lynn looked up. She was surprised to see me and opened the door quickly.

"What are you doing here?" she asked.

"I love you, Lynn. I came here to tell you I love you. I'm sorry I didn't tell you yesterday when you told me. I didn't want you to finish out this day without knowing that and hearing it directly from my mouth."

Lynn's eyes glistened with tears. "I love you too."

She grabbed my face with both hands and kissed me in the doorway of her classroom. Her entire class said, "Oooohhhh, Ms. Johnson is in love." They giggled and laughed. We laughed too. I held her in my arms, wanting never to let her go.

A week passed. It was the weekend, and Lynn would be meeting Perry and Jessie for the first time. I wasn't worried about Lynn and Perry getting along. I was more concerned with her and Jessie hitting it off. Despite Jessie being cordial at their wedding, I knew she still didn't like me.

We met up at Houlihan's on Route 110 in Farmingdale. Perry and Jessie got there before we did, so they were at the table already.

"What's up, guys?" I asked.

"You're late," Jessie said, rolling her eyes at me.

"Sorry. We got caught in traffic," I said, which was a lie. In reality, as good as Lynn was looking before we left, I couldn't come here without having her first.

"Perry . . . Jessie . . . This is my girlfriend, Lynn."

It felt weird saying, "girlfriend," but I liked it. I felt like I officially changed. Jessie mumbled something under her breath and gave Lynn a weak handshake. Perry got up and hugged her, but I knew exactly what he was doing. He was discreetly trying to check her out.

After the hug was over, he gave me a head nod and a thumbs-up. We shared a laugh. Jessie shot me a look and turned to face Lynn.

"So, how long have you guys known each other?" Jessie asked.

It was evident her inquiry wasn't to start a friendly conversation. It was meant to dissect our relationship.

"A little over five months," Lynn replied.

"Interesting. Where did you guys meet?"

"Oh, we met at the gym."

"The gym, huh? Yeah, Kenny has met a lot of his friends there."

"Jessie, be nice," Perry said with a stern and concerned voice.

"I'm always nice, honey. Anyway, so Lisa—"

"It's Lynn."

"Right, Lynn. Sorry. Kenny has had so many friends that it's hard to remember their names because after he's done with them, I know I'll never see them again."

I was furious. Jessie was embarrassing me. I was about to scream at her when Lynn slowly reached for my hand and held it.

"I know about Ken's history. Everyone's got things in their past they're not proud of. He's grown from it, and he's trying to move on."

"You know about his history? Did you know he fucked his friend's sister or that he fucked his other friend's ex-girlfriend?"

Jessie saw the confusion and anger on my face.

"Oh, you're wondering how I know about the whole Kim thing? Well, Perry called to invite Ray to the wedding like a million times. I knew he wanted him there, so I called Ray myself to try to talk to him for Perry. Ray told me he wouldn't come because you fucked his sister. He was still mad at Lucy for cheating on him—a trait of yours that probably rubbed off on her. Ray called her to curse her out one night when he was drunk. She told him she wasn't the only one getting fucked behind his back, and he should ask Kim how your dick feels. He confronted Kim about everything Lucy said, and Kim confessed the whole thing."

"Baby, you need to stop right now," Perry yelled. "I'm so sorry about this." He apologized to Lynn. "What is wrong with you?" he asked Jessie.

"What's wrong with *me?* What's wrong with me is that after all Ken has done and the people he's hurt, he thinks he's going to change. Guys like him *don't* change. She should be thanking me. I'm trying to help her out before she gets dogged out like the other chicks he's messed with."

"That's not up to you. Lynn already said he told her about his past. She's OK with it, so why are you causing trouble?" Perry asked.

The waiter came over. It was apparent he overheard our conversation and felt awkward about asking us for our order. We told him to give us a minute. I was ready to breathe fire, but Lynn stayed calm and kept holding my hand.

Jessie faced Lynn again. "I'm not trying to come off as a bitch, but I've seen him screw over two of my friends to the point where they don't even talk to each other anymore."

"I appreciate that. It was hard to hear about Ken's history, but I love him, I trust him, and nothing that you or anyone else says to me is going to change that or make me feel differently. So, let's order, shall we?"

Lynn opened up the menu and started looking at all the choices. Jessie looked stunned. Perry smiled, and I was proud I had a strong woman that believed in me.

Before I knew it, I had been with Lynn for a little over a year. I was utterly in love with her.

She had her quirks, no doubt, but everyone has those. I hated it when she left the toilet paper roll bare in the bathroom. You go in to do your business, and when you go to wipe—damn, there's no toilet paper. That pissed me off to no end. I hated it when she made tea and left the teabag in the cup while it's in the sink. Uh, that drove me crazy. I hated it when she wore sunglasses at night or when she went on her cleaning frenzy and threw stuff out without checking what it was. But despite all of those little things, I couldn't see myself without her.

There was only one major problem that genuinely bothered me: her ex-boyfriend, Sean. They had a close friendship and talked on the phone almost daily. They regularly texted each other and hung out from time to time.

I trusted her, but I didn't want history to repeat itself. Whenever I saw them together, they looked like best friends who had never argued in their lives. Whenever I asked Lynn why they broke up, she'd get upset, avoid the question, or told me she wasn't what he needed. She never went into depth or gave any more insight into the history of their relationship or why they broke up.

Whenever she talked to him on the phone, she always went to another room or went into the bathroom to speak with him. She rarely spoke to him on the phone in front of me. She got upset whenever I asked about him, which always made me think she still had feelings for him.

He was a pretty boy who looked like he could be a model. He worked with a production company on Broadway and did work with several popular Broadway shows. He was in good shape and had a similar build to me, which made me wonder if she fell for me because we had similarities. Was she thinking about him when she was sexing me? Paranoia reared its ugly head.

***

We were sitting in the audience for *Hairspray,* waiting for the musical to begin. Sean was one of the people responsible for bringing it back to New York, so, of course, Lynn wanted to support him.

"Babe, stand up. Some people are trying to get in this row," Lynn said.

I stood up.

"Sorry."

"Ken?"

I turned my head and couldn't believe who I was looking at.

"Hey, Ashley."

Of all places, I couldn't believe I was seeing her there. She was with one of her female friends. I thought there'd be some lingering anger seeing her again, but there was nothing. I guess I really had given my all to Lynn. "This is my friend, Melissa."

We shook hands.

"How've you been?" Ashley asked.

"I'm good, I can't complain." I reached for Lynn. "This is my girlfriend, Lynn."

Ashley looked shocked. "Girlfriend? Wow, it's very nice to meet you."

She turned and looked at me. I could see she was a little jealous. In a way, I was glad. Now, she knew how I felt when she would throw her boyfriend in my face. Lynn looked her up and down too. Lynn looked like an Amazon next to Ashley, and you could tell her tall, well-proportioned body made Ashley feel inadequate.

I told Lynn all about Ashley, so I'm sure she was curious about the woman I was so hung up on.

"I'm still single, but I'm happy," Ashley said.

"That's cool."

The lights started to dim. We all took our seats and got ready for the play to begin.

The play ended, and everyone gave the cast a standing ovation. Lynn and I waited in the lobby so she could congratulate Sean on the success of the play. She spotted him and immediately ran to him and hugged him.

I waved at him. He returned the gesture and went right back to talking with Lynn. I leaned against the wall, irritated that my girlfriend was staring into the eyes of her ex-boyfriend and smiling. Someone touched me and broke my thoughts. It was Ashley.

"So, your girlfriend seems to like that guy a lot," she said.

"That's just one of her friends, nothing more."

"Well, does she hug all of her friends like that? If she does, I might have to make friends with her. Sometimes I get lonely," she laughed.

I was getting irritated.

"So, is your number still the same?" she asked.

"Yeah, it's still the same."

"Maybe we can meet up. It's been awhile."

"I have a girl now. If we did hang out, she'd be coming with me."

"I'm not into girls, but, hey, maybe she could bring that guy she's talking to."

As always, she knew how to push my buttons and fuck with my head.

"Well, I'll call you soon so we can catch up on things," Ashley said.

I nodded, and Ashley surprised me with a peck on the mouth. I was worried Lynn would see that and get pissed, but she was so into talking to Sean that she didn't even notice. Ashley walked to her friend Melissa who was standing at the exit. Ashley said something to her that made her laugh, and they left.

Over the next two months, Ashley called and texted me daily. She would always ask me, "Did you leave your bubble butt girlfriend yet?" or "Do you remember how good my pussy felt on your dick?" I could've easily stopped this by ending all communication with her, but the truth was, she was my backup plan. If history did repeat itself, and Lynn cheated on me, I knew Ashley would be the first one I fucked to make myself feel better. It bothered me that I was doing this because as much as I thought I changed, I needed to know I had some sort of security blanket if things turned for the worse, as much as I wanted things to be different.

I had just made dinner. Lynn and I were about to watch the Knicks game when her phone rang. What pissed me off was I knew it was Sean because she had that Ciara song "Promise" assigned as his ringtone.

She answered the phone. "Hey . . . What? Calm down."

"Is everything okay?" I asked.

She waved at me and went into the bathroom with the phone. I put the food I made on our plates and placed them on the table. Then I sat on the couch, thinking all types of bad thoughts, wondering if she was disrespecting me in my own house and saying inappropriate things. I never listened to her conversations before because I wanted our relationship to be based on trust, but I said fuck that and put my ear on the bathroom door. It sounded like she was crying.

"Yes . . . I know . . . It's just . . . it still hurts me . . . I loved you . . . yes . . . I still love you . . . I'll always be here for you no matter who I'm with."

I couldn't believe that shit. She was telling another guy she loved him at *my* house. On top of that, Lynn openly admitted she'd be there with him no matter who she was with, which sounded to me like she didn't see us lasting long term.

My anger got the best of me, and I banged on the door. "Open the door," I yelled.

She opened it and looked at me like I had no sense. "I'm on the phone."

"I know you're on the phone. Hang up. We have to talk."

"Hold on, sweetie. I have to talk to Ken for a second."

Hearing her call him sweetie only infuriated me more. She covered the phone with her hand.

"What's your problem?"

"Hang up the phone."

"No. Sean is going through a lot of shit right now, and I'm talking him through it."

"Sean's a grown man. He can handle his own problems."

"What's your deal right now?"

"I don't like hearing my girlfriend tell her ex-boyfriend that she still loves him. I have a problem with that."

"Sean . . . Let me call you back. I have to talk to Ken."

"You really want to do this, Ken?"

Hearing that question scared the shit out of me. I didn't know where this was headed, but we were in too deep to get out of it now.

"Yep, I want to do this now."

"First off, you shouldn't have been listening to my conversation, to begin with. Second, if you're going to question what I say to my ex, maybe you shouldn't be getting messages from Ashley reminiscing on the times you two used to fuck."

Guilt was all over my face.

"Oh, you have nothing to say now, huh? The other day she sent you a picture of her pussy and asked if you missed it. I erased that shit immediately. I didn't care if you knew I checked your phone."

"So, you don't trust me? You were reading my phone?"

"Yup, I did."

I was hurt and angry. I thought Lynn trusted and believed me when I said I'd never hurt her, but apparently, she didn't. I felt like our relationship was bursting at the seams. I brought the argument back to her actions.

"She did write me text messages, but I never replied with any crazy shit or made her even think or expect anything would happen between us. You told this guy you love him in *my* house when *I'm* cooking dinner for you. You told him you'd always be there for him no matter who you're with. I shouldn't come second to your ex."

"You don't come second to him. You don't understand."

"Well, *make* me understand. You said Sean broke your heart—that he left you—yet you're best friends with him. You told the guy you love him. Are you still fucking him?"

She looked insulted that I asked the question, but she said nothing.

"Do you *still* love him? Do you love him more than me? If he asked you to come back to him right now, would you leave me?"

There was more silence. We stared at each other. I looked at Lynn with disappointment and disdain. Her lack of an answer made me feel the answer to all of the questions I asked was yes. I didn't care if this was my place. I grabbed my keys, wallet, and cell phone and left her standing there. I heard her crying through the door as I headed to my car.

I looked at my phone. While I knew I shouldn't and knew I'd probably regret it, I called Ashley and told her I was coming over. The entire ride to her house, I was at war with myself. A part of me was saying I shouldn't regress. I made it this far. I didn't need to do this to feel better. But the other half of me was saying I should do it. Lynn was probably screwing her ex this whole time while I was trying to be a one-woman man, so I should get mine too.

I got to her place, and she answered her door in her robe. "You got here fast. You must've wanted to see me badly, huh?"

She had that smile like she knew she had me—like this was all a game, and her victory was guaranteed. I didn't answer her. I walked inside and had a seat on her couch. She walked up to me and kissed me on the mouth. I felt nothing—no lingering feelings like I did in the past, and no desire for her. I knew even if I did fuck her, it would feel as empty as that kiss.

"I'm going to take a quick shower." She grabbed my crotch and kissed me again. "Get ready for me," she said as she dropped her robe and went into the bathroom.

While she was in the shower, I wondered if I should leave but ended up staying. Minutes later, she walked out of the bathroom with a towel in her hand. Her body looked as flawless as ever as she dried herself in front of me. I've always been attracted to her, so it was no surprise I was hard instantly watching her dry off. She walked over to me, mounted me, and kissed me.

"Doesn't this feel good?" she asked.

I said nothing. In my head, it didn't feel good. It didn't compare to the feelings I had for Lynn. She grabbed my crotch again, pulled my dick out, and stroked it while she kissed me more.

"Doesn't this feel so right?"

It didn't feel right. I wasn't sure if Lynn was playing me or if we'd even stay together, but I did know I didn't want this. I was only going through the motions.

"Doesn't this feel so familiar, like being home?"

When she said that last part, I thought of all the times I had been there for her and how she told me she didn't date Black guys. I thought about Bri and all of the other countless women I hurt. I pushed her off me. I adjusted my dick and zipped up my pants. I didn't want to be used by her anymore. I didn't want to go back to being the way I was before. I didn't know what type of future I had with Lynn, but I knew I wouldn't have a future with Ashley.

"What are you doing?" she asked, surprised and upset.

"I can't do this."

"Looking at your dick. Your body is saying you can."

"OK, let's say we fuck, then what? Would you date me?"

"Oh God, here we go with this shit again. Uh, pull your skirt down. Stop acting like a bitch. Why can't you just let it be? We're never going to be together. Why do you have to be such a bitch about being in a relationship? Any other guy would just want some ass and be happy, but you always want to be together."

"That's my point. You don't care about me. You don't even *want* me. You're doing this so you can feel like you have control over me—to boost your ego."

"You're right. I am, and you're going to cave in eventually, so let's save ourselves from this conversation."

She opened her legs and showed me her shaved pussy. I looked at her. I was tempted, but she had no respect for me. She, like Jessie and countless others, believed I could never change. If I did anything with her, I'd be proving them right.

I walked away.

"Where are you going?"

I didn't answer. I didn't speed up. I just walked out with my head up because I didn't let her manipulate me. I proved to myself I was better than the way I was before. I had willpower. She quickly put on her robe and ran toward me as I was walking out the door.

"It's OK. You'll be back. As soon as Lynn fucks you over just like Bri did, you'll be right back to me."

I looked back at her. "I won't go back to you. I used you up already. I don't need you anymore."

Her face looked furious as she slammed the door.

I got in my car. I was speeding, trying to get home as fast as I could. I hoped Lynn was still at my place so we could talk. It started to rain hard. I grabbed my cell phone and scrolled through my numbers to call Lynn. Not paying attention, I hit a big pothole. My tire blew out. Then my car spun and swerved all over the road. I gripped the steering wheel tight, trying to gain control of the vehicle, but there wasn't much I could do because I was speeding. I tried my best to avoid other cars. I hit a tree. Then I ricocheted and hit three more trees. My car began to flip over repeatedly. I screamed—and then darkness overcame me.

I woke up in pain. My head was killing me. My body felt numb and throbbed. I could barely see, but within a few minutes, everything became clearer. I didn't recognize where I was at first, but eventually, I realized I was in the hospital. I slowly looked around the room. My mother and Lynn were sleeping in padded chairs around my hospital bed. I called for Lynn. "Babe." My mouth was dry. My voice was scratchy. She didn't hear me. I tried a little louder.

"Babe."

Her head rose, and she looked at me. Our eyes locked. Lynn smiled through tears. She woke my mom, who was holding her old tattered Bible in her hand. My mom rushed over to the bed.

"My God, I thought I was going to lose you," she said.

"I'm so sorry we fought, baby. I'm so sorry," Lynn said.

"It's OK," I strained to say to Lynn.

I couldn't say much. I was in too much pain. The little I did say was a lot for me.

Mom said, "The doctors said you were lucky. You were in a coma for a week, but your brain stem and frontal lobe showed no damage. Even though your car was totaled, you didn't break any bones. It's a miracle you're still alive. Lynn was here the whole time with you. Perry came too. He just left not too long ago. He couldn't take any more time off from work."

Lynn called for the nurses and doctors to come in. They asked me a few questions and checked the readings on the machines I was hooked up to. My mom hugged Lynn and kissed her on the forehead. I was happy they were with me. The doctors explained to my mom that since I was still in a lot of pain, it would be difficult for me to talk, so she did most of the talking. She explained that after the car accident, the police found me unconscious in the wreckage of my car. They found my cell phone in the debris and saw that the contact page was on Lynn's number. They called it, expecting her to be my wife or another family member. They explained to her what happened, and she immediately called my mother and Perry. They all met at the hospital and had been there ever since. Despite everything, I still had some people in my life that cared about me.

Three days passed, and I was feeling somewhat better. I was still in pain, but it wasn't nearly as bad as it was before. Lynn was in the room with me alone. My mom finally went home to rest and go to church.

"I have to talk to you about something," Lynn said.

I didn't know if I had the strength to deal with whatever she was going to spring on me, but I nodded anyway.

"I know you always wanted to know the reason why Sean and I broke up. I know you felt like there was still something going on with us, but the fact is, nothing is going on because Sean is gay."

My eyes bulged out of their sockets. I couldn't believe it.

"I was embarrassed. Sean came out to me when we were dating, and it hurt me because he told me he never fully believed he was gay until he dated me. Deep down, I felt like I wasn't feminine enough or that, somehow, I did something to unlock that part of him. He had girlfriends in the past, but he never believed he was gay until he was with me. I cried, and he broke up with me to go to some guy he saw on the side. He hadn't told anyone, not even his parents. He was always scared to talk to them about it, which is why he always called me. The night we fought, he called me because he was suicidal. He had finally told his parents, and they disowned him. He felt alone and just wanted to end it all, so I tried to talk him out of it."

"Why didn't you tell me this before?" I asked as best as I could while in pain.

"I felt ashamed. I didn't tell any of my girlfriends about it or even my dad. I just told everyone I wasn't the right person for him. He wasn't ready to come out, and I wasn't up to feeling like I was the person that drove him to be gay."

I felt empathy for her. I understood her embarrassment, and if I were in her shoes, I would've probably done things similarly. Lynn cried uncontrollably, but I grabbed her hand and promised her we'd make it through this.

Lynn helped me heal physically, and we helped each other to recover mentally and emotionally. She accepted that Sean was gay and learned to understand that it wasn't anything she did that made him that way. It was always inside him. She helped me understand that while I did terrible things in the past, I had changed, and I needed to stop beating myself up. We were each other's support system.

Chapter Thirteen

Evolution

A year passed, and Lynn and I were still going strong. She still challenged me, and our relationship grew better every day. My mom was doing well too. She signed the divorce papers my dad sent to her. She met a man at the library named Ernest, who was educated and churchgoing.

I met him a few times. He seemed like a good guy, but as much as I hated my dad, I didn't like seeing another man being affectionate toward my mom. While I wasn't a fan of another man being around the house with my mother, I couldn't deny she was happy. She smiled, laughed, and the house was clean and not cluttered like it usually was when my dad would leave. Most importantly, she let go of my father completely. He wasn't even a thought anymore now that she had Ernest. One day unexpectedly, I got a call from my dad.

"Hey, son, how have you been?" he asked.

"I'm all right."

"You still seeing all of those girls?"

"Nah. I found one that makes me happy. I don't need more than that."

Lynn was lying down on the couch. When she heard that, she got up and kissed me.

"Well, that's good. That's good," he said. I sensed pain in his voice.

"How are your women doing?" I asked.

"I'm done with them."

"Even Janine?" Janine was the woman he left my mom for.

"Yeah, even her. Does your mother ever mention me?"

"Honestly, no. She's happy with her boyfriend, Ernest."

"Boyfriend," he said with disgust. "What does Ernest do?" he asked.

"He's a teacher like her, goes to church, never married, and no kids."

"Do you know if she got any of my letters?"

I knew she got them, but she never opened them. Once she met Ernest, she threw them in the garbage and never looked back.

"Yeah, she got them."

"Do you know if she's coming to my open mic tomorrow? You're coming, right?"

I knew for a fact she wasn't going. I didn't plan on going either. I guess my father was feeling regret now and realized this time around that he wasn't getting my mom back.

"I'll come. I don't think Mom is gonna go," I said.

"Oh," he said, sounding disappointed. "Well, try to get her to come. I'm dedicating the song to her."

"I'll try."

"OK . . . Thank you. So this girl you got now, is she a good woman?"

"Yeah."

"Good. Don't be stupid like me. If she's good to you, appreciate her. Don't mess it up by being selfish and trying to find something better."

"I won't."

"Good, well, I'll see you tomorrow."

"All right, until tomorrow."

I thought about not going, but I decided to keep my word since I told him I would.

I called Perry, and to my surprise, he was also going.

"I wasn't going to tell you because Jessie didn't want me to, but Krissy got signed by Def Jam."

"Get out of here.... Really?" I tried to act surprised, but I already knew. Sonia told me they loved her demo.

"Yeah, tomorrow's going to be her last time playing at Nakisaki's. I didn't want to say anything because I didn't know how you would feel seeing how you guys ended and all."

"Nah, I'm cool. I'm happy for her."

"All right, well, I'll pick you up, and we'll all go together tomorrow. Is Lynn coming?"

"Nah. She has her Parent/Teacher Conference."

"Oh, OK. Well, I'll see you tomorrow."

We walked into Nakisaki's, and the place was packed. There was a big banner that read, CONGRATULATIONS, KRISTEN, above the stage. As usual, Jessie was the typical bitch she was. She had a smirk on her face when we walked in, which made me realize this would be a long night. We took our seats at the middle tables, so we had a good view of the stage. The MC got on the stage and talked to the crowd.

"Ladies and Gentlemen, tonight, I'm happy but sad at the same time. One of our regulars and most popular open mic singers, Kristen Dos Santos, has made it to the big time and signed with a major record label."

The crowd roared for her.

"We're honored to be one of the places Kristen used to showcase her talent. Kristen, don't forget about us on your way to the top, okay?"

Everyone laughed.

"OK, folks, since this is Kristen's farewell night, we are allowing her to do the majority of the singing tonight."

Again, there was thunderous applause.

Three singers performed. They were okay. Each of them got decent applause. Next up was my dad. He got on the stage and looked as if he was checking to see if my mother was there. He spotted me. When he didn't see my mom, he looked disappointed.

"Good evening, everyone. I'm James Ferguson. This next song is dedicated to my ex-wife. I had a great woman, but I was dumb and didn't treat her right. Now I'm alone, and I wish I could have her back."

The crowd reacted sympathetically. Jessie looked at me and smirked. I ignored her. My father's voice sounded like he was getting emotional over his statement.

"This song I'm about to sing is an oldie but goodie. It's called 'If I Could Turn Back the Hands of Time.'"

The crowd cheered in anticipation.

My father sang that song wholeheartedly. Tears even welled up in his eyes as he sang certain parts. I realized he regretted all the things he put my mom through, but it was too late. He was paying the price and seeing my dad like that only reinforced my promiscuous days being over. I thought about Lynn and how much I loved her. My dad finished the song and got a standing ovation. While he was happy to get such a reception, the woman he needed to hear that song wasn't there.

He walked off the stage with his head down.

"All right, everybody, one more time, give it up for James." Again, everyone stood up and cheered for him.

"Next up is our headliner, Kristen Dos Santos."

The crowd erupted in applause. Krissy walked up on the stage, smiling. She looked amazing with her new slim figure and her wavy hair worn down.

"Thank you, guys, for coming out and supporting me. I wouldn't be able to fulfill my dream if it weren't for you guys constantly encouraging me," she said.

Krissy saw me in the crowd. We were in the front three rows, so she couldn't miss me.

She nodded, and I nodded back.

"All right, guys, you know how I love my girl, Beyoncé, so I'm going to do a few of her songs." She laughed.

The crowd laughed with her. The first song she sang was "Listen." Her voice was so beautiful that some women were crying from her singing. The song affected me too when I listened to the words. Krissy was a true entertainer, talking to the crowd between songs and telling what they meant to her. The next song she sang was "Best Thing I Never Had." The crowd was in awe with her voice, but that song hit me hard and made me feel like shit because of everything I put her through.

"This last song I'm going to sing is dedicated to my boyfriend, who rescued me when I was low and felt like giving up with everything. Baby, can you come to the stage?"

A big, dark-skinned, linebacker-looking guy got on the stage.

"This is Malik. Malik is my rock. He's the love of my life, and I'm so grateful to have found him. The last song I'm going to sing is 'Dangerously in Love.'"

That song was the song she sang when I first met her. I couldn't deny her last two song choices hurt me, especially when she dedicated that last song to *him*. I know I put her through so much, and I was happy she found someone she deserved, but I still felt bad about everything.

Krissy sang so passionately to him. She stroked his face and looked him in the eyes when she sang to him, and Jessie loved seeing me uncomfortable.

"She's finally over you. She got a record deal now, and her life is so much better with you out of it."

"Good, I'm happy for her. I'm not the same guy I was with her. I'm glad she found someone who appreciates her and treats her better than I did."

Krissy was looking at me when I was talking to Jessie. When the song was over, she got a standing ovation. The MC and her boyfriend handed her two dozen roses, and everyone was taking her picture. Krissy grabbed the mic again.

"Thank you, guys, for everything. I truly appreciate all of you. I just have to thank one more person because I honestly wouldn't have gotten my deal without him. He knew the right people, helped me make my demo, and put it in the right hands. Ken, will you please stand up?"

I couldn't believe she acknowledged me. Jessie's mouth dropped open. She had no idea I gave Krissy's demo to Def Jam. I stood up, and everyone cheered and clapped for me. She and her boyfriend nodded, and I returned the gesture. I could never make up for the stress I put her through, but I was happy that she forgave me.

"Um . . . so . . . You helped Krissy get her deal?" Jessie asked.

"Krissy got the deal by herself. I just gave the demo to the right people."

"Thank you . . . Thanks for helping my friend with her dream."

"She helped me realize I needed to change, so she deserved this."

Perry was smiling and glad Jessie and I weren't screaming at each other for a change. Malik kissed Krissy. She looked so happy and at peace. My dad watched the whole thing from backstage and walked out of the building. He didn't even say goodbye to me. I guess seeing Malik and Krissy in love and my mom not being there for him made him grasp that his days with my mom were truly over.

My mom married Ernest and was happier than ever. Ernest treated her like the queen she was, and they regularly traveled all over the world in their free time.

My dad found an apartment in Uniondale and finally settled down by getting a job at a bank. To satisfy his love for music, he also got a job as a wedding singer on the weekends. I forgave him. I let go of all the hatred I had for him all those years. I talked to him once a week to check on him, and we went out to dinner at least once a month.

I stayed in touch with Kim too. She kept me up-to-date on Ray, Lucy, and Adam.

Ray couldn't take living on Long Island anymore and moved upstate to Binghamton. He met a woman named Gloria and married her. They're expecting a son. I was glad he didn't give up on love and found someone.

Lucy, on the other hand, didn't have such luck. She tried to make things work with that guy, John, but he wouldn't leave his girlfriend for her. When Lucy heard Ray had moved and found someone else, it broke her heart. She learned the hard way that she made a huge mistake, and the grass wasn't always greener on the other side.

Adam finally found his queen, but she wasn't Ebony—she was Asian, to all of our surprise. He was happily engaged in California, where he landed a job working as a martial arts choreographer on movies. I was proud of my friend.

As for Kim, she finally stopped dating her usual type of guy and met a construction worker named Michael. The few times I talked to him, he seemed like a good guy. She and Michael lived together in her grandmother's house.

I'm grunting. My lungs are burning, and my legs feel like they're on fire.

"I can't believe you convinced me to do this shit," I said to Lynn. She was struggling too.

"I'm right here with you. It's almost over."

After a long time of doing marathons with Lynn, she finally convinced me to do the New York City Marathon with her. It was a grueling twenty-six-and-a-half-mile run. We were at mile twenty-five. Our bodies were in so much pain that we wanted to quit at times, but we kept encouraging each other along the way, pushing each other to finish this together.

During the run, I had lots of motivation. I reflected on all the wrongs I had done and the people I hurt. I thought about Tiffani and how I hadn't heard from or seen her in a long time. I thought about the events that led to that. I thought about Ray and Adam—two people who were significant in helping me become the person I was today—and how I lost them because I was young and stupid.

Besides reflecting, I thought about how I was scared about my future.

The day before the marathon, I saw Ron.

"I think I'm going to propose to Lynn tomorrow at the finish line. I bought a ring and everything."

"Damn, that's great. I'm proud of you," he said.

"I don't want to sound like a punk, but I'm scared. I'm scared that something will happen and I'll regress and end up alone like my father. I'm scared I'm going to hurt her and lose her like I lost all the other people who I felt were close to me."

"I'm going to give you this quote, and I want you to follow it. 'The truth is unless you let go, unless you forgive yourself, unless you forgive the situation, unless you realize that that situation is over, you cannot move forward'—Steve Maraboli," he said.

"I understand."

"Good, now let me see that ring."

Ron's quote was what I needed. I let go of the anger and hatred I had for my dad. I let go of my past and the bad things I had done. I could never forget them, but I needed to forgive myself and have faith that I had evolved.

"There's the finish line, babe. Let's do this together," I said.

Lynn looked at me, her face flushed and winded, and smiled at me. "I love you," she said.

"I love you too."

We crossed the finish line together, holding hands. I pulled her close to me, kissed her, and got down on one knee with the certainty I was ready for the next chapter in my life. I let go of that darkness inside of me.